Pictures

FROM AN

Institution

A Comedy by

Randall Jarrell

NEW YORK   ALFRED A. KNOPF   1954

Pictures

FROM AN

Institution

PICTURES FROM AN INSTITUTION *is a work of fiction. The details, the names, the characters, and the Institution are not intended to, and do not, relate to any existing institution or to any real persons living or dead.*

L. C. catalog card number: 54-5973

THIS IS A BORZOI BOOK
PUBLISHED BY ALFRED A. KNOPF, INC.

PUBLISHED MAY 3, 1954
SECOND PRINTING, JUNE 1954
THIRD PRINTING, JULY 1954

TO *Mary* AND *Hannah*

CONTENTS

I.

The President Mrs., AND Derek Robbins

1. Half the campus was designed by Bottom the Weaver, half by Ludwig Mies van der Rohe; Benton had been endowed with one to begin with, and had smiled and sweated and spoken for the other. A visitor looked under black beams, through leaded casements (past apple boughs, past box, past chairs like bath-tubs on broomsticks) to a lawn ornamented with one of the statues of David Smith; in the months since the figure had been put in its place a shrike had deserted for it a neighboring thorn tree, and an archer had skinned her leg against its farthest spike. On the table in the President's waiting-room there were copies of *Town and Country*, the *Journal of the History of Ideas*, and a small magazine—a little magazine—that had no name. One walked by a mahogany hat-rack, glanced at the coat of arms on an umbrella-stand, and brushed with one's sleeve something that gave a ghostly tinkle—four or five black and orange ellipsoids, set on grey wires, trembled in the faint breeze of the air-conditioning unit: a mobile. A cloud passed over the sun, and there came trailing from the gymnasium, in maillots and blue jeans, a melancholy procession, four dancers helping to the infirmary a friend who had dislocated her shoulder in the final variation of *The Eye of Anguish*.

In this office Constance Morgan had been, for a year, the assistant to the secretary of the President; this was her last day.

Her job was like most jobs, except for its surroundings: either she did what she did not want to do, or wished that she had it left to do. By four o'clock there was nothing left. She sat in uneasy content, in easy discontent—she could not tell, for a moment; then she remembered and laughed at herself. She picked an envelope from the top of one pile, put it on the top of another, and took a last last look through the drawers of the desk. Dr. Rosenbaum's old St. Bernard's voice came to her from the tennis courts, and she felt once more the pleasure she always felt at any reminder that he existed; she saved for him St. Augustine's best sentence: I want you to be. Two voices from the President's office— the President's, Gertrude Johnson's—she heard with different feelings; she could not have said exactly what they were.

2.

GERTRUDE JOHNSON was, of course, the novelist; she had come to Benton six and a half months ago, late in the fall, to replace a new teacher of creative writing who had proved unexpectedly unsatisfactory. Gertrude had, as her enemies put it, a hard heart and a sharp tongue, but her heart was softened a little, and her tongue dulled, at her first interview with the President of Benton, Dwight Robbins. He was a nice-looking and informal and unassuming man, a very human one, as he sat there on the edge of his desk, in the winter sunlight of his office; she felt—people could not help feeling as soon as they met President Robbins—as if she had just taken a drink. Everything was blurred a little with attractiveness, and she almost believed, as she did not ordinarily, in Friendship at First Sight. President Robbins wore a simple, grey flannel, undergraduate's suit; his fair

4

hair kept flopping in his face; in spite of once having been a diver in the Olympics, he gave an impression of slightness. He had what novelists used to call "an engaging grin," but it *was* engaging; one liked the way the skin crinkled around his eyes. Gertrude tried to think of a word for him, and did: the word was *boyish*.

The President, for his part, saw a short slight woman who was from head to foot, except for her pale blue eyes, a pale, pale, almost wholly unsaturated brown. Her lips were painted a purplish maroon; she had put on no other make-up. She wore her hair more or less as our mothers wore it; her features, as far as one could distinguish them, were undistinguished. Then one noticed that she had an obstinate Irish—or, perhaps, an obstinate apish—upper lip. Her face seemed a ground on which anything could figure: one felt that when she wore new earrings her husband, the children in the street, and the blind beggar on the corner would congratulate her on them. This is what you saw. Yet when you knew her how different it all looked; Gertrude's spirit shone through her body as though the body were an old pane of glass, and you thought, "My God, how could I have been so blind!"

They talked a little (Gertrude in her anomalous Southern speech, President Robbins in Standard American) about the job he was offering her. The salary was not what either would have wished it, but he explained why it couldn't be in a way that was new to her: his married alumnae either died before their husbands, who left money to their own colleges, or else on their husband's deaths left money to the husbands' colleges as memorials; and his unmarried alumnae left their money to cats and dogs and causes. Gertrude and the President laughed. Gertrude had not met a great many college presidents, but she knew from fiction, conversation, and Reason what all of them are like; President Robbins was different.

The job seemed unusually undemanding: one taught classes only twice a week, and did the rest of one's work in individual talks or "conferences" with the students. Gertrude smiled and said, "There's nothing I'd rather do than talk." It was true.

President Robbins laughed—he admired frankness—and said heartily: "Good! Then Benton is certainly the place for you." They both sounded a little too hearty, but they knew that one necessarily sounds that way in such circumstances: who comments on the weather with all the lack of interest that he really feels?

Gertrude was, as novelists say, "between novels"; she had taught writing once at an old-fashioned, high-schoolish college in Missouri, and knew that after it Benton would be a breeze. The President seemed to feel—several sentences implied it—that she would be a great acquisition to Benton; this was so, of course, but she was pleased that he both knew it and showed that he knew it. They arranged everything: President Robbins took her back to the station in one of the school's cars, and they had a drink on the way; late that week Gertrude and her husband found an apartment in Mount Pleasant, the little city that Benton lay at the edge of, and on Monday of the next week—a snowy Monday—Gertrude taught her first class at Benton.

Now she had taught her last class there, thank God! Suffused in summer, blind with bliss, she sat saying goodbye to President Robbins; and President Robbins, blind with bliss, sat saying goodbye to Gertrude Johnson. Constance, in the office outside, could not help hearing every word of their somewhat self-conscious, wholly delighting voices; they both sounded a little hearty, but they knew that one necessarily sounds that way in such circumstances.

3.

GERTRUDE AND the President's Friendship at First Sight had lasted only until they took a second look at each other. After this look Gertrude no longer felt as if she had just taken a drink, but felt as if she had a long time ago taken a great many: that look awoke both of them from their amicable slumbers.

What a pity it was that that party had ever been given! —the party that brought with it their first terrible quarrel, a quarrel that ended their friendship after eleven days. Without the party, they both felt bitterly, it might have lasted for weeks. One could not help blaming Gertrude a little more than one blamed the President; the President, like most people, behaved in a different way after he had had a great deal to drink, but Gertrude, knowing no other, behaved as she always behaved. But the drinks at the party, the almost unavoidable intimacies at the party, what they had said and what Mrs. Robbins had said and what people had said they all of them had said at the party—these, the memory of these, made Gertrude and the President look narrowly at each other, and their eyes widened at what they saw. George looked at the dragon and thought, *Why, that woman's a dragon;* and the dragon looked at George and thought, *That's no man, that's an institution.*

The word had come to Gertrude at the party, when she had found herself reflecting, "This institution's drunk." For days after the party the President felt, *Another such party and we are lost*—his ordinary disorderly executive existence had not prepared him for Life; Gertrude felt, yawning, *Another party.* It was one more pearl on the string of her existence, and she had come here to string pearls; when the pearls gave out, she knew, Godfather Death would come and cart her away.

But Dwight Robbins; President Robbins, that is; the President, that is—the President *interested* Gertrude. She realized, suddenly, that she was no longer between novels. She looked at the President as a weary, way-worn diamond-prospector looks at a vein of blue volcanic clay; she said to herself, rather coarsely—Gertrude was nothing if not coarse: "Why, girl, that Rift's *loaded.*" How can we expect novelists to be moral, when their trade forces them to treat every end they meet as no more than an imperfect means to a novel? The President was such invaluable material that Gertrude walked around and around him rubbing up and down against his legs, looking affectionately into the dish of nice fresh mackerel he wore instead of a face; and the dish looked back, uneasy, unsuspecting.

Mrs. Robbins, the Robbins' little boy Derek, the Robbins' two big Afghans: these and Benton—and Benton!—interested Gertrude too. Derek and the Afghans didn't really, except as properties: Gertrude thought children and dogs overrated, and used to say that you loved them so much only when you didn't love people as much as you should. *As much as you should* had a haunting overtone of *as much as I do*—an overtone, alas! too high for human ears. But bats heard it and knew, alone among living beings, that Gertrude loved.

If you loved people as much as you should, Gertrude told you that you should not "extend to or expect from created things the love that belongs to their Creator." Gertrude's wheel was fixed, everybody soon found; and yet most of us, fools that we are, could not resist going back to play at it.

Gertrude thought Europe overrated, too; she voyaged there, voyaged back, and told her friends; they listened, awed, uneasy somehow. She had a wonderful theory that Europeans are mere children to us Americans, who are the oldest of men—why I once knew: because our political institutions are older, or because Europeans skipped some stage of their development, or because Gertrude was an American—I forget. She would have come from Paradise and complained to God that the apple wasn't a Winesap at all, but a great big pulpy Washington Delicious; and after the Ark she would have said that there had not been the animals, the spring rains, and the nice long ocean-voyage the prospectus from the travel-agency had led her to expect —and that she had been *most disappointed* at not finding on Mount Ararat Prometheus.

Age could not wither nor custom stale her infinite monotony: in fact, neither Age nor Custom could do *anything* (as they said, their voices rising) with the American novelist Gertrude Johnson.

4.

IF GERTRUDE had asked Dwight Robbins what two times three is, he would have hesitated a fraction of a second and then spontaneously replied—or rather, would have replied with charming spontaneity, with a kind of willing and unconsidered generosity, of disinterested absorption in her problem—

What did it matter what he would have said? You could always find it worked out in percentages in the monthly poll of public opinion in *Fortune*, back under the heading Opinions of Liberal Presidents of Liberal Arts Colleges. He loved to say to you, putting himself into your hands: "I know I'm sticking my neck out, but. . . ." How ridiculous! President Robbins *had* no neck.

From *The Wealth of Nations* one learns that the interest of each is, in the end, the good of all; if one observed President Robbins one saw that the good of all is, in the beginning, the interest of each. We have read in the Gospels that the children of darkness are wiser in their generation than the children of light; but both, when they choose between God and the world, are stupider than those who know that we do not need to choose. President Robbins had no complaints about this Paradise, the world. The Tree of the Knowledge of Good and Evil *is* the Tree of Life, he knew; and President Robbins lay sleeping in its branches, his parted lips smelling pleasantly of apples.

About anything, anything at all, Dwight Robbins believed what Reason and Virtue and Tolerance and a Comprehensive Organic Synthesis of Values would have him believe. And about anything, anything at all, he believed what it was expedient for the President of Benton College to believe. You looked at the two beliefs and lo! the two were one. (Do you remember, as a child without much time, turning to the back of the arithmetic book, getting the answer to a problem, and then writing down the summary hypothetical operations by which the answer had been, so to speak, arrived at? It is the only method of problem-solving that always gives correct answers—that gives, even, the typographical errors in the back of the book.)

President Robbins was so well adjusted to his environment that sometimes you could not tell which was the environment and which was President Robbins.

Had it not been for Mrs. Robbins, President Robbins' life would have been explicable down to the last detail, and he himself the only existing human representation of the Theory of Perfect Competition: as one looked at him one could not help thinking of all the marginal producers who because of him must have been forced out of living or whatever it was they did. But why had he married Mrs. Robbins? It was a question to which there could not be an answer. Marianne Moore has said: *We prove, we do not explain our births;* and this is true of marriages.

5.

PEOPLE DID not like Mrs. Robbins, Mrs. Robbins did not like people; and neither was sorry. She was a South African —not a native, not a Boer, a colonial. She had been a scholar once, and talked somewhat ostentatiously of *her work,* which she tried *to keep up.* To judge from her speech, she was compiling a Dictionary of Un-American English: if lifts and trams ever invade the North American continent, Pamela Robbins is the woman to lead them. Often, when you have met a true Englishwoman—the false ones are sometimes delightful—you feel that God himself could go no further, that way. Mrs. Robbins existed to show what he could do if he tried.

For Mrs. Robbins understanding anybody, having a fellow-feeling for anybody, admitting anybody else exists, were incomprehensible vices of Americans, Negroes, continentals, cats, dogs, carrots. She was "half British phlegm and half perfidious Albion," according to Gertrude John-son, who loved to refer to Pamela as the Black Man's Bur-den; any future work on Mrs. Robbins will have to be based on Gertrude's. This *half . . . half* formula was Gertrude's favorite. She said that the President was "half *jeune fille*, half *faux bonhomme*." I hadn't liked her formula for Pamela, so I accepted her description of the President with bored matter-of-factness, as if she'd told me that he was half H_2 and half SO_4; but then I thought, "It's so; it's so." Sometimes Gertrude was witty without even lying.

For Mrs. Robbins life was the war of one against all; in this she was another Gertrude, a commonplace, conven-tional, jointed-hardwood Gertrude. (Yet her conception of this war was that of a Hessian prince of the eighteenth cen-tury, while Gertrude's was that of the director of some War of the Future, a war in which the inhabitants of the enemy country wake up one morning to find that they have all been dead a week.) Mrs. Robbins asked: "If I am not for myself, who then is for me?"—and she was for herself so passionately that the other people in the world decided that they were not going to let Pamela Robbins beat them at her own game, and stopped playing.

Once Mrs. Robbins had a long and, in its later stages, surprisingly acrimonious argument with several of her guests (to Americans English manners are far more fright-ening than none at all) about a book of Evelyn Waugh's called *Brideshead Revisited*. She believed it to be a satire on the Roman Catholic Church, since she was sure that its au-thor was "too intelligent a man" to believe in "all that." Her guests had few good arguments, and she many bad ones: yet, say what she might, the guests stayed unconvinced. Fi-nally she exclaimed, drawing herself up: "I have lived among the English aristocracy, and I know." I had always loved Cleopatra's "The man hath seen some majesty, and should know," but before this I had never really *heard* it.

Mrs. Robbins fought to acquire as much—not merit; what did she know about merit?—as much prestige or position or face as possible. Since, as everybody knows, the English never boast, there was nothing she didn't feel free, feel obligated, to tell you about herself: she was her own tombstone. For her mankind existed to be put in its place. She felt that the pilgrim's earthly progress is from drawer to drawer, and that when we are all dead the Great Game will be over. Mrs. Robbins poured tea as industrial chemists pour hydrofluoric acid from carboys.

To hear her was to be beginning to despair. Constance Morgan's beloved Dr. Rosenbaum once murmured, like the Spartan boy: "I do nodt like de tune she says zings to." Gottfried Rosenbaum, that kindly—or as some people said, that crazy—composer, could as easily have pronounced the Hottentot click sounds Mrs. Robbins had grown up among (though to hear her, she seemed to have been born in an airliner over the Cape of Good Hope, and to have arrived in Sussex on the second day) as he could have pronounced *th.* He said *d* a third of the time, *t* a third of the time, and *z* a third of the time, and explained, smiling, that after a few years, ass zhure ass Fadt, these would merge into the correct sound. It is true that his *d* and *t* and *z* were changing, but not in the direction of any already existing sound: his speech was a pilgrimage toward some *lingua franca* of the far future—"vot ve all speak ven de Shtate hass videredt avay," as he would have put it.

It was never the individual sounds of a language, but the melodies behind them, that Dr. Rosenbaum imitated. For these his ear was Mozartian. To hear him speak French, if you didn't try to understand what he was saying, was as good as attending *Phèdre:* he seemed a cloud that had divorced a textbook of geometry to marry Guillaume Apollinaire—when you replied, weakly, *Yes,* it was in the accents of Matthew Arnold appreciating Rachel. Without realizing it, Dr. Rosenbaum imitated for a few minutes the characteristic tune of whatever person he had been talking to—you could tell immediately whether he had been having a conversation with one of the professors educated at the City College of New York or with one begun at Indiana and finished at the Harvard Graduate School.

But even his Unconscious knew enough to refuse to imitate Mrs. Robbins. Her every sentence sang itself to a melody so thin-lipped, so emptily affected, so bloodless, so heartless, so senselessly and conclusively complacent, that it was not merely inhuman but inanimate, not merely lifeless but the negation of life—as you listened plants withered, the landscape grew lunar, the existence of *Paramecium*, of molds and spores, of the tobacco mosaic virus came to seem the fantasy of some Utopian planner; her voice said that there is nothing.

To understand what Pamela Robbins was one didn't need to listen to what she said, to understand English, to understand human speech; the Afghans, who had never learned to make the slightest sense out of, discrimination between, *Here* and *Get down!* and *Bad dog!*—they knew what Mrs. Robbins was, and as she fed them wagged their tails distrustingly. They ate like horses—no, that isn't fair, they ate horses; anything but horsemeat, in those quantities, would have been beyond the Robbins' means.

If I tell you that Mrs. Robbins had bad teeth and looked

like a horse, you will laugh at me as a cliché-monger; yet it is the truth. I can do nothing with the teeth; but let me tell you that she looked like a *French* horse, a dark, Mediterranean, market-type horse that has all its life begrudged to the poor the adhesive-tape on a torn five-franc note—that has tiptoed (to save its shoes) for centuries along that razor-edge where Greed and Caution meet. This dark French look was, I suppose, Mrs. Robbins' "Norman blood" coming out; for surely the Normans must have taken along with them on the Conquest some ordinary Frenchmen.

6.

A FRIEND of mine told me that, years and years ago, he had seen Dwight Robbins being introduced to Anthony Eden at a dinner of the League for the Promotion of Anglo-American Amity—or Unity, perhaps; he was not sure of the name, but the dinner had been at the Waldorf. My friend said: "As they shook hands Mr. Eden looked at President Robbins, and his face sagged; I realized for the first time that he is a man of comparatively advanced years."

This happened to everyone who met President Robbins: the freshmen of Benton thought the President younger than they. (Though they themselves were as old as Time, and wondered when the grown-ups—the other grown-ups—would see that they were.) President Robbins, because of the diving, had begun his real career several years later than those who are called *boy wonders* ordinarily do, so he made a point of looking, and looked, several years younger than they. He had been made President of Benton at the age of thirty-four, instead of at the age of twenty-nine. There was nothing he could do about this, he knew.

15

But it was foolish of him even to want to try: he possessed, and would possess until he died, youth's one elixir, Ignorance; he drank each day long draughts from the only magic horn, Belief. If you had said to people, "Dwight Robbins was thirty-four when he was appointed President of Benton," they would have said to you, "You mean he's *thirty-four!*"

He said to the World: *I believe—Lord, help thou mine unbelief;* but the World knew that it did not need to help, that he could not disbelieve in one button of it if he tried. He was a labyrinth in which no one could manage to remain for even a minute, because there were in it no wrong turnings. He fitted into things, things fitted into him. If, a soldier in the army, he had been given what is called a Good Conduct medal, he would have felt that he had received it for his own good conduct, and he would have felt, without wanting to, that his medal made him a little superior to the friend beside him who had received none. He believed.

Sometimes waking at morning, walking under the trees of Benton, climbing to the diving-board of its swimming-pool, he would say to himself with a flush of pure, of almost unbelieving joy: "I'm President of Benton!"—and at these moments his eyes were not boyish but a boy's.

7.

WHEN HE had first read *The Great Gatsby*—he was the kind of president that has read *The Great Gatsby*—he had felt a queer thrill of identification with Jay Gatsby; now and then he would mention the book in a detached way. For he too had begun very "low" indeed, among the very poor, and he would still once or twice a year do or say, or not do or not say, little things that made your face, before you could control it, go rigid with astonishment; and he was taught by that astonishment, and forever after kept a finger in that hole of the dyke. (In the end the dyke would have no holes left, and President Robbins would be in Holland for good.)

Once, making a money-raising tour among Southern alumnae, he had said one of these little things while being served breakfast on a tray in his room. It made the houseboy go back and tell the cook that President Robbins was not—and here he sounded embarrassingly like Uncle Tom or Aunt Jemima—was not quality folks. The cook replied, for-givingly, that he was only a Northerner, and beat her biscuit-dough with steady strokes.

But in a certain sense President Robbins was right: in a certain sense he was like Gatsby. There was a part of Gatsby that his bank, the company that insured him, and other institutions knew—a part that was in love not with Daisy but with the bank; and this part of Gatsby President Robbins shared with Gatsby. The World and President Robbins were in love with each other.

This earth carries aboard it many ordinary passengers; and it carries, also, a few very important ones. It is hard to know which people are, or were, or will be which. Great men may come to the door in carpet-slippers, their faces like those of kindly or fretful old dogs, and not even know that they are better than you; a friend meets you after fifteen years and the Nobel Prize, and he is sadder and fatter and all the flesh in his face has slumped an inch nearer the grave, but otherwise he is as of old. They are not very important people. On the other hand, the president of your bank, the Vice-Chancellor of the—no, not of the Reich, but

of the School of Agriculture of the University of Wyo-
ming: these, and many Princes and Powers and Dominions,
are very important people; the quality of their voices has
changed, and they speak more distinctly from the mounds
upon which they stand, making sure that their voices come
down to you.

The very important are different from us. Yes, they have
more everything. They are spirits whom that medium, the
world, has summoned up just as she has the rest of us, but
there is in them more soul-stuff, more ego—the spirit of
Gog or Magog has been summoned. There is *too much*
ectoplasm: it covers the table, moves on toward the laps of
the rest of us, already here, sitting around the table on
straight chairs, holding one another's hands in uneasy trust.
We push back our chairs, our kinship breaks up like a
dream: it is as if there were no longer Mankind, but only
men.

8.

PRESIDENT AND Mrs. Robbins' little boy was named
Derek. All the children at the nursery school thought that
he was named *derrick*, but this did not seem to them an odd
name for anyone to have—after all, Peter Rabbit . . . and
isn't the Lone Ranger named the Lone Ranger? Derek was
a very ordinary little boy, but he had not always been so.

When Derek was nineteen months old his mother went
to a psychiatrist—no Freudian, but a homely, American,
social-worker sort of psychiatrist; he specialized in children.
He asked Mrs. Robbins the psychiatric equivalent of *What
seems to be the trouble?* Pamela Robbins answered him with
the reserved dignity of people who have won and lost an

empire; but after two sentences her racial stiffness dissolved in grief and dismay and astonishment; she said, in the voice of Eve telling Adam about Abel: "He growls at people and —and they just growl back at him! Oh, Doctor, he'll *never* learn to talk."

Absurd as this sounds, it was true: Derek did growl at you—he had a wonderful growl, an astonishingly deep growl for so young a child—and unless you had a heart of stone you growled back. Not even Lotte Lehmann has made sounds that have bewitched me like that growl: when I heard it I not only believed in the Golden Age, I was in it—I felt for a moment that life was too good for me.

The psychiatrist said that talking is "simply a matter of maturation," but advised, as a precaution, "a thorough physical check-up." He went on to say that Carlyle's first words, delivered at the age of three, had been *What ails wee Jock?*—that Lord Macaulay's first words had not come until he was four; a lady had spilt hot tea on him at a party, and he had said, drawing back a little from her solicitous caress: *Thank you, Madam, the agony is somewhat abated.* The psychiatrist seemed to have specialized in First Words as others do in Last. He went on to tell Mrs. Robbins about a famous case of twins one of whom was taught to roller-skate at the age of seven months—the other was not; but the other, after a week's practice at the age of fifteen months, had. . . . Here Mrs. Robbins' attention wandered back to her own troubles: she knew which would win at the age of fifteen months. The psychiatrist's next case, that of the baby gorilla which, reared with a psychologist's baby, had for many months outstripped the child—this case helped her only a little more; she went home bowed under her weight of reassurance.

But Nature, which suffers fools gladly—which, indeed, does almost nothing else—went along with the psychiatrist, and in a few months Derek was talking like everybody else; his first words were, "Ma-ma!" I was away from Benton for a little, and when I got back Derek had turned into an ordinary, a drearily ordinary child. He was, so far as the Robbins were concerned, almost ideally disappointing: when you looked at him playing by the sand-pile it would never have occurred to you that his father was President of Benton and his mother a connection (with the right books, a good light, and a free evening you could trace the connection) of the Marchioness of . . . better not to say.

About Derek's badness, his disappointingness, there was neither distinction nor sweep; he seemed just a dopey little boy. He was worse than the Afghans—at least they looked exemplary. You looked at President Robbins, and then at Derek, and you said to yourself: "The fathers have eaten Cream of Wheat, and the children's teeth are set on edge." I suppose that Derek's abject ordinariness was a kind of defense against his world and its two pillars, Dwight and Pamela—he had been taught to call them by their first names. I never saw under his shell except once when I heard his mother reciting him a fairy tale before he was sent upstairs to bed; he made her repeat all the parts of the story in which giants or dragons or step-mothers were killed. He seemed to need these repetitions: that commonplace little boy by the sand-pile was only Derek's imaginary playmate.

But later I met, at a picnic, a teacher at the nursery school, and she told me a story which lifted Derek's crust of ordinariness as the hood of a car is lifted. At the nursery school the children painted and modelled and cut out; and Derek was different from the others, from the beginning, in one way—he painted, modelled, and cut out nests of snakes. By the end of the year he had improved a great deal: the snakes in his paintings were smaller, and pushed down into the left-hand corner of the paintings, next to the feet of a big little boy; he modelled cows and bears, though their legs *were* snakes; and he pasted together his cut-out snakes into links, and made a construction-paper chain out of them.

The nursery teacher asked me despairingly: "Now what, may I ask you, is the prognosis for a child like *that?*" The growls and snakes—and Derek—had made me like Derek so much that I hated to say it, but I replied: "I guess he'll turn into a grown-up in the end, one just like you and me." The teacher said, "But I'm not joking"; and I said to myself, "But I'm not joking." But what both of us meant to say was, I think: "Poor little boy! poor little boy!"

9.

BUT EXCEPT for Derek and except for Pamela, President Robbins had what people call a rich, full life. He had so many friends that, as Gertrude said, "they fell over each other going out the door." She also said, smiling subtly, that she used the word *friends* in a Pickwickian sense. They did not seem to me to resemble any of Pickwick's friends, so I replied that I did not know what she meant; and she said to me, quoting Aristotle—for she was far too well informed: "My friends, there are no friends!"

Of course the President's friends didn't like him as well as many of our enemies like *us,* but they took pleasure in his misfortunes, were confidential with him when they had drunk so much of his liquor they couldn't see who he was, accepted favors willingly—they were normal Presidential friends, the mean or median or average friends of all very important people.

Ordinary people think that very important people get along badly with one another—and this is true; but they often get along worse with you and me. They find it difficult not simply to get along with, but to care about getting along with, ordinary people, who do not seem to them fully human. They make exceptions, real or seeming, for school friends, people who flatter them enough, relatives, mistresses, children, and dogs: they try not to bite the hand that lets them stroke it . . . but all power irritates—it is hard for them to contain themselves within themselves, and not to roast the peasants on their slopes. But they eye one another with half-contemptuous, half-respectful dislike: after all, each of them *is* important, and importance, God knows, covers a multitude of sins.

Gertrude Johnson could feel no real respect for, no real interest in, anybody who wasn't a writer. For her there were two species: writers and people; and the writers were really people, and the people weren't. But unless we are very uncommon men, you and I split up the world in some analogous way; as Goethe has said, *But who is so cultivated as to refrain from cruelly stressing, at times, the qualities in which he excels!* And in this connection, no quality is so popular as that of having no particular qualities at all. The great—who may or may not be very important people—do not seem to most of *us* fully human.

President Robbins, judge him as you please, was not human. He had not had time to be; besides, his own gift was for seeming human. He had taught sociology only a year, and during the last three months of that year he had already been selected to be Dean of Men at ———; two years later he was appointed Dean of the College of Arts and Sciences at ———; in six years he was President of Benton. *They* had selected him. But how had *they* known whom to select? Would someone else have done as well? Why had they selected *just him?*

If you ask this, you have never selected or been selected; you would know, then. Such questions are as ridiculous as asking how stigmata know who to select—as asking, "Wouldn't somebody else have done just as well as St. Francis?" A *vocation,* a *calling*—these words apply quite as well in secular affairs as in religious: Luther knew. Have you yourself never known one of these *idiots savants* of success, of Getting Ahead in the World? About other things they may know something or they may not, but about the World they have forgotten—in previous existences for which, perhaps, they are being punished?—far more than you or I will ever learn.

President Robbins was, of course, one of these men. He "did not have his Ph.D."—but had that bothered one administrator upon this earth? All had been as refreshingly unprejudiced about his lack of one as the President of Benton now was about anybody's possession of one. But at Benton all of them were like this: they looked up your degrees so they could tell you that, whatever the things were, they didn't mind. President Robbins had an M.A. from Oxford—he had been a Rhodes Scholar—and an LL.D. granted, in 1947, by Menuire. (It's a college in Florida.) To make the President dislike you for the rest of his life, say to him with a resigned anthropological smile: "I've just been reading that in 1948 Menuire College gave the degree of Doctor of Humor to Milton Berle."

President Robbins had brought seven former Rhodes

Scholars to Benton during his first two years there. Benton thought him in most ways an ideal President, but about this they felt as the constituents of a Republican senator do when he appoints seven former U.N. officials to postmasterships. An ounce of Rhodes Scholars was worth a pound of Rhodes Scholars, in Benton's opinion.

10.

BUT WHEN the President spoke to them they could have forgiven him a wilderness of Rhodes Scholars. Benton had a day for parents and alumnae which was, or was not, called Founder's Day—I have forgotten. Yet surely it was not: who could have founded Benton? Benton is a Category like Time or Space or Causality.

I have forgotten the name of the day, but I remember its lunch. The day before, a third of our luncheon had been a salad of uncooked spinach, a midnight-green salad with, here and there among the leaves, an eye of beet: a yew-tree's notion of a salad: a salad that was exactly like a still-life by Soutine—had I not been poor I should have had it varnished and framed. But on parents' day we had, among other things, lobster and shrimp in little crumbling shells—no, *big* crumbling shells—of pastry. The girl with whom I used to play tennis was waiting on our table; she mumbled to me, "Gee, what's up?" I flickered my eyes toward the longest table: the President sat there among matrons. Had I been hatted, had I been gowned, had I been shod as were those matrons, I should have sold myself and made my fortune; but alas! they had had the idea before me.

That night we came together to hear President Robbins: the matrons, the girls, the teachers, Constance, Dr. Rosenbaum, Gertrude Johnson, I. "Good God," Gertrude whispered to me when she had looked around her; for once she was wordless. We suffered our way through a long program, and then President Robbins began to speak.

After two sentences one realized once more that President Robbins was an extraordinary speaker, a speaker of a —one says *an almost extinct school,* but how does one say the opposite? *a not-yet-evolved school?* He did something so logical that it is impossible that no one else should have thought of it, and yet no one has. President Robbins *crooned* his speeches.

His voice not only took you into his confidence, it laid a fire for you and put out your slippers by it and then went into the other room to get into something more comfortable. It was a Compromising voice. President Robbins was, in Shaw's phrase, "a man of good character where women are concerned," and he had never touched a Benton girl except in a game of water-polo; yet as you heard him speak something muttered inside you, "To a nunnery, go!"

He would say to you in private in his office, about the teachers of Benton: "We like to feel that we educate [there was a slow, chaste separation between the next two words: they seemed youths and maidens who have become strong and sublimated through remaining apart] each . . . other." If his voice was tender then, consider what it became in public: for that voice did not sell itself to the highest bidder, it just gave itself away to everybody.

President Robbins made a speech that—that—as Gertrude said, you had to hear it not to believe it. When he finished (and not a minute too late; the audience wolfed that speech down the way the Afghans ate their horse-meat) he finished by thanking the students, parents, and faculty of Benton for the experience of working with, of learning from, and of growing to . . . love . . . such generous and intelligent, such tolerant and understanding, such —and here he paused quite a long time—such . . . good . . . people. As he said . . . *good* . . . there was in his voice so radiant a freshness, so yearning a transfiguration of all created things—how *chromatic* it was!—that the audience rose from their seats and sang, like Sieglinde: *Thou art the Spring!* No, they didn't actually, insensate things, but they wanted to: you could look at them and see that they were Changed.

Gertrude said softly, "Let's go in and wring the dew out of our stockings; mine are soaked." I thought, "Good old Gertrude"; but as soon as I realized what I was thinking, I stopped.

11.

AT OUR nation's capital, hidden away by legislators, there is a colossal statue of George Washington—seated, antique, naked to the waist; he looks as awful as Ingres' Zeus, but good. I sometimes thought that this statue, rather than the Smith shrike-tree, should have been put at the center of Benton as a representation of President Robbins Being the Spirit of Benton. But the shrike-tree was good too.

People really did think of the President in a costume somewhat similar to the statue's: *Time* and *Life* and *News-Week,* just after his appointment, had all carried pictures of him taken in the days when he had not yet thought of becoming an educator, but was only a diver at the Olympic Games. People would say, "Did you see where they appointed this diver a college-president?"—plenty of presidents had been football-players, but a diver was something new. (The picture in *Life* showed him standing between Johnny Weismuller and Eleanor Holm; and I heard a little boy say about it, in the most disgusted voice I've ever heard: "They've made *Tarzan* the president of an old girls' college!") When the President went on money-raising tours among his alumnae and his students' parents and grandparents and guardians—

Poor man! he spent half his time on these, and half making speeches, and half writing articles for magazines and appearing on radio forums and testifying before Congressional committees that it would be unwise, in time of war, to draft the girls of Benton into the Women's Army Auxiliary Corps, and half . . . as you see, he had learned the secret of busy and successful men: that there are thirty-six hours in every day, if you only know where to look for them. If he had known where to find one more, an hour for himself, a kind of Children's Hour for the boy Dwight Robbins, who can say what might have become of him? But he had never known.

His appeals for funds were nowhere more successful than in Hollywood. Several Benton alumnae were stars, socially-conscious script-writers, wives or daughters of producers. President Robbins appealed to them sitting in somewhat Hawaiian swimming-shorts at the grassy verge of swimming-pools: as he looked thoughtfully into the thoughtless water he seemed to the alumnae some boyish star who, playing Tom Sawyer, fancies for the moment that he is Narcissus. Not to have given him what he asked, they felt, would have been to mine the bridge that bears the train that carries the supply of this year's Norman Rockwell Boy Scout Calendars. They felt this; it seems far-fetched to me.

He was, in sober truth, in awful truth, a dedicated man (the really damned not only like Hell, they feel loyal to it); and if his dedication was to the things of this world, to this world, should we scorn him for it any more than we scorn some holy *faquir*, some yellow-robed disciple sitting cross-legged among those whom the Buddha addressed as *Bhikkus?* If it were not for men like President Robbins, how could this world go on? *Everything* would be different.

And yet one must admit that such men are in long supply.

12.

THE PRESIDENT'S conversation was, as Gertrude said, a lecture interrupted by silences of pure appeal. (Why did he say he wanted to *go back* to teaching?) He wanted you to like him, he wanted everybody to like him—it was part of being a president; but talking all the time was too. When he and Gertrude met they did not, shouting *A Roland! An Oliver!* set out to see which could talk the whole time: each knew what his opponent was. One would talk for five or ten minutes while the other, all smiles and *rapport* and inattention, stared out the window or, better still, at a wonderful reflection which each of us can sometimes see in the windowpane; then they would trade parts.

Gertrude said, in private to the world, very ingenious things about President Robbins; if you have ever heard any you will think me another Parson Weems. Gertrude not only told big lies like Hitler's, she also told a kind of lie that she had learned, I think, from Chekhov—a kind of this-must-be-true-for-who-in-God's-name-could-have-made-it-up lie. Anybody could have told how President Robbins' first wife turned the gas on herself and her babies after he had gone off to Bermuda with another man, though not just anybody could have made up that suicide note; but how many of our novelists could have matched Gertrude's account of how President Robbins was expelled from the nudist camp? How her eyes rolled when she had him say, "Believe me, *I* have nothing to hide," when really. . . . Surely you have heard that story; Gertrude has told it five hundred times. Once, after it, I heard someone say quietly to a friend: "She may be a mediocre novelist, but you've got to admit that she's a wonderful liar." But this was unfair to her; her novels, too, were wonderful lies.

One of Abraham Lincoln's stories ends with the words: *Go it, old woman! Go it, bear!* I suppose one should have felt so about Gertrude and the President; yet, sometimes, my mortal standards broke down—the two were such fun to watch that I blessed them unawares.

But once President Robbins was no fun at all. He was talking to me in his office—telling me about Donne's being more popular this century, or about the cartoons in the last *New Yorker,* or about how much better girls from Benton do at graduate school than girls from Vassar—and after a moment he smiled at something he said, and I smiled back, relishing as I always did the little crinkles in the skin around his eyes. But when he stopped smiling the crinkles did not go: they were wrinkles, now.

Time had come not with a scythe and an hour-glass but with an engraver's needle, and had worked hard, many hours in many years, on that cobwebby frost-tracing radiating from President Robbins' boyish eyes. . . . —But why hadn't the President seized him, offered him a rank and a salary, one course in freshman history and one in the

Cultural Interrelationships of Asia and the West, sat him down in the President's office while they educated each other, smiled at him, put him on committees, on committees, on committees? I said to the President, silently, in wordless anguish—for he was a joke, a joke, it wasn't fair to have anything happen to *him:* "Oh, don't get old! Oh, please don't *you* get old!"

But just then Eve Trembath, the President of the Student Body—a fine girl, one of the President's best friends at Benton—came in to ask him something, and instead of calling him *Dwight* she called him *Sir;* and President Robbins, looking at her absently, did not correct her.

13.

THE ROBBINS had two Afghans, Yang and Yin. They were enormous Afghans, very pretty and very bad—Yang was more than very bad, he was awful. They chased cars and bit at their tires, they ran by girls and jumped up and snapped at their legs and tore their shorts, they chased poultry and howled all night, they lay down in the middle of the tennis court and chewed tennis balls, and Yang swam in the swimming pool; once he was in it he couldn't get out of it by himself, but stood there trembling and silent—if he hadn't shown up before the Robbins went to bed the President would say, "O, God, he's in the swimming pool!" They would call the night watchman or set out for the swimming pool. . . . There he was.

Yang stood up to his neck in the shallow part of the pool, looking yearningly out over its tiled walls, shivering, doggedly silent.

"Why does he like to get in the swimming pool,

Dwight?" said Derek. "Why doesn't he bark, Dwight?"

The President answered, as he strode toward Yang: "They're all overbred. You can see their portraits in Egyptian tombs."

Derek did not know what the first sentence meant; how were Afghans over bread? But the second sentence he understood too well: he *could* see that portrait, a terrible picture, of Yang and Yin standing in the tomb, up to their necks in something dark, in something that came higher, higher. . . . He thrust the picture from his mind: its white head emerged for an instant from the darkness, panted, was jerked down.

. . . But goodness, they were beautiful dogs!

II.

The Whittakers

AND

Gertrude

1. One night that winter Constance Morgan, President and Mrs. Robbins, Flo and Jerrold Whittaker, and my wife and I had dinner at Gertrude Johnson's.

The Robbins and the Whittakers were there because they were going to be in Gertrude's book about Benton. Gertrude was never polite to anything but material: when she patted someone on the head you could be sure that the head was about to appear, smoked, in her next novel. And she appreciated the advantages of Creation: "It's nice not to have to lie out at some water-hole with a flash-bulb," I heard her say once, "but just to be able to ask your eland home to dinner." The listening elands laughed and swallowed.

My wife and I were there because we were very old acquaintances—I would say *friends,* but Gertrude had no very old friends—of Gertrude's. And we were not only old acquaintances, we were New York acquaintances. She could remember meeting us at the City Center, the Museum of Modern Art; when she and Sidney said *back home on Bleecker Street,* we knew what that meant—we too had lived on Bleecker Street. Or if we hadn't, it was almost as if we had; Gertrude told my wife one day, in a moment of confidence, that she and Sidney kept forgetting that we weren't really New Yorkers. "We keep remembering," my wife answered.

"What did Gertrude say when you said that?" I asked. My wife said, "I forget. But she looked at me the way you'd look at a chessman if it made its own move."

Sidney was there because he was Gertrude's husband; or perhaps he had asked, "Gertrude, may I come?" as I had asked whether Constance might come. I asked just after I had said that she thought *These Mortals* Gertrude's best book. Other people thought *These Mortals* Gertrude's last book.

"She'd give a lot to come along with us," I admitted.

"Tell her I'll be glad to let her come," Gertrude said in a handsome voice. "I never see any young girls. Except these students—and they never seem to *say* anything. I suppose, as a novelist, I ought to see more young girls."

I agreed with her. I generally agreed with Gertrude; the rest of the time I never seemed to *say* anything. Someone has said, about people: "Let us act as if they were real; who knows, perhaps they are." I never made this mistake with Gertrude. Men go thousands of miles to see the Grand Canyon: to look down into Gertrude I was willing to pay, and be silent.

Constance hadn't liked *These Mortals* or thought it much good, but as she had looked into its hard eyes she had turned pale and still, which was a tribute to Gertrude, in a way. "What is its title from?" she asked me. "It—it has that reminiscent, sententious, elevating sound titles have."

This sentence is impossible for anyone to say, so Constance said it with difficulty. After serving me her made dish, she blushed. I almost did—was this the way I sounded to *Constance?*

I didn't want her to sound like me, I wanted her to sound like Constance; I wanted her simply to be. But she was

growing up—no, not growing up, she was about to be ready
to grow up; and since she lived in a world where there were
people like Gertrude—though this may be unfair to people
—I got her invited to Gertrude's as she wished to be invited.

I answered Constance's question; I said, "It's Puck—
What fools these mortals be!"

I had known Constance since she was seven. If someone
had seen us together and had asked me about her, I'd have
answered, "Why, that's Constance." I don't know how I'd
have gone on: perhaps to say, "Constance Morgan—you
know, *my* Constance"; perhaps to explain that she was a
little girl, used to be a little girl, whom I had known for a
long time. But if the person had said, "But what *is* she?" I'd
have said that she was a pianist, and worked at Benton, but
I'd have felt like saying, "No, no, you don't understand: it's
Constance." There is always someone to whom your rela-
tions are indescribable; Constance was this someone.

So I repeated to myself, why I hardly knew: "What fools
these mortals be!"

My wife and I drove by for Constance. Before we got
her we were a youngish—we would have said—couple going out to dinner; after our first look we sighed, and saw
stretching before us a short, safe, uneventful pathway to the
grave. It was like having the moon get into our car, the new
moon: we looked at each other by her thoughtless light.

Gertrude's apartment-building looked like any other.
"It's not fair," I said. "Not even a plaque by the door in
commemoration. They do these things better in France."

Constance said, "What?"

"Don't you mind," said my wife. "He's just being a
writer for us. Writers want their sites marked."

We climbed the stairs and rang the bell; Sidney came to

the door. He peeped at Constance like a rabbit: her looks frightened him, so that he glanced back over his shoulder for reassurance. Gertrude got our coats into Sidney's arms, and us into the apartment, without noticing us or Sidney or the coats; and Sidney, reassured, hung up the coats.

We stood in a little lighted hall. Before us was a big room, dark enough to look bigger than it could have been—we stepped out into it uncertainly. There was a low bench or coffee-table, fairly close to me, that had on it a—I looked hard at it, because it seemed to be a model teepee or wigwam, an enormous one. Gertrude went over to it, felt at its base, and switched it on. Its lodge-poles were of black cast-iron; a merciless light fell from it, illuminating on a table across from it the first icosahedron I had seen since Solid Geometry. "Why, you have an icosahedron," I exclaimed; Gertrude went over to it, felt at its base, and switched it on. You could see everything, now.

Gertrude said that it was silly to have moved their furniture here just for—she supposed—six or seven months, but that it hadn't cost much, if you considered how much cheaper unfurnished apartments were. "Those furnished ones!" she said. "Anyway, I can't stand working in surroundings I can *see*. I've long ago stopped seeing these."

"It's nicer with your own things," Sidney said. We said we thought so too, and looked around us at the things. As I looked I appreciated—and not for the first time—what a gift for decoration Gertrude had: she and Sidney had gone into a bare apartment and after a few days had got it looking barer.

Some people have in their living room, encased in bronze, their child's first pair of shoes; the Bacons had had plated the first thing Sidney had ever been afraid of, a sweet potato. I had never seen a bronze sweet potato before, but I liked it: its ramifications were so alarming as almost to make it (what they said it was) sculpture.

Gertrude and Sidney had, instead of pictures, two reproductions from the Museum of Non-Objective Art, in frames or containers half of plastic, half of mirror. One was romantic, and showed a kidney being married to the issue of a sterile womb, amid trailing clouds of mustard—or Lewisite, I am not sure; the other was classical, and showed two lines on a plain—or plane, perhaps.

"Is that a Mondrian?" Constance asked politely.

Gertrude looked at her as if she had asked whether it was a Landseer. It was plain that Mondrian's day was past.

Sidney said, saving things: "No, but it *is* influenced by Mondrian, I think."

I did not want them saved. I said, "How can anything be? If it's influenced by Mondrian it's a Mondrian."

There was a silence. I looked around me.

Gertrude was sitting in a chair exactly like a sweatered cocktail sausage on skewers. Sidney sat on a felt hassock, and I was distributed, rather generally, over a broken plywood beaker, a giant one. How I wished that it had had skewers!—then I should have been nine inches from the floor, not three. A man with heart disease would have found climbing the staircase of the Eiffel Tower scarcely more dangerous than getting up from Gertrude's plywood chair; I heard, or fancied that I heard, a ghost muttering to his fellows: "It was Gertrude. She did it with a chair."

Constance and my wife had come off better: they sat on a great something that lay there

> *As a huge stone is sometimes seen to lie*
> *Couched on the bald top of an eminence;*

39

> *Wonder to all who do the same espy,*
> *By what means it could thither come, and whence;*
> *So that it seems a thing endued with sense:*
> *Like a sea-beast crawled forth, that on a shelf*
> *Of rock or sand reposeth, there to sun itself.*

Someone had dyed it raspberry; my own chair was a vibrant, mutant lime; Gertrude's, and Sidney's hassock, were ochre. And these colors were, as Marxists say, "no accident," they were a scheme. I grew fonder and fonder of the classical picture—whose lines were, after all, only black; whose plane was, after all, only grey. If it had had a patch of white I would have proposed to it.

2.

BY NOW President and Mrs. Robbins (Dr. Robbins, really; she had her Ph.D.) had come; so had Flo and Jerrold. Jerrold Whittaker was almost famous, and the President had had to pay for him a sociologist's ransom. But it was worth it: he was the man who had said of President Robbins' first paper, years and years ago, "That young man writes like —like Mannheim." He himself wrote like—but sociologists, when they speak of each other's styles, make one feel tone-deaf as Gertrude; one has to suppress a child's wondering, "How can you *tell?*"

We were given drinks, and drank them, and talked while we drank them. But *talked*, here, is a euphemism: we had that conversation about how you make a Martini. The people in Hell, Dr. Rosenbaum had told me once, say nothing but *What?* Americans in Hell tell each other how to make Martinis.

We got up and trailed from the room, trailed back into the room: once for, once with, our dinners. As she served us Gertrude had—sporadically, and not paying much attention to them—the manners of a Southern hostess: by this I mean that she made you refuse anything three times. But her cooking was neither a Southern cook's, nor a Northern cook's, nor a cook's: it was the cooking of a child.

There was very little of Gertrude's dinner, but what there was was awful: it was a dinner you would not have invited a dog to. You felt with naive resentment: "You'd think if she'd wanted to have people to dinner she'd have cooked them more than *this*"; ah, but she hadn't wanted to, not really. She felt, somewhere in the depths of her Lucy Stone-ish heart, that cooking is a man's job; and, soon, so did you. After her dinners guests had often wanted to pay Gertrude the simple tribute of a sampler, one bearing in chain-stitch or lock-step the words *Kinder, Kirche, Küche*.

While we ate we talked. People say that conversation is a lost art: how often I have wished it were!

Gertrude felt that the rhythms of academic conversation have been neglected by novelists; that whatever you say against novelists, you have to give them credit for *that*. Professors and their wives, like almost everybody else, have *a general conversation:* they talk about their business, their common acquaintances, politics, the weather; they tell you the thing that amused them most in last night's newspaper, last week's magazine. And, often, someone on the edge of the conversation, saying something else to someone else, has not heard; what she has not heard is repeated to her, things or people in it are identified for her: a general conversation is something that can go on indefinitely and still wind up back of where it started—it is, as Gertrude said, the only vacuum that reproduces its kind backwards. Gertrude didn't want conversation, she wanted an audience.

Benton people were not much fun for Gertrude to talk at, sometimes. Nothing spoils malice like explanation. She had whispered to her husband one night, during a party full of footnotes: "If I have to tell these fools who George Barker is *just one more time. . . .*" At home on Bleecker Street the delighting ear outstripped the wicked tongue, but here, here! She and Sidney left. How good it was to be home with Sidney, who understood and appreciated and asked for every last story. (When Sidney died they would read upon his heart, "Tell them your story about——, Gertrude.") But these people! She was sitting on the edge of the bed, undressing. Flinging down her garter-belt, she stood up and said to her husband, in a consummation of despair: "These people don't know Paul Goodman from Charles Henri Ford!"

The conversation during Gertrude's own dinner was worse than usual, since Gertrude felt that she had to be—and after that dreary cooking, enjoyed being—a real hostess. If Lazarus, the grave-clothes swinging from his limbs, had cried to Gertrude that he had come to tell her all, she would have answered: "Mrs. Robbins, you *still* haven't had one of my rolls. Go on, Lazarus, we're listening."

All of Gertrude's guests greeted with delight the imposing dessert, a cake like a baroque altar, a cake bought at a nice bakery. It was good to eat something that had felt a cook's transfiguring hands. Besides, we were hungry; we ate every bite of our helpings, and would willingly have said, like soldiers: *Any seconds?* We looked at the platter on which that lovely dessert had towered. The platter was empty now; and we too were empty.

3.

WHEN THE dishes had been shut away in the kitchen Gertrude sighed, as a horse sighs when you take its saddle off. She felt: "Now, they're fed!" She looked around at her guests, little islands in a sea of unwaxed floor (a tall chromium-and-Patapar floor lamp rose from one group like a robot palm) and shook her head in wonder at herself and life. One scrap of childhood remained to her, the feeling that everything is absurd. That she could have been so foolish as to ask these people here, that they could have been so foolish as to come, seemed to her impossible. Then she remembered why she had asked them, and went over to the President, her eyes dutifully shining.

At first President Robbins talked a little stiffly and warily, but then he warmed to himself. He liked to say: "The secret of good conversation is to talk to a man about what *he's* interested in." This was his Field Theory of Conversation. He always found out what your field was (if you hadn't had one I don't know what he would have done; but this had never happened) and then talked to you about it. After a while he had told you what he thought about it, and he would have liked to hear what you thought about it, if there had been time. He did this with everyone: when he met a school-child, he told him what he thought about lessons; when he met a topologist, he told him what he thought about topology, or related fields. Conversation is expression, not communication, he knew; he listened only for endowments. He talked to Gertrude about novels.

Normally she would have let a sentence or two fall on him, looked out over his squashed shape, and passed on; but now she was Collecting for the Book. She nodded; nodded; nodded again and again; nodded until she could hardly remember whether she was agreeing or falling asleep. Now and then she would say *Yes* or *Yes?*; once when the President said something unusually absurd, she gave him a startled, grateful smile—one could see her lips move as she memorized it.

A voice asked: "Does Derek like turtle-eggs?" The voice, the speaker came up suddenly in their midst: a raw, honest, earnest voice that jumped up on them like a big wet dog; a speaker who looked like a shooting-stick, like the woman children make from Tinker-Toy sets. It was Flo Whittaker.

Flo always made me think: It is necessary that good come, but woe to him by whom it cometh. She was as public-spirited as the sun. She thought of others night and day, and never about herself—but if she had thought about herself, she would have done something about that too. She worked for causes; she really *worked*. Yet she did not neglect her family for them; she didn't neglect anything for anything. She treated you, no matter who you were, exactly as she treated everyone else, so that after she had talked to you a while you almost doubted that you existed, except in some statistical sense. Except when she was indignant, she was cheerful; she was good, honest, and sincere; and she was so thin you could have recognized her skeleton. Sometimes it seemed to you that she was not a person, not a thing, but an idea, and a mistaken one at that. A badly mistaken one: she always said not the wrong but the wrongest, the most wrongest thing—language won't express it. Benton people knew fifty or sixty of her worst sentences, and recited them as if they had been the catalogue of ships in the *Iliad*. But nobody held them against her or felt, as people usually do, that she had meant them all the time—she lived before Original Sin, and could only make mistakes.

She was a sketch for a statue of Honesty putting its foot in its mouth, in Old Red Sandstone: even her skin was so raw and forthright that her daughter had said to her once, as she was putting on her bathing suit, "Mommy, you have dishpan hands all over"—it was one of Flo's favorite stories. She explained everything to you, was reasonable with you, as though you were a child; and you weren't vexed but—as you looked at her poor, thin, functional arms and legs, her safe, tame, certain face—you were troubled. After a few minutes with Gertrude you wanted to be good all day every day; after you had been with Flo you didn't know what to do—honesty and sincerity began to seem to you a dreadful thing, and you even said to yourself, like a Greek philosopher having a nervous breakdown: "Is it right to be good?"

When well-dressed women met Flo they looked at her as though they couldn't believe it. She looked as if she had waked up and found herself dressed—as if her clothes had come together by chance and involved her, an innocent onlooker, in the accident. If a dress had made her look better than she really did, she would have felt guilty; but she had never had such a dress.

Mostly she wore, in the daytime in the winter, a tweed skirt, a sweater-set, and a necklace. The skirt looked as if a horse had left her its second-best blanket; the sweaters looked as if an old buffalo, sitting by a fire of peat, had knitted them for her from its coat of the winter before; the necklace (sometimes it had earrings to match) was made of seeds or acorns or sea-shells that had been gathered and varnished by her children, if you were lucky—by her charities,

if you were unlucky. These necklaces were worse than con-
versation-pieces, they were collection-boxes; admiring one
was as good as signing a check. As my wife said, "It was a
black day when Quakers first made jewelry." (Flo was not
a Friend, but a friend of Friends.)

Flo wore, in the daytime in the summer, faded blue denim
pedal-pushers, a faded blue denim halter, and a pot hat, a
round white hat like a little girl's, that she bought each
spring at Peck and Peck. She wore these except on the
beach: there she wore flowered cretonne (or chintz) dressmaker bathing suits that would have fallen off her if she had
not borrowed, to hold them up, some thumbtacks from her
next-door-neighbors—one felt this. She looked in them,
always, as if she were leading six or seven little children up
a sand dune. She was, surely, the least sexual of beings; when
cabbages are embarrassed about the facts of life, they tell
their little cabbages that they found them under Mrs. Whittaker.

At night, winter or summer, she wore dirndls and, above
them, raw sultry peasant things that looked as if an em-
broiderer of little girls' frocks had made a blouse for Mata
Hari. From the enormous opening at the top of one of these
her little neck looked out like a fawn; her wan hair fell
about her ears in helpless locks; from her nice good scare-
crow's face (that looked not literally, but figuratively,
cross-eyed) she stared candidly into your face, blinked, and
swallowed.

She had to repeat her question about the turtle-eggs. The
President replied stiffly—he hated to be interrupted, and it
seemed to him that he was always being interrupted—"He's
never eaten any." Then he said, his face lighting up: "I've

read that they're quite good, though, fresh. I was reading just the other day—where was it I was reading—"

"In the *Swiss Family Robinson*, I'll bet," Gertrude broke in. "There's a place where—"

"Not to *eat!*" Flo cried, laughing. "To *collect!* John has I don't know how many. And seventeen grown ones. In a pile in the back yard. They're asleep for the winter. If Derek would like one I'm *sure* John would—but I suppose Derek isn't old enough to take an interest in such things, yet."

The President said, "Derek is—"

Flo said swiftly: "But John *was* interested in them at Derek's age. We couldn't let him have snakes then, though. (He catches them, you know.) He has four now. Two are rattlers. One has seven rattles. *They're* all asleep now, too."

"Seven," thought Gertrude dreamily. "Seven books." She realized that she wasn't paying attention. She would have made the perfect naturalistic novelist, so far as memory is concerned—and that is very far—except that she got bored and wouldn't listen, and then had to make things up; the novelist's greatest temptation, Gertrude felt, is to create.

Flo was continuing her conversation about Derek. "He was a biter, wasn't he?" she asked.

"A biter?" the President said helplessly.

"Didn't he bite? Oh no, of *course* not; how foolish of me! *He* growled." Then she said to Gertrude, in an informative voice: "He didn't talk until he was almost two. For a while they thought he—"

But here she stopped. She stopped all over, like a locomotive. Then she said to the President, gently: "Biters is what we mothers used to call babies when they bit. I remember

47

my mother saying I was a biter." She remembered this for a moment, with a tender smile. Then she said, frankly: "How *is* Derek?"

The President said, "Derek's fine."

"I'm *so* glad," Flo said. "I've always liked Derek."

Gertrude was looking at Flo narrowly, like a hydrogen bomb staring at an Act of God. "Have you ever read *Le Misanthrope?*" she asked Flo.

"I don't *think* so. No, I'm almost sure I haven't."

"It's a play by Molière about—"

"Oh, *that* one! Of course I've read it," said Flo. "I read it in fourth year French."

"Sometimes you—sometimes one of the characters reminds me of you. Do you remember a character named Alceste?"

"Oh, *no*," said Flo. "I just read it in fourth year French."

"Read what in French?" asked Dr. Whittaker, who had come over to the group. He stood looking down on them like a crane—a scrap of the mist through which he had flapped to the party still blurred his glasses, so that he took them off and polished them on the sleeve of his coat. Without them he could see almost nothing; and yet somehow this didn't seem to change him, to make any difference at all to him.

They explained to him about *Le Misanthrope*. (Dr. Whittaker spent his life either explaining things or having them explained to him.) He listened in earnest good-humor; this was a party, he wished to laugh whenever he should. The curve that his arm described, from his shoulder to his Martini, seemed to have been taken from some graph, or table, in a study called *Vector-Diagrams of Good-Fellowship.*

After hesitating for a moment, he replied. He always hesitated before he spoke, like a child who has to translate everything from the vernacular into English; but with him, of course, it was the other way around. He was every inch a sociologist.

He said in a deprecating voice: "Most of my own reading in French has been in scientific French, I am sorry to say. But for a scientist to be *only* a scientist, I have always felt, is—is worse than a crime, it is a blunder." A charming happy smile lit his gentle grey face; as he would have said, his quotation was quite *à propos*. "You will agree with me, I know," he said to the President.

"I do, I do indeed," the President answered. Talking to Dr. Whittaker was like living abroad: your English changed.

"To have read a certain proportion of Molière's works is indispensable to a valid understanding of the cultural background of the French," Dr. Whittaker said. He always talked like this. He spoke reasonably even to pets. He talked the way a windmill would talk, the way a sentence would talk—as he spoke, English seemed to have been dead for many centuries, and its bones to have set up a safe, staid, sleepy system of their own, in respectable secession from existence.

He went on: "I *have* read *Le Misanthrope*, I am happy to say. It is a work of true sociological insight." His eyes flashed, and then softened as he said: "Unhappy Alceste! Those sacrifices, necessary but onerous, which the social organism has always exacted, must always exact, from its individual cells, those—if I may coin a phrase—intra-social subtractions, are indeed, in *Le Misanthrope*—" but here he seemed very human and attractive, for he lost his way in his sentence. The sentence was bewildered: it had begun so promisingly, and now had to finish with a lame *depicted by the pen of a master*. In the classroom, where Dr. Whittaker was almost as much at home as in his study, this would not have happened; there each sentence lived its appointed term, died mourned by its people, and was succeeded by a legitimate heir. His voice—he had raised it to the elevation of his sentence—came across the room to me quite clearly, and I remembered the pretty girl who had said to me, "It's not just classes, it's Dr. Whittaker! I can stay awake in my *other* classes."

After a little more about *Le Misanthrope* ("I have read that the *aesthetic* effect of a work of literature is lost in translation; now in your experience has this been the case?") Dr. Whittaker went on to Balzac. Sociologists love Balzac—sociologists of the old school, that is; and if Dr. Whittaker's school had been any older he would have been dead. He had once been on a camping trip or a field trip—I forget which, but the camping trip seems more likely—with Lévy-Brühl, and would tell bewildered comparative psychologists anecdotes (third-hand, I hope) about Charcot and Janet. He was a sort of last link between Sociology, Anthropology, and Psychology, and sociologists and anthropologists and psychologists looked at him with respectful impatience, knowing that they would be happier apart. He was much older than his wife; but this didn't matter, he had been even as a child, and had played with his tops and marbles with the same gentle, sober, trusting smile with which he now raised succulents, collected rocks: Flo arranged the best ones for him in a shadow-box.

His audience had been reduced to a joyous Gertrude, who was listening like—like Sidney; but suddenly the thought pierced her: "I can't *use* him, he's no good to me at all! My readers would never swallow that gorgeous creature."

At a little distance Flo was saying to the President—but in a low voice, tactfully: "I'm surprised to see *you* here. I heard you and she—" here she nodded at Gertrude—"had had a big fight."

The President said, "Oh no, it was only a friendly discussion." He started to say this, and then it was more than he could do: he compromised with, "It was only a heated discussion." He went on to say, with a smile at his homely metaphor, that Gertrude's bark was worse than her bite. This was foolish—Gertrude's bark *was* her bite; and many a bite has lain awake all night longing to be Gertrude's bark.

My wife and I were talking to Sidney; in the farthest corner of all, Mrs. Robbins was telling Constance about Sussex. "Are *all* the English like Mrs. Robbins?" Constance asked my wife later that evening.

"No, no, of course not," said my wife soothingly. "If they had been, we'd have all died out long ago."

She reminded Constance that Mrs. Robbins wasn't an Englishwoman at all, but a South African. "All that sunlight," she said. "And cosmic rays—I'm sure there're more cosmic rays down there. Mrs. Robbins is a *mutation*."

My wife was fairly long-suffering about Mrs. Robbins, but she did make a point of asking her, whenever they met, something about South Africa. As the years went on Mrs. Robbins replied with increasing, with engaging vagueness, as a woman will say about the 'Twenties: "But my goodness, I was a baby then!" I always felt that if it hadn't been for her Achilles leg, that unlucky South Africa, Mrs. Robbins would have conquered more territory than

Genghis Khan, and would have wound up being called the Mother of Gods and Men.

4.

THE PRESIDENT, by now, was talking to Flo about furniture. Her fields were politics and furniture, and he and Flo knew each other's politics by heart.

I too used to talk to Flo about furniture—listen to her, that is: what did I know about furniture? But she was so much better, when forced back upon blacksmiths and glassblowers, than she was on what the changes in the composition of the C.C.F. party in Alberta really *mean*, that I had developed a question that began: "Just the other day, in an antique shop. . . ." Then I would describe the queerest chair or table or plate or mug that I could make up on the spur of the moment; and no matter how queer it was—I grew confident with the years—there was always a real one like it that Flo could tell me about. It was almost like going to the zoo.

Going to the Whittakers' was almost like going to the zoo. Part of the house, of course, was merely functional: they had a bulletin board for the children, and pinned to it, like butterflies, their children's schedules, their doctor's telephone number, their senator's telephone number, the dates you could see the Perseids and the Leonids, and the first red leaf; the food they ate when they were well, the medicine they took when they were ill, the clothes they wore when they were dressed, the sheets they lay under when they were undressed, all had been recommended by Consumers' Union—if you had taken them for a trip on your new yacht, they would have told you how you could have got it at Sears Roebuck under a different brand name and saved four thousand dollars. But the rest of their house was *different*.

Jeremy Bentham's stuffed body would not have been ill at ease in their house. You went into a warm dark cozy morass or labyrinth or limbo of fire-dogs, dough-chests (full of old numbers of the *Journal of Social Psychology*), Delft pepper-mills, needle-point footstools, barometers, chess-tables, candle-molds, Holbeins (their motto was, *If it isn't a Holbein it isn't a picture*—and Dr. Whittaker himself looked like a Holbein of the aged Émile), quilts, counterpanes, comforters, throws, Afghans, stoles (that had got in among the others by mistake), hooked, knitted, quilted, tied, crocheted, and appliquéd rugs—my favorite was a Pennsylvania Dutch one with some sort of animal on it and underneath, in German, *Don't Tread on Me*. The sampler had been done by an indentured servant of eleven. And there was weeping willow china, bone and luster and Belleek and beaded and bumped and brown-landscaped china, glass enough for a history of glass; the chair-legs (all the chairs were either *very* big, *very* little, or *very* oddly shaped) wore ruffled pantaloons, the doorknocker looked like a brass Toby jug, and the weathervane was a reproduction of a Shaker weathervane that Jay Gould, or Mike Fink, or somebody like that had killed himself at not getting for his collection of American primitives; the ashtrays had French proverbs on them; and there were mats woven by poor blind people, brooms (or carvings of foxes) that Southern Highlanders had made at a school when they weren't learning to read and write—

Believe me, after the Whittakers', other houses looked pale.

Dr. Rosenbaum particularly loved their house; he had said to me after his first visit, almost stammering in his delight: "Idt iss like Troy. Idt iss like a barrow, a—a mitten."

"A mitten?" I asked, puzzled.

"No, no, I misbronounce. *D, d*—a *middten*, a *kidt*chen *middten*."

At first I hadn't understood why the Whittakers' house was the way it was, but then I learned that Flo was not only the daughter of an English professor but also had been engaged for several years to an English professor. (He had gone to England on research, and never come back.) Flo said to me one year, when I had done something for a cause of hers: "Tell me, would you have any use for—now promise me to be frank; remember, I *don't* want you to feel you have to take them just because I've offered to give them to you, if you don't really *want* them—remember now, you've promised; *would* you have any use for some bound volumes of the *PMLA?*" The *Publications of the Modern Language Association* is referred to by its initials or not at all.

I said, "*I?*"

"They're complete up to 1938."

I said that I thought Miss Batterson would like them even better than I would. Miss Batterson was still Benton's teacher of creative writing in those days, and Flo was her best friend among the faculty wives. She forgave Flo her causes for her china; but if Flo had made popovers of her husband and children Miss Batterson would only have said comfortably, "In my day, of course, no lady would have done that"—she never judged anyone born after 1905.

Flo said, "How foolish, how *foolish* of me! I suppose I must have taken it for granted, deep down in my subconscious, that Camille already had them." She was right.

The Whittakers were not like their house, and lived in it rather as modern man lives among the Ruins of the Cultures of the Past. As a young wife Flo had wanted to have a pair of scissors in every room: she was well along on her second pair, now. But they made no difference to her: if Atropos had lost her scissors, Flo would have given her hers; Flo's real possessions were where rust couldn't corrupt or moths consume or anything do anything to them. If you had met her naked on a raft she would have said to you: "I suppose we'll just have to face the fact that we *are* going to have to get used to being together with no clothes on. I was saying to Jerrold just this morning—Jerrold is my husband, you know—I said to him, 'Sweetheart—' " And after you had been on the raft with her for two weeks and on the island with her for two years, sharing mussels, you would have known her no better than you knew her then; but then, how could you have known her better than you knew her then?

The other three Whittakers were not, like Flo, without atmosphere, bare well-meaning asteroids in a blue-black sky. Jerrold was almost courtly, like a wooden leg of the old school; Fern smelled, surely, of brimstone and sulphur; and John was like a saint—a saint of the future, perhaps.

He was no more trouble around the house than a Field Book of North American Reptiles. This is a heartless way to put it: he was a good and agreeable, if inhuman, boy. His sober, absorbed, and private face was as spare as his father's, as upright as his mother's. From the khaki shorts in which he roamed the forest, seeking snakes, his knees stuck with a kind of indomitable rectitude—they looked like a penny with Abraham Lincoln on both sides. In school John was so far ahead of his classmates that it took him a minute to remember which grade he was in, this year; during his study periods he made, with a crowquill pen, in India ink, zoological drawings of . . . but you can guess without my telling you what John made drawings of. The walls of his room were covered with these coiling visions, except where some fairy-tale character, or little boy sitting in the sun with a sand-pail, survived from earlier matriarchal cultures.

In my whole life I had known only two children who drew snakes, John and Derek Robbins; both were Benton children. Sometimes I wondered uneasily about this, and wanted to ask other parents at Benton whether their children drew snakes.

John found relaxation from his primary avocation—this is his father's phrase—in several hobbies: he played chess (by correspondence with a little Danish boy), collected stamps, diagrammed football plays, made hand-dipped chocolates—there was usually a rack of them drying in the refrigerator—and read science-fiction stories: not the kind in which a man rescues a girl from a big extraterrestrial being who is about to, to do Heaven knows what to her, but the kind in which you have described to you the civilization of organisms that utilize in their metabolic cycle, instead of oxygen, fluorine, methane, or ammonia. He said to his mother one morning: "I dreamed I was married to a girl with blue blood."

"We Americans don't believe in things like that any more, dearest," Flo answered in a worried voice; she was relieved when things explained themselves.

But he was a boy no one could worry about, really: as long as there were reptiles, he was all right; and if they had become extinct, he could have studied their fossils. Without his sister he would have been in Paradise. But Fern was, as people say, a Little Manager; Fern wanted, as people say, Her Own Way. (That was all she wanted, but it was enough: the Milky Way was small beside Fern's.) This was hard on John, just as it was hard on Dr. Whittaker, on Mrs. Whittaker, on the cocker spaniel, on the turtles in the back yard, even, who dreamed that Something Was Happening as Fern arranged them in a pile with a better shape to it. John spent half his time at home saying absently, paying as little attention to her as he could: "Mother, make Fern stop!" As this did no good, he would try to reason with her, saying pathetically: "How would you like it if I bothered you all the time?"

"Mother, tell Brother not to put his feet up on the bed! He's got them right up on the bed!" Fern replied. "MothER! MothER!" Her "MothER!" was a high, brutal, peculiarly penetrating sound, the noise a piglet possessed by demons would make to catch up short a backward sow. When my wife would come home from an afternoon at the Whittakers' she would sometimes say, sighing: "It's a shame Mrs. Robbins doesn't have Fern."

Fern was a thorn in the flesh to remind the Whittakers that they had flesh; but they weren't reminded. If Fern had been an imperialist or an international banker or something like that Flo could have understood her being so bad, but as it was it didn't make sense. I thought of saying to her: "Look at it this way, Flo—Fern is a proto-Fascist."

To the Whittakers Fern was a poltergeist, a fit, the chance at the bottom of the universe, and they slid their eyes across her as fast as they could. Everything, to Jerrold, was the illustration of a principle; Fern suggested to him no principle. I thought this very clever or *very* stupid of him. As for Flo—

As for Flo, Flo was a voter, an Informed Voter.

Once there was a man named Peter Bell; a primrose by the river's brim a yellow primrose was to him. If you had told Flo this she would have exclaimed, "What an attitude to take! We mustn't blame it for its *color*"; she would have explained that the spots on its petals were, after all, only the results of its environment—everyone knows what the waterfront is like; and she would have preserved an open mind about it while she determined the real facts of its case.

Was it a Common primrose? (Flo liked for primroses to be Common.) Was it a registered or unregistered primrose? an organized or unorganized primrose? Had it voted at the last election (been in the last war)? voted (been) on the right side? known what it was voting (being) for? That primrose, after a while, was so much trouble to her that if she'd been anybody but Flo she would have wished she'd never heard of it. Even Flo felt that something was wrong: after determining that her primrose was a random or representative primrose, she from then on, till the day she died, dealt with primroses in lots of a hundred thousand, and remained on macroscopic or molar terms with her universe— she oversaw it with systematic benevolence. She really *was* benevolent, and efficiently so: if I were a town, there is no one I should rather have by me in a disaster.

Fern was a black primrose by Brother's snakes, and Flo's methods were a little large-scale for dealing with such an anomaly. It didn't bother Flo: her daughter's faults were, after all, only private. Almost everything that happened to Flo and her family and friends was, after all, only private; and to her real life was public, what you voted at or gave for or read about in the *Nation*. Life seemed to Flo so *petty*, compared to real life. The trouble with women, people say, is that they take everything personally; Flo took nothing personally. If she had been told that Benton, *and* Jerrold, *and* John, *and* Fern, *and* the furniture had been burned to ashes by the head of the American Federation of Labor, who had then sown salt over the ashes, she would have sobbed, and sobbed, and said at last—she could do no other —"I think that we ought to hear *his* side of the case before we make up our minds."

This is absurd, of course; no one would say such a thing; but Flo did say such things. Saints are necessarily absurd— and Flo was a saint, of a poor kind; almost all saints are saints of a poor kind. She lacerated not simply the flesh but the heart, all the instincts and prejudices and fancies, base or bewitching, of the human animal. What a world it would be if everybody were like Flo! And yet—what a world it would be if nobody were like Flo. . . . When we cancel out everything that is divisible in this world, the sides of the equation balance; and without Flo that would have been impossible—she cancelled out half-a-dozen good Republicans.

She was a kind and a selfless and a ludicrous woman. I used to look at her with wonder and exasperation. (It is not every historical epoch that can support a Flo.) I felt for her, sometimes, a despairing tenderness: I wanted to say, "Don't you mind, Flo," to pat her poor bare bony shoulder. But it was a shoulder armored with something stronger than steel, more impervious than adamant: with righteousness; my hand fell away from what it could never touch.

She said to me once that she couldn't bear to read Old novels, novels written before the last fifty or sixty years. I asked, "Why is that?" She answered: "I get too upset at the status of women in those times. It was so *degrading*."

But why tell you any more about Flo? You know Flo. She did and believed—and Jerrold made for her, whenever he conscientiously could, clear abstract formulations of why she was right to do it, right to believe it; and the years went by, shifting the continents in their places, scaring the blind fish in the caves of Ocean, till the years themselves were changed—only Flo and Jerrold were not changed. He floated over her like a cirrus cloud, clear and far-off in the air of heaven; and she blew on below greyly and busily, bringing the crops rain, and little children balloons, and stirring the ballots as they fell into their boxes.

5.

OUTSIDE, THE long evening was drawing to its close. Owls caught mice, and fish, and rabbits, and brought them home to their babies; people turned off their television sets and went to bed; people woke, turned over, and went back to sleep; the girls of Benton, their hair in metal hair-curlers, their limbs in ski-pajamas or black nylon nightgowns, slept like dormice, their mouths open to the big soft stars. No longer educating each other, no longer doing anything at all, the teachers of Benton lay curled in their nice warm beds. For the hour they only were.

There was one enclave of hungry consciousness: Gertrude's apartment. Gertrude's guests had been going for hours—how many times some couple had got up to go!— and yet they had not gone. In a corner of the sofa Mrs. Robbins slept. Sleep, settling on her hard face, had begun to soften it; begun, and got nowhere, and dropped off to sleep. Constance and my wife, their shoes off, huddled at the other end of the sofa, feebly looking from face to face. The rigors of the evening had aged Constance and made a child of my wife: she looked as if she had been waked to see Santa Claus and couldn't remember who Santa Claus was. Sidney just sat there, looking contentedly at Gertrude: he knew who Santa Claus was. Gertrude listened—listened As A Novelist. (Gertrude and Sidney, fortunately for them, didn't know that it was late; at home on Bleecker Street no one in the memory of living man had left a party this early.) And I— as Saint-Simon says, I was on my side of the table: I couldn't see how I looked.

We were talking about education for democracy. Flo and the President talked, mostly. Occasionally one heard, below their shriller tones, a grave sustained note, the sound of the cello: it was Jerrold. He did not seem to be sleepy; he had never been sleepy, I think; but sometimes he slept, because he needed to—was, after all, supposed to. *First*, he would say, touching his first finger; *second*, touching his middle finger; *third*, touching his ring finger. . . . The day before, at lunch, I had heard him telling Dr. Willen about the dream he had had that night. He began: "I dreamed that the Winter number of the *Journal of Sociometric Studies* had come early, and it was all tables. . . ."

Said President Robbins: "What I always say is, the privately endowed college is a two-way street." He went on to say that something—I missed the word—was a commitment, and it was a commitment we must implement. My sinuses ached as if they had never slept, but I could not think of them for thinking of the grains of sand under my eyelids, which—if I could take them out and put them into an hourglass, and turn it over when the eggs were done, and take the eggs, and the sand, and the hourglass off before they—

I pulled myself back into being. Flo was saying: "Take the average fifth-grade child today—he may not spell as well as he did yesterday, but he's a *citizen*." I thought, *Why be?* and didn't pull any longer.

And yet after a little, a little more, the evening was over; this time, after we had said goodbye, we went. Outside, the world was dark and cold and silent; in fifteen minutes Constance and my wife and I were eating hamburgers and coffee and hot mince pie at an all-night restaurant in Mount Pleasant.

"Isn't it *good!*" said Constance. "I was never so hungry in my life. I kept looking at that candy-box—you know, the one on the shelf over the bookshelves—" we nodded—"and I'd say to myself, If it's full that's four, no, four and a half for every one of us; even if it's only half full that's two; even if it's only a fourth full—but that would depress me, I couldn't *bear* to think it was only a fourth full. I'd keep remembering the last box of candy I bought at Candyland and wishing I'd got more chews."

I said, "More what?"

My wife said, "More chews." Constance said, "Could I have another piece of pie?"

. . . When the guests had gone, Gertrude went numbly to her bed, hardly able to take her clothes off; Sidney turned out the lights in the living room. He said to her as he climbed into bed, smelling of toothpaste, warm and cozy in his cotton flannel pajamas: "It was a nice party, Gertrude, I thought. Wasn't the dessert good!"

Gertrude did not understand what he said, she was so tired. But the sound of his voice stirred in her a sort of feeble consciousness, and she said despairingly: "Aren't they *dull*, Sidney?" In another minute she was fast asleep.

6.

ALL THE days of that winter Gertrude Collected for the Book. She had never had a subject that pleased her as Benton pleased her. It seemed to her absurd beyond the dreams of avarice; she would say to Sidney, in wondering terror: "Wouldn't it have been *awful* if I hadn't accepted? To think I thought it was only a job!" Sidney would answer, in wondering terror: "Awful."

Sometimes Benton irritated her, of course. She phrased her irritation well, I thought: "When I first got here I said to myself, *How well all the animals get on together!* But then I saw they were vegetables." Benton could not help seeming to her a bog of virtuous and complacent dullness. "My heavens," she exclaimed to Sidney, "more happens at home on Bleecker Street in a week than happens here in— than ever *will* happen here." At Benton there were hardly even scandals. (At home on Bleecker Street there were hardly even scandals either, but for a different reason.) Occasionally one of the professors of Benton would fall in love with one of the students of Benton, but this happened distressingly seldom—that winter it didn't happen at all. Gertrude waited, as an astronomer waits for a good nova; but it was no use, she had to make up her own. And Benton was not only loveless, it was plotless; there too she had to make up her own. Life at Benton was a routine affair—and if you had told life that, it would have replied indifferently, "It's life, isn't it?"

But Gertrude did what she could with what she had; it

was surprising, really, how much she could do with it. She was a thorough Freudian (though one of the blaming kind): she knew without half trying the secret of every alcove, and could hardly look at a baby without saying to the mother something about polymorphous perversity. She would say about Benton girls, all alone with Benton girls: "What a pity it is that just at the most impressionable age, at the very edge of heterosexuality, just when their precarious new patterns of behavior need to be stamped in most firmly—" you can imagine without difficulty how Gertrude went on. This was an injustice to the girls of Benton, who did everything but attend classes at Harvard, Princeton, and half a dozen other schools for men.

Gertrude's remarks were resented. Benton people preferred the Freudianism of those Freudians who believe in anything except what Freud did. And it was social maladjustments that most of them were interested in, not sexual: sex would settle itself in the World of the Future. . . .

But usually Gertrude made them, made everybody laugh. She was a continually witty and occasionally humorous woman. She loved to make people laugh, just as she loved to shock them. Both gave her a sense of animation and assurance: she was sure, then, that— What was it she was sure of then? Of something; she was not sure what. But her sense of assurance was real.

She was, as people always said, a *wonderful* story teller. She could even remember whether she had told you a story before—would even, sometimes, not tell it to you again. *Mots* she scorned to repeat; to someone who asked, after she had said something especially good: "Did you think of that *right now?*" she replied contemptuously, "If I don't think of it *right now* I don't say it."

It was true. And it was certainly not because she couldn't remember it. What a memory Gertrude had! I have heard her narrate for an hour and a half a Christmas dinner that she had had six years ago at the home of her publisher; if she did not reproduce each speech of the publisher, his wife, and their nasty little nine-year-old daughter, it was only because she suppressed some in order to place the speakers in a more unfavorable light. And how she looked as she remembered! or invented: there was a possessed and lying, a visible gaseous inspiration in those shifty protruding eyes, the eyes of a Pythoness—those poor, rolling, faded, baby-blue eyes. . . .

She was a mousy woman till she smiled: her teeth bared themselves, counted, and their lips went over them. Her smile was, I think, all that people have called it: it was like a skull, like a stone-marten scarf, like catatonia, like the smile of the damned at Bamberg; the slogan of the company that manufactured it *was* "As False as Cressida"; torn animals were removed at sunset from that smile. And yet it was only a nervous grimace, her one attempt to establish an ephemeral rapport with her world: "One would have said her body thought," and her body had kinder thoughts than she. That skull's grin was no *memento mori*, but Gertrude's admission that she too had to live.

Life had been hard for Gertrude from the beginning. She loved to tell Sidney stories about the South; he said to her after one of the most terrible, his eyes huge: "It's like *The House of the Dead!*" Gertrude started to say impatiently—how *naive* Sidney was!—that of course things weren't *really* like that, but she caught herself before she said it.

Every place was like every other to her; she saw the difference, but she didn't feel it. Wherever she went, she went in Gertrude.

Her voice had lost little of its original Southernness: she was what she was, and would be—she had made up her mind. *If I can stand myself, by God, you'd better,* she could have said; must often have said. When she felt good her voice was just one more Southern voice. But when she was dispirited and spoke, a strange thing happened to you. It seemed to you that the worst thing you had ever read about the South was a day-dream, a wish-fantasy, the doting euphemism of a senile mother, compared to what the South really was. The Southern past, the Southern present, the Southern future, concentrated into Gertrude's voice, became one of red clay pine-barrens, of chain gang camps, of housewives dressed in flour-sacks who stare all day dully down into dirty sinks; and the sinks (I do not know how her voice did this, but it did it) were not only rusting, they were rotting. Her voice was the voice of a small-town librarian pushing back from her forehead a strand of hair—a damp strand, that is—and going wearily at evening to a room with a bed, a chair, a bureau, wallpaper; it was the voice of hominy, of turnip-greens, of light-bread, of that dessert which men call ambrosia but which the gods call—oh, heaven knows what!

One unwilling auditor of Gertrude's, a well-known Southern writer, had said of her, biting his lip: "She's the worst Southerner since Jefferson Davis." If she had not been a woman—a lady, I mean—he would have challenged her to a duel. One felt that.

7.

BUT AFTER a while Benton seemed to Gertrude a little different from other places because Dr. Rosenbaum lived there.

Gertrude was tone-deaf. She disliked music so thoroughly that she did not even talk about it much. She had that worst virtue, omniscience, and would at the drop of a hat have contrasted for you the latent class-consciousness of Inigo Jones with that of Capability Brown; yet she was so ill-informed about music, relatively speaking, that she used to confuse Reger and Busoni, and had a half-mystical, half-subliminal conviction that one or the other was a twelve-tone composer, or a precursor of twelve-tone composition, or something like that. Her own favorite composer was that most laconic of musicians, Anton von Webern: forty-five seconds seemed to her an ideal time for a piece to last, and what if there were no tunes in it?—she had never heard a tune.

She could almost have sympathized with the Whittakers about Classical Music. Flo and Jerrold loved folk ballads. Their house was always ringing—twanging, rather—with Colonial songs, and ballads for Americans, and songs of labor unions, and some songs called Dust Bowl Ballads; they loved these Dust Bowl Ballads best of all. But they knew that they should like Classical Music, and they knew that many of their friends listened to it a good deal of the time; so they decided to listen themselves, and give it a fair trial. They started out by buying the *Nutcracker Suite;* for a few weeks after that they would play, every third or fourth night, the *Nutcracker Suite,* and listen to it silently; then they stopped. I asked them once how they had liked it. Flo said: "It was very nice." She paused, and then said quickly: "It was very nice but—but it wasn't like the Dust Bowl Ballads!"

To Gertrude it *was* like the Dust Bowl Ballads. She liked to define music, in her unaging, undifferentiating voice, as a "sonorous scheme"; she would go on to say that, emotionally speaking, there was no difference between the *Manzoni Requiem* and *Tales from the Vienna Woods*, and would finish, with a blank, fanatical, considering stare: "They're both *essentially* experiences in pure duration." (And truly, for her, they were.) This angered some people and impressed others; but when at one of her first parties at Benton she repeated this to its Composer in Residence, Gottfried Knosperl Rosenbaum, he burst into laughter, and then said to her in his confidential wheezing bass: "Dere iss no autobiography like Stravinsky's, eh, Mrs. Bacon?" He knew.

People had always seemed to Gertrude rather like the beasts in *Animal Farm:* all equally detestable, but some more equally detestable than others; but from then on Dr. Rosenbaum stood out among his kind. His eyes—or as Gertrude said, *those odious little pig eyes of his*—had a disconcerting matter-of-fact understanding. A correct answer is like an affectionate kiss, Goethe said; a correct answer, Gertrude would have said, is like a slap in the face. Dr. Rosenbaum pigeonholed Gertrude, made her feel somehow put in her place; and Gertrude knew that there was no place for *her* in all the universe.

He was the one thing at Benton that couldn't be dismissed with *of course*. Gertrude felt that nothing she said even shocked him. He behaved, pretended to behave, as if he had

68

heard it all before, and treated her with playful good-humor. At parties—at committee meetings, even—he would whistle to her the *Harmonious Blacksmith* or *Humoresque*, and then murmur like a river full of stones: "*Schön, schön!* A posdthumous fragmendt of Webern's, Mrs. Bacon." Gertrude *knew* that this could not be so: it was too long. . . . She replied once, with wonderful intensity: "You and Paderewski's parrot!"

"*Vot* parrot?"

"That parrot that sat on his foot when he practiced—that parrot that kept saying, *Ach Gott, wunderschön!*"

Dr. Rosenbaum chuckled delightedly, and said with a look of deep respect, "You are mosdt vell-readt in music for a layvoman"; and his little eyes twinkled at her. . . . Gertrude was brave as a wolverine, but sometimes, in that unequal struggle, she despaired; when she would meet Dr. Rosenbaum lumbering to the tennis courts, wrapped in a cable-stitch sweater the size of an ordinary overcoat, accompanied by three devoted music students in cut-off jeans and men's pink Oxford shirts, all four singing happily *Ich armer Tamboursg'sell*—when she saw this she would turn aside, or stare rigidly into the hedge, or shut her eyes, unwilling to tolerate the sight. She wanted to—to unravel his sweater, to make the girls' jeans long and new again, to reveal that the song they were singing had really been written by Sir Edward Elgar. She was even sorry that Dr. Rosenbaum was a Jew (he had got his fair hair and the name *Gottfried Knosperl* from his mother, a braided Austrian type, all *himmelblau und zuckerl-rosa*), since this made it impossible for her to say what she felt was somehow really true: that he was a Nazi, *the* Nazi. She said, instead, that until she had met Dr. Rosenbaum she had never begun to appreciate the full potentialities of the anal-sadistic type; translated for the Germanless, in a tone of contemptuous forbearance, the name of this God-Pacified Bud of the Rose-Tree; said, in a wonderfully considering voice, that there was something extraordinarily *dated* about his type of music, wasn't there?—all that decadent, sensual (once she said by mistake, *sexual*) Viennese chromaticism. It was no wonder that his music wasn't better known. And she liked best of all to say—her eyes narrowing a little, distending a little—that Dr. Rosenbaum and Wagner had *a great deal in common*. Her tone indicated that they had had in common, at the least, a suicide-pact at Mayerling. Later on, when Gertrude knew more about Dr. Rosenbaum, she thought of better things to say—things so hair-raisingly better that she felt real humiliation, real remorse, at having started out with such pap.

Gertrude was almost like Hugo Münsterburg, who never in his whole life had a dream: she had had two. But one night she found herself in darkness, a queer greyed darkness that stretched off without end, or ended an inch from the hand that was raised to ward it off—she could not tell. The grey silvered; she was walking on a lonely shore. Sand sucked at her bare feet, she went on patiently. Finally it seemed to her that she could not go on. She looked out at the sea, and there was nothing on the sea; she looked for a long time, and there was still nothing; then the sea mounded a little, and she saw emerging from it, beyond slow phosphorescent breakers, a steely side. The steel was parted into a kind of door: from it there pushed out a round rubber boat; and in this—she watched for a long time as it slowly came nearer, and the tiny heaving blurred blob inside it turned into a man—and in this, his little eyes shining with victory, his breasts huge as a manatee's, sat Spy Rosenbaum. Gertrude felt a surge of such elation, of such justified and righteous joy, that she jerked all over, and awoke bolt up-right in her bed.

The world around her was different from her dream. Bands of moonlight from the Venetian blinds lay on the bedspread as innocently as if they had been the colors of children's blocks; her husband lay there like a log, his face innocent as the designs on children's blocks; only she sat there outside this tender and foolish universe, with its shared silly secret. . . .

She made a movement that pushed from her everything. How *could* she have been so foolish as to— She felt for humanity, at that moment, an emotion that it is hard to express exactly, but that was the equivalent of Caligula's *If they only had one neck!*

8.

BUT USUALLY, those weeks, she was happy. When the nomads' scant pasture is burnt up by drouth, and they come down on peaceful villages like the wolf on the fold, destroy-ing all that is in their path, they *do* enjoy it; and while the flaming roofs of Benton soared like red-winged blackbirds into the sky, and the grandmothers of Benton hid under haystacks, Gertrude looked around her joyously. She was pleased to see the effect she was having: part of it, of course, was only the general one that writers always have; but part of it, she could not help feeling, was a particular, almost a peculiar effect: the effect of Gertrude.

For those weeks she did not hold Benton's faults against it. It was, after all, only material, only Life; and Gertrude was almost as good as Henry James, whom she would quote, at complaining of poor muddling niggling silly mixed-up Life. She said, like him, that the life of man is poor, mean, nasty, brutish, and short without a writer to change it.

How Gertrude wrote! Some of her best days came early in the book, when she had hardly any notes—had *no* documentation, really. But for once she didn't care. She was so carried away that she made up, made up, went on making up; she could check up later and, if the reality didn't agree, so much the worse for it! But it was the reality she was grateful to: sometimes when she had just invented some peculiarly revolting and ludicrous and revealing situation for the President to find himself in, and he had responded to it as only he could, she would meet the real Dwight Robbins hurrying to a committee meeting, or out walking with a pipe and an Afghan, and she would look lovingly into his simple face. He was her President, and he worked.

But her tenderness was mixed with a kind of impersonal awe at the difference between what he was and what she had—what had been made of him. The President himself used to feel almost the same awe, when he thought of what he had been and what he had become. He approved of, gloried in, his every action; yet he wasn't vain, exactly, and he wasn't the hypocrite that Gertrude said he was. He had not evolved to the stage of moral development at which hypocrisy is possible. To him the action was right because it was his—he had never learned to judge his own act as though it were another's. If he had told you that he would do something he did it, unless there was some reason for him not to do it. He had the morals of a State; had, almost, the morals of an Army.

Morality, to him, was making a good impression on

everybody, selling himself (that accurately ambiguous phrase) to everybody. He praised himself to his face just as he would have praised you to yours, except that he did it more modestly, with a kind of demure grace. You almost expected him to speak of himself in the third person, as a child or a mother does; to say, "Let the President try now." President Robbins could remember singing in school, "To think of all my young delight/Fills the heart with memory bright." He felt this young delight, this inexhaustible interest, in everything that he did—and when he had done it, it filled his heart with memory bright. He felt about *his* school, *his* career, *his* life almost as Gertrude felt about The Book. She couldn't wait for it to be done, so that she could read it and cry out, "My God, what a genius I was when I wrote that book!" And why wait? She didn't.

Some days Gertrude was so brimful of the book that she could hardly bear to talk to the girls about their silly stories. These were happy days for the girls, who told her how they had got their inspiration, explained the subtle parts to her, talked about their philosophy of life: she listened unhearing, her eyes fixed before her like a sibyl's, and then flung praise over the girls with oblivious generosity. At the end of a conference she would scrawl down what notes she could (a word or two to the sentence—with her memory that was enough) and then, stretching enormously, rubbing her blurred eyes, her lips still working, would go to the door of her office to let in the next girl.

Home at last, she wrote as fast as she could, abbreviating, leaving out words, hardly gesturing at the letters—it was still too slow. Time itself was too short, and before she knew it Sidney was there, had been there; was there listening, there laughing, there looking at Gertrude with wide delighting eyes. Saturdays and Sundays and holidays were best—Sidney was home all day then. If days are heaven-sent, those days were heaven-sent; her muse brooded over Gertrude with calm eyes and snaky locks. As she read, Sidney listened; as she wrote, Sidney waited to listen; and Homer himself never had a better listener than Sidney. But sometimes on week-days with no conferences, no muse, no Sidney, the bare apartment looked bare even to Gertrude, and she would think, staring out of the window into the grey day: "I wish I made enough from my writing so Sidney wouldn't have to work."

Sidney went behind her like a shadow, useless and waiting to be used. If people could have remembered him they would have called him Mr. Johnson. He was—to identify him from the covers of her novels—"at present engaged in research on documentary films"; last year he had been "a member of a public opinion survey"; the year before—how could anybody remember what Sidney had done the year before? Some people live; some people exist; he subsisted.

And yet Sidney and his wife—"that beige snake," "that— that *soul*less girl," as her two last best friends had called her —were the same penniless homogeneous *écru*, the color of last year's seedcases, of lost haystacks: they always looked a little ghostly in their clothes, as if their clothes had bought them at a bad store. People were fond of wondering why Gertrude had married Sidney. (Nobody ever wondered why Sidney had married Gertrude.) Gertrude had married her first husband for his brains and her second husband for his money, and both of them had married her, as often happens, for her books. People knew this, just as they know everything about everybody except perhaps themselves; why she had married her third husband they did not know. Certainly he himself did not; he had too much respect even to guess. No reason would have seemed adequate to *him:* he would still pause now and then, in the midst of his accustomed happiness, and feel once again his old astonishment at the good-fortune that is possible to man.

Gertrude would say to him, "Don't interrupt me, Sidney!"—but then quickly, sometimes: "I'm sorry, Sidney." She betrayed toward Sidney, alone among mortals, a rudimentary and anomalous good-nature; one could see that, to her, there were people and Sidney. It was absurd of her to waste herself on Sidney, but as she said to herself, "Sidney needs me." There was something soothing about Sidney, Gertrude felt; it was absurd of her to feel that way, but she felt that way. She had made her living, her life, out of the rejection of the absurdities of existence; Sidney was an absurdity she had grown accustomed to—accepted willingly, almost.

The Bacons' household, with Gertrude thoughtfully typing, and occasionally bursting into laughter and reading something aloud to Sidney, who stood at the sink drying the dishes, laughed at what she had read, and looked at her with admiration and devotion—the Bacons' household was, as Gertrude herself said after catching an unexpected glimpse of it in the mirror, "a sort of Elves' Workshop." She went on: "You know the elves' motto, Sidney?"

"No, what?"

"Every little elf helps."

The little elf laughed—and it wasn't a pale or a forced laugh, either. "That's *good*, Gertrude," he exclaimed, and began to hang the cups up in the cupboard. Gertrude looked at him with a queer pitying understanding smile; it was queer because one could see, at its hesitant heart, something tender and indulgent—loving, almost. Gertrude started to say—she stopped herself.

III.

Miss Batterson

AND

Benton

1. Gertrude had replaced at Benton Manny Gumbiner, a writer who—as he himself said when, early his first winter, he left Benton—was too advanced for it; when his name was pronounced at Benton one distinguished after it a caesura of pure awe. If Gertrude had made her writing students take off all their clothes, pile them on the table with the chairs, and then had had them burn the next classroom's Spanish teacher on the pile, the old students would only have said to the new, with a smile: "You should have been in *Manny's* class."

Before Manny, for as long as anyone could remember, Benton had had the same teacher of creative writing, Camille Turner Batterson. When she had begun to teach it it had not even been called creative writing. She was of a generation almost inconceivably remote. She wore tweeds that were part sachet; she used an intermediate *a;* she had kodak pictures of the Lake Country—in them she stood in gorse with a timid smile, her hand extended to a Dawn Horse or Highland pony. She believed, or had believed, in ladies, in gentlemen, in the poor; once only a few years ago she had said that something was "common." She had never married; neither had her mother, her grandmother, any of the Battersons—one felt that.

She remembered the old days, the first days, of Benton, when several of its students would have had difficulty writing *cat*, and this not only because they had been to progressive schools and learned to print, but also because—rich as they were, pretty as they were—they were *slower* or *difficult* children: there was a submissive sadness in the slowing of the voices, the softening of the voices, of the mothers and fathers as they pronounced these words that the world had so carefully selected for them to use. Nowadays Benton picked and chose: girls who had read Wittgenstein as high school baby-sitters were rejected because the school's quota of abnormally intelligent students had already been filled that year. (The normality of the intellectual environment of Benton was rigorously maintained.) When teachers complained of the docility, the commonplaceness, of the girls they got in their freshman classes, Miss Batterson would repeat to them a sentence from the first theme she had ever graded at Benton—in those years they had still had grades. The writer had been to church the Sunday before, and remarked: "I could not but help think of the World War when it was mentioned that a soldiers' faith is even strong when he is fighting for something which he knows not what for." Miss Batterson remembered the trial—it had amounted to that—of a mathematics professor who had given an examination. This was a little later: progressivism had dawned at Benton like—like thunder.

Her office was full of ferns, her desk was of golden oak, she wore sprigs of flowers in the buttonholes of violet suits; her gentle face, that of Undine grown old, kept about it a dreamy, dazzled aura, the look of something in a painting by Odilon Redon. She was a diffused, Salon photograph; and yet she must have had in the depths of her wistful soul a Gift or Daemon that once or twice a year awoke, whispered to her a sentence she could repeat—to the world's astonishment—and then turned back to sleep. Dr. Rosenbaum had first been aware of this Daemon when Miss Batterson retorted, to a colleague's objection that all Benton students read *that* in high school: "There is no book that all my students have read." Dr. Rosenbaum knew that it is in sentences like this, and not in the pages of Spengler, that one has brought home to one the twilight of the West. He gave a brotherly laugh and agreed: "*Ja*, dey haf de sense dey vere born vidt."

Yet Miss Batterson had truly belonged to Benton, had had her own genteel isotopes of all its attitudes. She had long ago become accustomed to dividing—consciously or unconsciously, who knows?—all literature into writing and Benton writing. If Katherine Mansfield's stories (they were for Miss Batterson the precarious consummation of Fiction) were more brilliant and universal, still at the same time there was something more directly expressive, therapeutic, about the work of Benton girls: one could see that it had helped them more. Her point of view about student work was that of a social worker teaching finger-painting to children or the insane.

2.

I WAS impressed with how common such an attitude was at Benton: the faculty—insofar as they were real Benton faculty, and not just nomadic barbarians—reasoned with the students, "appreciated their point of view," used Socratic methods on them, made allowances for them, kept looking into the oven to see if they were done; but there was one allowance they never under any circumstances made—that the students might be right about something, and they wrong. Education, to them, was a psychiatric process: the sign under which they conquered had embroidered at the bottom, in small letters, *Canst thou not minister to a mind diseased?*—and half of them gave it its Babu paraphrase of *Can you wait upon a lunatic?* One expected them to refer to former students as psychoanalysts do: "Oh yes, she's an old analysand of mine." They felt that the mind was a delicate plant which, carefully nurtured, judiciously left alone, must inevitably adopt for itself even the slightest of their own beliefs.

One Benton student, a girl noted for her breadth of reading and absence of coöperation, described things in a queer, exaggerated, plausible way. According to her, a professor at an ordinary school tells you "what's so," you admit that it is on examination, and what you really believe or come to believe has "that obscurity which is the privilege of young things." But at Benton, where education was as democratic as in "that book about America by that French writer—de, de—you know the one I mean"; she meant de Tocqueville; there at Benton they wanted you really to believe everything that they did, especially if they hadn't told you what it was. You gave them the facts, the opinions of authorities, what you hoped was their own opinion; but they replied, "That's not the point. What do *you yourself really believe?*" If it wasn't what your professors believed, you and they could go on searching for your real belief forever—unless you stumbled at last upon that primal scene which is, by definition, at the root of anything. . . .

When she said *primal scene* there was so much youth and knowledge in her face, so much of our first joy in created things, that I could not think of Benton for thinking of life.

I suppose she was right: it is as hard to satisfy our elders'
demands of Independence as of Dependence. Harder: how
much more complicated and indefinite a rationalization the
first usually is!—and in both cases, it is their demands that
must be satisfied, not our own. The faculty of Benton had
for their students great expectations, and the students shook,
sometimes gave, beneath the weight of them. If the intellectual demands Benton made of its students were not so
great as they might have been, the emotional demands made
up for it. Many a girl, about to deliver to one of her teachers
a final report on a year's not quite completed project, had
wanted to cry out like a child: "Whip me, whip me,
Mother, just don't be Reasonable!"

3.

DR. ROSENBAUM's saying about Benton was not unjust.
It went: The Patagonians have two poets, the better named
Gomez; the Patagonians call Shakespeare the English
Gomez.

The faculty of Benton, the true faculty, felt that if
Benton were gone it would no longer be possible to become
educated. They were a little awed by this, and cast their
eyes down, but it was a truth that, in the end, they looked
seriously at. They felt toward, say, Oxford, as the kinder
members of the Salvation Army used to feel toward the
Established Church: they would have been forgiving except
for all the harm it did without meaning to. They said, over
and over and over: *What is the good of learning about
Spinoza if you do not learn about Life?* (And this is true:
how much better it would be if we could teach, as we
teach Spinoza, life!) They had heard intelligent people

say, as intelligent people say with monotonous regularity, that one gets more out of one's reading and conversation at college than one gets from college itself. Benton decided, with naked logic: Why not let that reading and conversation *be* college, and let students do the ordinary classwork on the outside?—if they felt that they needed to; for some of it might profitably be disregarded, all that part that is, in President Robbins' phrase, *boring*. So the students' conversation and reading and "extra-curricular cultural activities" and decisions about Life were made, as much as possible, the curriculum through which the teachers of Benton shepherded the students of Benton, biting at their heels and putting attractive haystacks before their even more attractive noses: they called this "allowing the student to use his own individual initiative." There was more individual initiative of this kind at Benton than there was in Calvin's Geneva.

Benton teachers pointed out that they were preparing their students for Life, which is not spent in classrooms listening to a teacher lecture; and it would have been obvious to reply that it is not spent in offices listening to a teacher talk, either—or for that matter, at Benton: even the most individually initiating student went at last, and spent the rest of her years in Life. There she would say, as people do about the army, that no book had prepared her for *this* —would, finally, write a book to prepare people for it.

Dr. Rosenbaum had said, about Benton, to Camille Batterson: "Idt iss nodt fair, nodt to ledt in boys; boys, too, *dey* must be educatedt. O, if I only couldt haf been a liddle girl, and go to Benton! You vould not catch me being vot I am now"—and he sighed with bright eyes, what he was now, but sorry for it. He was always in good spirits with Miss

Batterson. He looked at her, whether she talked or whether she listened, with benevolent delight; and as she made her tentative way down the walks of Benton, he would pad along beside her like some big animal friendly to man. When he walked on one side of her and Yang on the other, the three looked like a Victorian illustration of a fairy tale. Whenever Yang met Miss Batterson he stuck with her, if he could, for the rest of the day; you would come on him waiting patiently outside her office, now and then snapping at the girls who tried to pet him.

Often Miss Batterson, out for a walk, would meet the President, out for a walk with Yang; they would speak a few friendly sentences and then leave each other, the President out for a walk and Miss Batterson out for a walk with Yang. The first few times this had happened the President had done all that he could to keep it from happening: he had spoken winningly to Yang—so winningly that the trees of Benton would willingly have followed him, but not Yang; he had lost his temper with Yang—Yang snarled and bared his tremendous teeth; he had even tried to drag Yang off by the collar—he could have put a collar on a polar bear, dragged at it, and had as much effect. After a while the President came to take these scenes (I used to think of him as a planet rending its garments and crying, "Ah, sharper than a serpent's tooth is an ungrateful satellite!") for granted, and acted as though they were little attentions he was paying to Miss Batterson, who would say, "Dogs love me, I'm afraid." They—and cats, and cows, and children, and the other unthinking lives of the world— didn't love the President, I'm afraid, but lay under his feet so that he stumbled over them, or drew away from him, or spoke or growled or mooed or purred so that he couldn't understand them; if it hadn't been for grown-ups, I don't know what President Robbins would have done.

The teachers of Benton were *very* grown-up. To work as hard as they worked, they had to be. They had a half-hour conference once a week with each of their students—they conducted them over the *pons asinorum* one by one; they taught a couple of long classes; each was the adviser—they had a stranger name for it—of a number of girls, and the girls were encouraged to have problems (one famous student had so many that her adviser said to her at last, *If I were you I'd commit suicide;* but he was not one of the real faculty); instead of writing down grades for the students they wrote out, for the work of each girl in each class, analyses, protocols, brochures; they were expected to enter into the political and social and cultural life of the community, all the group activities of the school; and there were reports, studies, reorganizations, plays, lectures, clubs, committees, committees—ah, how they searched each other's souls!

And that was all? No, there was more, much more—I have not the heart to write it down. At Benton it was not the students alone who had nervous breakdowns. How glad Dr. Rosenbaum was that he was only a Composer in Residence, less use than ornament, almost; he would say this, but he worked hard with the class he had. For weeks at a time Gertrude would hardly refer to herself except as Aunt Tom or Old Black Gertrude.

When the President said, about the faculty of Benton, "We like to think that we educate each other," he had every right to think so—they spent as much time with each other as with the students. (After her first three weeks at Benton Gertrude said with a nasty smile, "I am allergic to big families." She said that, so far as committees were concerned, she was going to get an excuse from her psychoanalyst that the President could sign; and God knows her psychoanalyst would have given her this or anything else she asked for—he had had a transference to Gertrude, and listened in dumb awe while, upright on the couch, she talked.) At Benton a few "produced"—works of scholarship, works of art, in the summer; but most of them, after they had been at Benton a while, produced Benton girls. And Benton did not look down on these "mere educators," as most schools do all the time they are saying they don't. One teacher had last had something printed in a 1928 *Dial;* they respected him for that article, but they respected him more for having put away such things and gone on to where they were.

Sometimes you meet, coming down the leafy path along which you are walking, a man dressed as Napoleon; as he talks to you you look at him with distrust, pity, and amusement—carefully do not look, rather. But as the two of you walk along, and people come up with wallpaper designs full of Imperial bees, rashly offer their condolences on the death of the duc d'Enghien, ask for a son's appointment as Assistant Quartermaster-General of the army being sent to the Peninsula, you realize that it is not he but his whole society that has "lost touch with reality."

But Benton was not only a delusion, it was a gratefully primitive one: at Benton the members of the faculty had an importance, a dignity and significance, that we have lost. They were archetypal; as they debated whether, for therapeutic reasons, Bunny Macready should be allowed to go ahead with her project of making mobiles from Meccano sets—or words to that effect—they had the look of men from Plutarch. One of the professors—it was Dr. Crowley

—looked exactly like someone whom Mrs. Rosenbaum had once seen, and it took her three years to remember who it was: the Patriarch or Metropolitan who had supervised, in St. Petersburg, the first Easter service she could remember. His robes and beard were gone, but otherwise he was as of old. The shadows of the men and women of Benton swept from their shoulders like togas; from time to time, conscious of their destiny and of how their poor tired shoulders ached, they rearranged them.

Benton people felt, like Paul: I am a Roman, and a citizen of no mean city. They felt, too, that that gave them the right of trial at Rome. They said to the outsider judging them that they appealed to Benton, and he replied or was supposed to reply: "You have appealed to Benton, and to Benton you shall go." There the Bentonians got that special justice with which we ourselves judge ourselves—a very lenient justice, the outsider would have said, mocking them; yet was it really so lenient as it seemed? They reminded one of that horrid aphorism that the Day of Judgment is a summary court in perpetual session: they were their own judgment. One looked at them and thought of another saying: *Whose bread I eat, his man I am;* and this is most true when the bread is, as it was at Benton, the bread of Life. And yet —and yet. . . . At Benton, too, men ate their bread with tears.

4.

WITH HER brightest students Miss Batterson was always on terms of uneasy, disappointed admiration; their work never seemed to be helping their development as much as the work of the stupider students was helping *theirs*. Every year there was a little war—an eighteenth century one, though—about whether the school magazine was printing only the work of a clique. Miss Batterson was perfectly good-hearted in this: if you cannot discriminate between good and bad yourself, it cannot help seeming somewhat poor-spirited and arbitrary of other people to do so. Aesthetic discrimination is no pleasanter, seems no more just and rational to those discriminated against, than racial discrimination; the popular novelist would be satisfied with his income from serials and scenarios and pocket books if people would only see that he is a better writer than Thomas Mann. I knew in the army a case of one of the rarest things in the world, completely achromatic vision: to this soldier (he used to go on Wednesday night to preach guest sermons at the prayer meetings of a small Baptist church in Tucson) the world was the color of the pages of the *Daily News*. He said to me one glistening rain-soaked night, as we looked out over the bombers and tar-paper barracks of the base: "I like rainy nights the best of any time, it's so bright then. Everything's so much more. . . ." He hesitated, because he was embarrassed about his color-blindness; but we were friends, we had often been on K.P. together; I would understand. He said: "Everything's so much more *colorful* then." I have often had occasion to remember this sentence.

Miss Batterson's Unconscious, going back to childhood for the word, felt that it was mean of the best students so plainly to dislike the others' work; the others liked theirs, didn't they? And certainly all work, dropped into the mechanism by which she had learned to judge, did look extraordinarily alike. Her critical vocabulary (derived mostly from the elder classics, all called *How to Write*

Short Stories, all authoritative and archaic as the Elder Eddas) sounded as if some poetic student of hydrodynamics had wandered into Creation. The terms she had! Miss Batterson would have said of Jonson's alchemists that they had the right *feel*, but lacked a real critical vocabulary.

Miss Batterson was of only a little value to the students she taught, and that mainly in the *go thou and do otherwise* way in which teachers most often are, but she was of considerably more value to the students she advised. Her advice to her students was always—so to speak, so to speak: "Do whatever your grandmother would have done in your place"; and then quickly, those beautiful untroubled eyes— they were almost violet—clouding over with a doubt: "Whatever my grandmother would have done in your place." There was almost nothing you could safely ask her advice about, except perhaps thank-you letters. *Safely* meant, without injuring Miss Batterson's understanding of the world: all the students she served as adviser to thought a good deal, and talked to one another more, about what it would be safe and right and good to ask Miss Batterson's advice on; and they had almost killed with unkindness the one student who had ever been cruel and senseless enough to ask Miss Batterson's advice about a real problem. Miss Batterson, alone among the advisers of Benton, really did develop in Benton students both individual initiative and social maturity.

How Miss Batterson's eyes would light up at anything about Dr. Johnson or Charles Lamb or Fanny Burney or the Brontës or . . . She was the exact opposite of the people who like any foreign book better than any Anglo-Saxon one; she liked for writers to come of sturdy English stock, and she kept them among pomander-apples when they did. As she read their books her very bones felt that there was in the whole world no burglar under any bed, no Negro in any woodpile; her bones sighed and settled back in grateful luxury, as if into their grave: they felt safe.

Until I met Miss Batterson I had never seen an office with a cobbler's bench in it. The bench had lost its shoes and wax and thimbles, and wore maidenhair ferns now: ferns, and an annual called *A Virginia Calendar*, an engagement book full of photographs of houses you wanted to buy and live in and landscapes you wanted to walk through and die in, and of bliss at that. Sometimes one would meet, there in Miss Batterson's office beside the cobbler's bench, a student whom she not only taught, not only advised, but also protected. People who know what they are like often dislike anyone who resembles them; Miss Batterson, who did not know at all—she had a Platonic Ideal of womanhood, but didn't know that she had become it—was attracted to any girl who might be going to become Miss Batterson. There was a *she did not know what* about their stories: when you heard her talk about the stories of her protégées, trying to say what it was, you did not think as usual, *She's a true systematic critic*, but were impressed with how subtle she could be. She was all wrong, of course; but as someone says, acumen deserts intelligent men least when they are in the wrong. You realized that she had more mind than you had thought, than she had thought; if only she could have found it possible to break her way through to it, to get it out into the world. . . . But she had never had the heart to.

When one of these protégées went out into life, no one ever said of *her*, "She's a typical Benton girl." People said instead, "You went to *Benton?*"—being careful to stress the *Benton* and not the *you*. These young women settled

down into libraries, the English departments of quiet backward colleges, the society pages of small newspapers; or if
they settled down into marriage, they became some of those
mothers to whom people say in wonder, "You don't mean
to say those four great big boys are *yours!*"

Miss Batterson had a code, and passed a little of it on to
these girls. She had got it in exactly the way in which she
had got the name Camille Turner Batterson. It was a code
that had earlier been evolved to hold at bay or keep under
partial submission the fierceness and dominance and self-
will, the naked aggression of men in ninety-pound suits of
armor; and it was absolutely necessary to them, protected
them from each other just as the suits of armor did. Over
the centuries a great deal of sublimation and aetherialization
had gone on, and finally you got Miss Batterson, who had
been sublimated into air, thin air: she was trapped in that
armor as Ariel was trapped in the hollow tree.

One can hardly help being primitively attracted to the
Romantic belief that potentiality is always better than
actuality, that Nothing is always better than Anything; yet,
looking at Miss Batterson, one could not help doubting it,
just as we cannot help doubting the war-monument-orators
who tell us how lucky the dead soldiers are not to be growing old and fat and dull like us. Miss Batterson was poten-
tially anything and actually almost nothing. She was still,
after so many years, taking her first look at life; that first
look was her vocation. She had made trembling-on-the-
verge-of-things a steady state, a permanent one: she lived
in the State of Innocence.

When she died the Recording Angel would look at her
accusingly and she would say defensively, "I haven't done
anything," and he would close his book and sigh—she had

not understood at all.

She had not done anything; she had not, truly. That she loved Browning, and would read "The Statue and the Bust" to her girls with mild ladylike fire—this was one of those ironies of which the world is composed. There are other elements in its composition, of course; but one must look for those.

Yet perhaps the Recording Angel would reach out to Miss Batterson and touch her with the tip of his finger, and the poor dew would at last thaw, the seed in the tomb begin to sprout.

5.

IT RATHER surprised me that Gertrude would talk to me about her book; and she was surprised, I could see. She believed in the saying, *Never show a fool anything unfinished* —believed in it so thoroughly that she felt an uneasy resentment at having to show anybody anything, finished or unfinished. In a more reasonable world she and Sidney could have read her book when it was done, given it the Pulitzer Prize, and stored it away in a vault under the Library of Congress. She did not tell the people at Benton that she was writing a book about them: it would make them nervous if they knew, she said to Sidney, and they wouldn't be able to behave as they normally do. For that matter, she didn't tell me—she just asked me questions about Benton. She asked me more questions than I knew there were; after a while we found that we had been talking to each other about the book, quite openly, for weeks.

This would not have happened if I had been a novelist. Then I might have stolen Gertrude's ideas, might have looked at them with a colleague's bright awful eye. But I was only a poet—that is to say, a maker of stone axes—and she felt a real pity for me because of it: what a shame that I hadn't lived back in the days when they used stone axes! And yet, why make them now? Every once in a while she would say to me, "Haven't you ever thought of writing a novel?" I would shake my head and say that my memory was too bad; later I would just say, "That again!" and laugh. She would laugh too, but it puzzled her; finally she dismissed it from her mind, saying to herself—as you do about someone who won't go on relief, or mind the doctor— "Well, he has only himself to blame!"

I always answered her questions. If I hadn't, someone else would have—and it was appropriate that she and Benton should meet and, each in its own way, preserve the memory of the other. But sometimes I felt sheepish—felt like a flock of sheep, that is—as Gertrude sheared from me (with barber's clippers that pulled a little) my poor coat of facts, worked over it with knitted brows, and then, smiling like Morgan le Fay, cast over my bare limbs her big blanket conclusions. Benton and I certainly couldn't complain that we hadn't been understood; so that we—if I may speak for Benton—complained that we couldn't recognize ourselves for so much understanding, that we had been understood out of existence, and that, to make it worse, it had been done with the facts which we ourselves had furnished. Poor moths attracted to the lepidopterist, who trade him their soft wings for the hard conclusion that they are typical specimens of genus A, species B, sub-species C—and who murmur with their last breath that he is a typical lepidopterist!

Gertrude and I had many conversations about the book. She sat there absently fingering her side, as if she were con-

sidering dieting. (My wife called this *rubbing her rib*—
"What does she want to rub her rib for like that?" my wife
asked; I didn't know, and answered: "It's the one they
made Adam from. She wants it back.") Gertrude began,
once: "Who'll I marry to Flo Whittaker?"

"You don't think Jerrold suited to her?"

"Jerrold! Don't be *absurd*," Gertrude said in one of her
customary tones, a tone of impatient astonishment at the
stupidity of the world. But then her face changed, and she
went on almost wistfully: "I'd give a lot to use him. Seventy
or eighty years ago I could still have got away with him, but
nowadays—not a chance! He's just too good to be true."

I quoted:

> "*Ah! what avails the classic bent*
> *And what the cultured word*
> *Against the undoctored incident*
> *That actually occurred!*"

"What's that?"

"Kipling."

An unchristened expression—if it had been christened it
would have been called What-A-Writer-To-Quote! Johnson—went over Gertrude's face. She got back to Jerrold:
"He's all art and no nature. He's not even a type, he's a type
of types."

"Lots of people are. A—"

"Lots of people are *anything*, but that doesn't mean you
can use them in a book. You know as well as I do what
Aristotle says about the improbable and the impossible. My
readers wouldn't believe in that man for a minute. If you
and I were back on Bleecker Street, think how improbable
he'd seem to you!"

"More improbable than Bleecker Street?"

Gertrude sat up straight and said with real, not habitual impatience: "Living around colleges the way you do, you've just lost your sense of what's probable. If you believe in Jerrold Whittaker you'd believe in anything."

I could have said defensively, "I don't believe in *you*," but I didn't. But I said what I could for the probability of Jerrold: "You think he's a fool when you meet him, but he isn't—he's only the most literal-minded man that ever lived. But he's as unprejudiced and disinterested and objective as a scientist in an old novel—you can convince him of something in an argument, even, and you know how rare that is. And he can do a certain sort of book, not a very good sort I admit, as—"

Gertrude said with a weary smile, "That's got nothing to do with it. Just look at the way he talks! And you yourself said, before you'd said three sentences about him—I'll quote you word for word: *as a scientist in a novel* and *you know how rare that is* and *the most literal-minded man there ever was.* Believe me, *that* bird's too rare for any novel of mine."

I said, "I guess you're right. They are pretty wild, some of them—professors, I mean. Have you met Dr. Willen, in the psychology department?"

"The one with her hair dyed black?"

"That's the one. She's Camille Batterson's best friend. She lost her job at Morford for cooking a hen on a Bunsen burner."

"For *what?*"

"She was doing experiments in visual perception, stuff with color wheels, and spending most of her afternoons and evenings at school. She got tired of having to go home so much, so she just slept on the cot in her office, half the time, and cooked dinners in her lab. But she was domestic, and the dinners got pretty elaborate. One night she was so proud of a hen she'd roasted, with dressing and everything, in a sort of Dutch oven arrangement over some Bunsen burners, that she went along the hall and knocked at all the office doors that were lighted and got two graduate students and a professor to come have dinner with her. They talked quite a lot about it. Of course, that hen was just the—the straw that broke the camel's back; she'd done plenty of queerer things. . . . But it was bound to happen with *some* psychologist: psychologists love teas. And physiologists—biologists in general. Though mostly they're sort of graham cracker and banana teas."

"Are they all so—eccentric?"

"Psychologists? Pretty often—some of them are odd to begin with, and that gets them interested in psychology. But the rest are the—the—the soberest of men."

"I didn't mean psychologists, I meant professors in general."

"Most professors aren't a *bit* eccentric. They're just like—" *just like you and me*, I had started to say, but somehow this seemed the wrong thing—"businessmen who've gone into teaching and got unbusinesslike. Or tame Roman emperors—they *are* sheltered, in their later days. I knew one old one that—you'd know him, he edited *The White Devil* —that put up the window and called to some boys that were making too much noise: 'Begone!' One of them right here —Dr. Savitt, the one that's the expert on Lincoln—has made a lot of money in real estate, and is a bank director; and I knew one who was paid by the National Association of Manufacturers to go around making speeches to Chambers of Commerce, and never washed; and the man I took geology with lectured in iambics, and used to talk about Geological Determinism. And I knew one who raised mocking birds from their shells, without their mothers, so as to prove their songs were inborn—and to prove the inheritance of acquired characteristics he raised two dachshund puppies that sat up and begged before he or their mother taught them, but they died. But *people* are that way, a lot of the time: every tenth person is making a house out of bottle-tops, or words to that effect. People are much more eccentric than they're supposed to be. But dully so. Of course, some professors are—" then I paused, feeling that I should have done so hours before, and said more sensibly: "It's like people. People aren't like anything, there are too many of them. Professors aren't like anything, they're like everything. I'm a professor; why, Gertrude, right now, you're a professor."

It was a queer thought: Gertrude looked at it, moved it with her paw, and let it stay there. She said drily, "You're quite eloquent on the subject." She was not used to my talking so much: she seemed to feel that I behaved to her, usually, almost as everybody should behave to her. One day when she was particularly satisfied with my behavior she said to me, "You know, you *remind* me of someone." She thought and thought about it, but couldn't decide who it was. I couldn't either, but that night it suddenly came over me who it must be: Sidney.

6.

MY GRANDMOTHER, like other grandmothers, used to tell me fairy tales; when she was tired she would just reminisce.

I used to say, when I couldn't get a story: "Nanny, tell me some Facts." As Gertrude's book grew, that phrase kept recurring to me. Finally I told it to Gertrude, and Gertrude got in the habit of saying to me: "Tell me some Facts. Some facts about—"

She said it, always, with the same smile, the smile of a suspended, autonomous intelligence, of a steady and sufficient state. There was a firm, floating, comfortable gaiety about the smile: it belonged to nothing, not even itself, and it was glad that it didn't. As I looked at it I would think of her awful ordinary smile, the smile of the flesh to which she was subject, and I could not help wishing that this other smile of hers, the Declaration of Independence of the intellect, were true.

Often the facts Gertrude asked me for were facts about Camille Turner Batterson. "It's like following Louis XIV," Gertrude said, after her first weeks of listening to Benton's reminiscences of Miss Batterson. Her listeners smiled politely, and Gertrude herself gave a short light laugh as she saw that, in her simile, the duc d'Orleans could take the place of Manny Gumbiner.

Miss Batterson, back from her new job out West, had spent half her Christmas vacation home in Virginia, half of it home at Benton. Gertrude, inside an hour, was looking at Miss Batterson almost as she used to look at the President. She said to me, in a quoting tone, something about thought always limping trembling behind reality. It was a sidelong preoccupied sentence, and Gertrude's eyes and ears returned to Miss Batterson as soon as they could, and stayed there.

That a real writer of fiction should be interested in *her* pleased and astonished Miss Batterson, that systematic critic and veteran collector of fiction: it was as if a giraffe had come to a taxidermist and begged to be stuffed. Miss Batterson did not realize which of them was the taxidermist, which the giraffe.

I asked Gertrude, genuinely puzzled: "If you can use Camille Turner Batterson why can't you use Jerrold?" She answered: "I've *explained* to you why I can't use Jerrold— do I have to go over it all again?" Then she explained to me why she could use Miss Batterson: the difference seemed to be that Jerrold was so generalized that it made him a too-peculiar type, one her readers couldn't believe in, but that Miss Batterson had so many particular, specific, peculiar qualities that readers would believe in her as a recognizable general type. Gertrude said, finally: "If you can't see for yourself I just can't explain it." She could look at someone and tell immediately whether or not he would support a plot: people were caryatids or they weren't, and that was all there was to it.

Miss Batterson had for Gertrude a fascination that she did not explain to me either. Underneath her amused understanding of Miss Batterson there must have been some unamused, unadmitted, un-understanding awe: Gertrude's subliminal self felt that Miss Batterson was a real lady, someone Charlottesville would send, with letters and commissions, as its representative to Charleston. Gertrude *knew* better than this, of course, but we all know better than we know better, or act as if we did.

Miss Batterson's being a real lady had neither helped nor hindered her at Benton: it had seemed, to people there, one more piece of eccentricity on her part. It had always astonished me to see how little fame or class or money mattered at Benton. Jerrold Whittaker was about as famous as

American sociologists get, but there were a dozen professors who were more honored at Benton—who seemed, to Benton, far more famous. He lacked the bright cloud of challenge and uplift, of social significance, that enveloped *their* famous ones; and they may have resented his having become famous in the world outside without first having become famous at Benton—they grew their own great. There at Benton Flo was better known than he, both for her Work and for her Sayings; as they said, "Flo's so civic-minded," "Flo *does* so much," "What Flo doesn't know about organization work. . . ."

Two of the faculty families were in the Social Register; they could as well have been in the Code of Justinian, for all the good it did them at Benton. Kim says, "There is no caste where men go to look for—" salvation, I suppose I should say; it was not salvation, though, but righteousness. It was a mark of the caste to which they belonged not to believe in caste, and I did not like them any the worse for that; I was amused at the divergence between practice and theory, though, when their sociologists talked gravely about *upper upper* and *lower upper* and *lower lower* classes in the world outside. *In the world outside*—some such phrase, or the thought that corresponds to it, often occurred to one at Benton.

As for the Benton bank director, as for the professors who had money of their own—how little it mattered in their life at Benton! They had caviar on their crackers at cocktail parties, instead of good red herring roe, and that was the end of it. The teachers of Benton were like sheep, where money was concerned, and the President was their shepherd: he had to scramble around looking, and worrying, and leading them to greener pastures if he could see any, while they walked on munching their scanty feed and baaing—piteously, but contentedly and accustomedly, too. Sometimes the President seemed to me not a shepherd but a scapegoat, and a willing one: the sheep had all the inconveniences and vexations of doing without money, but all the guilt of getting it had been put on his own diver's shoulders. Because the President smiled and spoke for money, I did not.

It was amusing to contrast the respectable casserole'd poverty of a professor and his wife with the matter-of-fact opulence—for Benton was a *very* expensive college—of some of the girls who sat on the floor at his feet, with more oil wells to their or their family's name than he had students. Several of the Benton skiers used to go, over the Christmas holidays, not to Sun Valley but to Davos or Kitzbühel; as one of them said to Dr. Rosenbaum, "It's only eleven hours more." And I heard one student, arguing with another girl about how good a Matisse reproduction was, end the argument with this extraordinary sentence: "I *ought* to know: it's in my step-father's—well, not my step-father's any more, but my mother's second husband's bedroom." But she could have said to me, with perfect truth: "What's extraordinary about it? The people I'm used to just have more marriages and more Matisses than the people you're used to." All the airplanes their families owned were considered part of the family business—for as one of them told me, with an inflection I had not heard her use before: "It's the only way you *can* own anything nowadays, after taxes."

But there were many more who were just comfortably well-to-do; and there were poor girls, too, on scholarships which paid part of what they had to pay—though they too were richer than most of the professors. And there were what I used to call to myself token students: black students, brown students, yellow students, students who were believers of the major creeds of Earth—one or two of each. If there is in Tierra del Fuego a family of fire-worshippers with a daughter of marriageable age, and a couple of thousand dollars a year to spare, they can educate her at Benton.

And all these people lived together in amity and complacency. It was like, in many ways, some little community in the Middle Ages: there was a most homogeneous public opinion, a most homogeneous private opinion—almost all the people there were agreed about almost everything, and glad to be agreed, and *right* to be agreed. They made you feel alone venomous among the beasts of the field, or like a spy on the Ark, and you argued helplessly and uselessly— there is no argument against righteousness—or held your peace and went off outside to the Waters of the World, content to drown there.

A professor who had been away from Benton for several years, a rather imaginative man, told me: "Now that I'm not at Benton any more, I dream that I'm back sometimes, the way you dream you're back in the army. In the army dream—it's touching—I always tell myself, 'Now you've been in the army a long time, you know your way around, there's not a thing for you to worry about,' and I go by the supply sergeant's and get myself some stuff, and get a couple of books at the Post library, and settle down to wait. But when I dream I'm back at Benton it's as if I were in a hothouse or a—or with the Lotus-Eaters: I can feel Benton all over me like a warm bath, and I try to move my arms and legs, and I can't, and I say to myself, 'You've got to get out of here. You've got to get out of here!' And then I wake up."

Most of the people of Benton would have swallowed a porcupine, if you had dyed its quills and called it Modern Art; they longed for men to be discovered on the moon, so that they could show that *they* weren't prejudiced towards moon men; and they were so liberal and selfless, politically, that—but what words of men, or tongue of man or angel, can I find adequate to this great theme? In the world outside one met many people who were negatives of the people of Benton: exact duplications, but with the whites and blacks reversed. There were people who thought anything but calendars and official portraits Modern Art, and spoke of it with exasperated hatred; people who wrote to the Chicago *Tribune* to denounce it for the radical stand it had taken on some issue; people who said resignedly, when their big summer houses, on cliffs overlooking the sea, had fewer closets than they liked: "But that's not the architect's fault—*that* just comes from being poor." They moved you to moralize, almost: as you looked at them you realized better the quixotic charm of the people of Benton, whom you could laugh at with an untroubled—a less troubled heart. You felt about the people of Benton: *If only they weren't so complacent! If only they weren't so*—then you stopped yourself, unwilling to waste an afternoon on *if only's*, and mumbled a summary *If only we were all dead or better!* Though this was unjust to the great mass of people, normal in-between people with nothing much wrong with them, people like you and me; well, not us exactly, but us if we were different.

Gertrude said about Benton, in the voice of a digital computer nagging at cash-registers: "Americans are so conformist that even their dissident groups exhibit the most abject conformity." I reflected, "Once upon a time, Gertrude, you'd have been ducked as a common scold." But then she said cheerfully, in the style of hers that I liked better: "A Group for Everyone and Everyone in His Group is the slogan for *their* sampler." There was some truth in what she said; I had felt its truth, I know, At Home on Bleecker Street. And Gertrude's slogan pleased me for another reason: it reminded me of a sentence of Freud's, about love-affairs, that I could apply to Gertrude and Sidney— they were *a group of two*. Yet this didn't sound right, somehow. I compromised with: they were a group of one and a half.

Benton was, all in all, a surprisingly contented place. The people who weren't contented got jobs elsewhere—as did, usually, any very exceptional people—and the others stayed. They didn't need to be exceptional: they were at Benton. One felt that they felt that all they had to do was say, "I'm at Benton," and their hearer would say, raising his hand: "Enough!"

The ranks of the teachers of Benton were fairly anomalous, their salaries were fairly similar, and most of what power there was was distributed; being the head of a department, even, was a rotated chore. What mattered at Benton was the Approval of Your Colleagues, the respect of the community of Benton. The most important man at Benton was the most respected man at Benton, a man called, simply, Dr. Crowley. (They used his first name about as much as one uses El Greco's.) I think that it surprised Benton people that he had never been given a Nobel Prize—a Peace Prize, say. They would have picked him to arbitrate a dispute between Earth and some other planet or solar system, and he would have decided for Earth because it was more progressive and had Benton on it, and the other planet would have seen that this was right and given in.

Gertrude could *see* all this about Benton, but she was unwilling to believe it, and she had the theoretical, manipulative skill by which she could explain it or anything else away. To her the most powerful professor in a department was always just about to expose the head of the department's love-affair with one of the students, in order to get the head's rank and salary and power for himself: or if it wasn't like this on the surface, it was at bottom. Sex, greed, envy, power, money: Gertrude knew that these were working away at Benton—though in sublimated form, sometimes—exactly as they work away everywhere else. *Though in sublimated form, sometimes:* the interest of the judgment lies there. The same water runs a prayer-wheel and a turbine. But to Gertrude this proved that a prayer-wheel is a turbine: under the ramifications, the multifoliate variegations of Gertrude's analyses of human conduct, there was a crude kind of economic, psychoanalytical determinism. She knew that there are good reasons and real reasons, and that the two never coincide. She knew, and told you, the real reason for everything—for everything, that is, except her *having* to know, *having* to tell you. And if you had asked her the real reason for this she would not have been taken aback, but would have said with a mocking grin, "I am the Scourge of God," or any of a hundred things, depending on how she felt at the moment; and then she would have told you why you had asked her what you did. She didn't care what you said, but only why you said it: so, in the end, you might just as well have said nothing at all. She was far too sophisticated to speak of Human Nature, Which Never Changes, but her novels spoke for her: they were as suspicious as an old woman, and their suspicions were as easily and as depressingly and as uniformly satisfied. Gertrude felt about Benton: "It's a place like any other." But like so many places, it wasn't.

7.

THE PRESIDENT had inherited Miss Batterson, and there was nothing he could do about her. Nothing, that is, that wouldn't have been cruel and inexpedient—and the President was always, I think, as kind as he could afford to be and as expedient as he could manage to be. But when, early the summer before, the University of Iowa, or Illinois, or Indiana—I remember it began with an *I*—had offered Miss Batterson a better job, a Chair in fact, he had not tried to meet their offer, but had told her that Benton was too grateful for all she had done for it in the past to stand in the way of her happiness and increased usefulness in the future. The President felt for an instant, as administrators always do, *If somebody else wants her don't I?*—but it was only for an instant. Having her teach creative writing was too much like having General Lee and his horse Traveller teach it.

It took several days for Miss Batterson to make up her mind. During those days, whenever the President thought of her, he breathed like a waiting man. Miss Batterson decided to leave Benton. The President gave a deep sigh: now one more part of Benton would be his. But he hid the joy he felt, and expressed, a little shortly, the sorrow he did not feel. Miss Batterson's offer was not anything that Miss Batterson had expected—was more, she was sure, than she had had any right to expect—and it had made her look, for the days she considered it, even younger than she usually did; now for an instant she looked a little older.

The President managed, as administrators do, to find out

why the other school had wanted Miss Batterson. I had
read poems there the winter before, as poets do; years ago
I had made my living by teaching English there, as poets
also do: I already knew.

The Head of this school's Department of English was a
round, just, equable man; he was better-humored, almost,
than I had believed a man could be. He had a cheek—but
words are wrong for that cheek: as you looked at it you
felt as you do when, on a summer's day, you look at the side
of a watermelon.

He had a wife, too. The Head had been guided by his
wife for as long as he could remember, and by his mother
before that. He had become Head of his Department in an
unusual way. His field was Cowper. Scholars are sown over
their fields almost at random, but after a time they begin to
resemble what they inhabit, and it all seems to the new-
comer Design. But the Head had resembled his field from
the beginning; he would have remained in it, as a lump of
sugar remains in a cup of tea, except for one thing.

When you pronounce Cowper properly, you say Cooper.
People who read about the Head knew that he was an authority on Cowper; if a Frenchman at the University of
Manchester had died, he would have been the authority on
Cowper. But when people who didn't know how to pronounce Cowper heard the head referred to by people who
did—in speeches, or in conversation, or during the inter-
changes of professional information that are called by scholars conversation—*they* thought him an authority on Cooper,
and spoke of him as such. The Head—he was only a professor in those days—did what he could, but there was not
enough that he could do. He explained, but most of the
world wasn't there to be explained to; people cared little

for Cooper, but less for Cowper—deep down inside, they would *rather* have had him an authority on Cooper: so that advertisements of textbooks of American literature, anthologies of frontier humor, reproductions of Currier and Ives were always there in his pigeonhole in the English office, there in the mail-slot at his office, there in the mail-box on his front porch—people were always stopping him on the campus and asking him Colonial questions, frontier questions, saying to him with a smile, "As an authority on Cooper you'll be interested in this man Winters: he says Cooper is one of the greatest novelists in English."

"One of the greatest novelists in English!" the Head exclaimed to his wife, the evening after he had been told this for the second time. "As well say it of Aphra Behn!"

His wife said, "I don't *understand* how people can be so—"

"I hope I never hear the name Cooper again!" He had quite raised his voice; but then he said with an apologetic shake of his head, "I'm afraid I interrupted you, my dear."

He found himself taking more and more interest in the administrative side of teaching. People had always thought him sound, they began to consider him useful; before long he and his wife were spending evenings with deans. He, far more than its chairman, was the informing intelligence of the committee that revised the English curriculum of the secondary schools of his state; he had a disproportionate share in the work that was done on a core curriculum for the Humanities Division, when the President of his University had the University adopt General Education. He talked less, now, about editions; quotations from Burke began to appear in his lectures, and his students miserably tried to distinguish between Canning and Chatham and Castlereagh, the Elder Pitt, the Younger Pitt; one day he said to his wife, looking at the engraving of Cowper that hung above their mantelpiece: "I wonder what he would have thought of *Emma*." The stocking-cap on the poet's head, the tea cup in the poet's hand had to him a look of limitation, of almost feminine restraint. Cowper's life seemed to him a sheltered one: it did no good to remind himself that Cowper had been, for a good deal of his life, insane.

After he became Head of the Department he seldom thought of Cowper; he let two graduate students finish his concordance; and when, a few years later, he overheard the Dean of the Graduate School saying to someone at a party, "It and the Department of Chemistry are the two soundest departments in the University—" when he heard this, and realized from the next sentence that it was his department that was being referred to, he felt a pleasure that he hadn't felt even when he had first held in his hands, fresh from the Cambridge Press, his own edition of *The Task*.

Nobody except the English Department had thought it sensible of him to be interested in Cowper; now everybody thought it sensible of him to be interested in the English Department. Each member of the Department did something that seemed to the world impractical at best, idiotic at worst; to be in charge of the whole idiocy and impracticality seemed impractical or idiotic to no one. He had never been what intellectuals consider an intellectual, but other people had thought him one, and he had had to suffer the consequences of their mistake. Now he had a pay roll to meet. His university was a large or, as people say, great university: the pay roll was a big pay roll. He had always been just and literal and thorough; nothing, now, was too small for him to oversee, too absurd for him to take seriously, too labyrinthine for him to find a reasonable way out of. Too much work, much too much work, made him grey before his time, but it was a grey of a rosy cast, a warm grey—you felt good as you looked at that grey. The Head not only *was* goodhumored and goodhearted, he looked it: his cheeks had calmed, with their soft compromises, his eyes had beguiled, with their sober literal blue, many a deadlocked, pigheaded committee, many a man or woman swept into a corner and left there, to grow separate and miserable and half-insane; and full Professors of thirty years, men who sat in their hillside towers like semi-autonomous states, manifesting themselves only in absent thunders, definitive editions—these, even, came, and spoke, and heard, and went away consenting.

He was a dull speaker, but a sincere and convincing one; he memorized jokes and, at the right spots in speeches, told them with an ecumenical smile, as though he were the Evening Star shining on the just and unjust. He made these speeches to associations, clubs, alumni; he wrote on the problems of American education, the administrative ones especially; he went to baseball games with the Dean of the School of Education, and talked to the coaches and Educators who sat around him. When the Head thought of his old life, it seemed to him a sheltered one; when the presidents of smaller colleges grew old, retired, or died, he was interested.

All this had pleased his wife, a daughter and granddaughter of judges—of Justices of the Supreme Court of Virginia. If she had married an English professor, it had been not because she wished to, but for love; when the years turned the English professor into an administrator, it was a joy to her, though not an unlooked-for joy—she had done all that

III

she could to help the years. She had given little dinners, she had . . . but it wasn't what she did, but what she was. She was—it was something you felt at first glance—a real lady; she was the sort of lady whom real ladies consider a real lady; beside her most ladies seemed hardly even women.

She was Miss Batterson's oldest and dearest friend. The two of them had had to give up going to Milford Academy together, going to Sweet Briar College together, but each summer they still went to bathe at the seashore together, to buy furniture in the country together. She had heard her grandfather's stories of Miss Batterson's great-great-grand-father—the one his slaves killed—had heard Ellen Glasgow refer to Miss Batterson as "a woman of the finest sensi-bility." She was able to spend only three months of each year in Virginia, and she knew that, until her husband re-tired, they could never go back for good, since there was no English department in the state of Virginia comparable to theirs. He could go back to Virginia only as a president.

The plains around the University—so full of snowflakes in the winter, so full of cornstalks in the summer—held nothing that could remind her of Virginia except the Vet-erinary Clinic of the School of Agriculture, a copy of the Governor's Palace at Williamsburg. Having Miss Batterson there would be like having a maze of box in her back yard—a maze in which the two of them, as little girls, had drunk cambric tea together. She said to her husband, when their Chair became empty: "Think of what it would mean to *these* young people—" she paused there: a great deal had been compressed into that *these*—"to *these* young people to come into contact with someone like Camille."

"More than they themselves would realize," her husband said thoughtfully.

"At the time, perhaps. But later on . . ."

"That's so."

"I wouldn't say this to Camille for anything in the world, but no matter what *she* thinks of it, you and I know that Benton is no place for Camille."

After a moment her husband said: "One reservation comes to my mind. You understand, I must think of the Department. *Is* Camille—for such a Chair as this, I mean—well enough known in her field?"

His wife said, "Well enough *known?* She's certainly one of the most respected teachers of creative writing—of short story creative writing—in the whole country. Think how well received her paper on Katherine Mansfield was at the M.L.A.! Her anthology may not be as much used as it once was, but it was one of the standard anthologies in its day. And you know yourself that Hoad, Batterson, and Hill is one of *the* textbooks on the short story."

"That's so," he said thoughtfully. He was not sure that it was, but when he asked others, it seemed to be. He did not have an easy time: part of the Department wanted Katharine Anne Porter or William Faulkner—it didn't seem to matter which—to have the chair, and it did no good to tell them that neither would take it. The rest of the Department wanted—but in the end it didn't matter whom they wanted. The Head of the Department, in such matters as these, had a wife of his own, a wife of iron.

. . . None of the people at Benton could understand why Miss Batterson was going to leave—could believe that Miss Batterson was going to leave. It was a more important position, other people would have said, but Benton people knew better than that. She would be getting more money, of course, but *she* didn't care about money; Miss Batterson wouldn't have said this, except under ether, but anyone could see that it was so. Her leaving Benton—her even considering leaving—made me uneasy; I remembered a saying, a saying I didn't believe or want to believe, about what to expect when the old change their ways.

That fall Miss Batterson went, shy, breathless, and—to begin with—sad, to a new world. She sent many letters and postcards home about it: home to the little Virginian town where she spent her summers, home to Benton. The tone of her letters—of her speech, when she talked to us at Christmas vacation—was extraordinary: it was as if she were attending the University, not teaching at it. Somehow, after almost sixty years in it, the world had still not happened to her, and she stood at its edge with a timid smile, her hand extended to its fresh terrors, its fresh joys—a girl attending, a ghost now, the dance to which forty years ago she did not get to go.

In March, the first spring after she left Benton, she died. Miss Batterson—who ought surely to have died, like the heroine of an old novel, of a brain fever—died instead, in the newest and largest of hospitals, petted by all her nurses, of a kind of corpuscular deficiency that ten years before had not even been identified. It was as Gertrude said: "What a thing for *her* to die of!" Her demands on life had been too small: they had not got her, even, her own death.

"To think I'll never see her again!" Gertrude went on. Her voice was full of personal sorrow: that windfall, that dispensation, that ornament of the Book of Benton was gone for good, and anything more about Camille Turner Batterson would have to be got at second hand or else invented. In Gertrude's voice there was no trace of any impersonal sorrow, sorrow for Miss Batterson and man; but she grieved for what Miss Batterson had been to her, so that there was in her response a kind of truth—of attractiveness, almost—that was absent from the President's suitable sentences. She behaved badly in her own way, and the President behaved well in his: he expressed grief in its Instant or powdered form.

It didn't seem possible to me that Miss Batterson had ceased to exist. I felt: if Miss Batterson goes, none of us are safe—and of course, none of us are safe. She had left Flo the cobbler's bench, two of the luster pitchers, and some china with brown landscapes on it that was much better, I remembered, than if the landscapes had been blue; she had left my wife a Tree of Life quilt, and me the old Macmillan edition of Chekhov's short stories—I had often borrowed from her the volumes the library didn't have. She had left Dr. Willen enough to furnish her laboratory in the style of Benjamin Thompson, Count Rumford. But I didn't enjoy my Chekhov, and when I saw the cobbler's bench in Flo's living room, it was a grief to me to see it there; I made some noticing remark and Flo, replying, began to cry, and her red face was redder than ever, her raw voice rawer. She had learned to think of people only in hundred-thousand lots, but she couldn't help feeling for them, sometimes, one at a time—so that I thought once more, in uneasy perplexity: How shall I feel about Flo? That figure of fun, that pillar of righteousness, that type of the age, that index of the limitations of the human being, that human being? Flo was so sharply delimited, her bounds were so harshly and narrowly set, that you were aware as you seldom were of your own limits, and said to yourself: "To someone I am Flo."

Jerrold spoke of Miss Batterson just as one would have expected him to speak of her, but there was something pinched and sad and—I realized sadly—old about his sober grief. He called her a "lady of the old school," and finished by saying, "From my association with Camille I gained, I could not but feel, an almost personal insight into the South's post-Reconstruction days." I looked at the cobbler's bench, the luster pitchers, the brown china, and wondered what they had gained from their association with Miss Batterson. Whatever it was, they didn't say. Nor did John and Fern. John, coming in, said hello to me as politely and matter-of-factly as ever, and Fern, going out, gave me the look of malevolence she saved for the world, and said nothing. And Yang, like her, said nothing. Sometimes, out walking with the President, did he vaguely expect to meet someone he could desert the President for, and feel a vague disappointment when no one came? I couldn't know.

8.

A GOOD many people at Benton felt that Miss Batterson had died "as old people so often do when they go into retirement." To Benton other colleges, the world itself, were retirement. When Dr. Rosenbaum first heard this feeling expressed, at lunch in the cafeteria, he turned his head away from the man who had expressed it, and his face looked more thoughtful and more forbidding than most people would have believed it could look. Outside, going home, he repeated to himself Bismarck's *You can do anything with children if you will only play with them.* It was almost his favorite saying, but he took no pleasure in it now: knowledge, even if it is power, is still not consolation.

The next day, when the first girls came to Dr. Rosen-

baum's office for their conferences, there was only a note
on the door postponing these, in Mrs. Rosenbaum's angular
impatient hand. Dr. Rosenbaum was looking out the window of a plane going into the airport at Charlottesville, on
his way to a funeral.

He had come home and said to his wife, after sitting there
silently for a while: "I believe that I have not been to a
funeral since Mayr's."

"There was never a funeral like *that*," Irene answered,
observing him. Dr. Rosenbaum continued heavily: "It is a
long time since I have done something as foolish as I can. It
is hard to be foolish here. Middle age is creeping on me like
a thief in the night."

She started to reply, but was cut short by Dr. Rosenbaum's, "You would not love my Middle Ages."

She said to him with her most dazzling smile: "But of
course not! . . . Not since Mayr! Do you remember how
we—truly, this is not a world in which the buds stay buds
for long. Except for you—except for you. You and I must
hurry to get some funerals in before our own."

"And it will be interesting to see Virginia," said Dr.
Rosenbaum, smiling back; his big body had a grateful domestic air, each pound of it understood. "The best of all
the heroes of the novels of Friedrich Gerstäcker, because he
had spent his childhood in Virginia, was nicknamed—ah no,
that was another, one named Tennessee. But you could not
possibly have pleased me more, when I was nine, than to tell
me that someday I should go to Virginia and ride a—a
mustang."

Mrs. Rosenbaum said, "We should have gone to see her
in the summer as she wished us to go. That poor Camille!"

Mrs. Rosenbaum didn't make the trip herself, but she

called the airline, and talked while Gottfried packed, and ate breakfast with him just before, drove him to the airport just after, the next day's dawn. For half the flight Dr. Rosenbaum worked away at an article on *Kat'a Kabanova* that he was writing for *Music and Letters;* the rest of the time he looked at cloud formations, which are different from the world. He mumbled to himself with mocking sententiousness that the more he saw of cloud formations, the less he thought of human beings, but he did not mean it; he was going to the funeral of a cloud formation, and he wished for her sake that she had been an ordinary human being instead.

He went on to Miss Batterson's home town in a bus. He looked characterizingly at the countryside, and dismissed it with a disappointed "English!" But the other passengers on the bus, their slow ruminating sentences, were not anything he could dismiss with *English:* he understood only a part of what they said, but relished all of it. "There is something about these peasant dialects that makes me feel at home," he would have said to you, with a laugh that hadn't grown in any fields wilder than those along the River Salz; and he wouldn't entirely have understood why the phrase *peasant dialects* would have amused you—though if you had explained, your explanation would have amused him.

Before the bus could enter Stanhope it had to get by a giant Consolidated School, one that could have taken under its wings the children of many a county. The school was of the school of Williamsburg; it had serious maroon bricks, but its doors and windows were yellow as daffodils. Beneath this school, as some little Rhenish village shelters itself beneath its crag and castle, the town lay, protected; it had one house less, as they told Dr. Rosenbaum, than it had had

at the beginning of the Civil . . . but what is one saying!
of the War Between the States. In its courthouse Patrick
Henry had had, with somebody of whom, alas, Dr. Rosenbaum knew nothing, a debate on—but this too Dr. Rosenbaum knew nothing of. He was in another world, but a
world that went some distance back: the churchyard held
women killed by Indians (Dr. Rosenbaum breathed faster)
in the seventeenth century, and it held, too, the dead of the
wars of four centuries. Four centuries are yesterday, but the
church itself was called Buffalo Church. Not even the Indians had prepared him for this: Dr. Rosenbaum, who was
as sensitive to buffaloes as all Europeans are, felt a pang of
pure believing bliss—oh, if Friedrich Gerstäcker had been
there to see the name: it would have crowned all his work.

The day, there at Stanhope, was a raw rain-washed blue.
It was cold enough for your knuckles to burn a little, but
you could see in borders along the walks green and yellow
prongs, like the tips of garden forks, that in two or three
days would be—jonquils, as we would say; buttercups, as
the people there would have said. Miss Batterson was the
only person buried there that day—the second to be buried
there since 1940: the churchyard, except for the burial plots
of a few of the oldest and smallest families, had long ago
been filled, and people were now buried in a larger ceme-
tery, implacable with sward and box and machine-polished
granite, that lay just beyond the Consolidated School.

In her family's plot, after Camille Batterson had been
buried in it, there was a place for one more Batterson, but
there was no Batterson left to fill it. Dr. Rosenbaum saw for
a last time, but with the eye of the mind, the dead woman.
Her face had had such "good bones" that the gazer had always reflected, "She must have been quite pretty as a

girl—" and then had stopped, ashamed: she was a girl. Now in his vision of her, her vague half-silvered hair floated above her good ghostly bones, her clear absent eyes —floated lightly, lightly; but no more lightly than it had in life.

After the ceremony Dr. Rosenbaum walked for a few minutes among the stones of the churchyard. The earliest inscriptions were rude work, as if the carver had been holding a chisel in one hand and a rifle in the other, but they soon arrived at an eighteenth-century elegance which, for some decades, they maintained; there set in then, to Dr. Rosenbaum's regretful eyes, a gradual aesthetic deterioration—by 1900 there were monuments which, to judge from their lettering, figures, and finish, had beneath them a dead bathtub. But all the people had been alive, and all of them were dead: he felt for them the undifferentiating sorrow, the elegiac, unforced acceptance, that man feels in the end for all his kind.

One marker of ordinary stone, very beautifully carved, told you that there had perished here the mortal part of JOHANNES MÖRIKE, who had been born in the Palatinate in 1747 and who had departed this life, in 1785, at Stanhope. Dr. Rosenbaum had written several songs—rather uncharacteristic ones—to the words of the poet Mörike, so that he half-laughed to himself, half-groaned to himself, "Nature is witty." America might not have its basalt and castles and tales of ghosts and knights and robber barons, but it had its Mörike. Dr. Rosenbaum said to him in mocking wonder, "What are *you* doing here, Johannes Mörike?"—and the gravestone replied to him, in mocking wonder: "What are *you* doing here, Gottfried Knosperl Rosenbaum?" Dr. Rosenbaum did not answer.

That afternoon he was shown the homes of, that evening he ate the dinner of, the nearest surviving relatives of Miss Batterson; when they had learned that he was a colleague of hers at Benton, come all this way for the funeral, they would not hear of anything else. Their surroundings were old and interesting, but Gottfried was used to rather older and rather more interesting surroundings than theirs. He did not want things to be European, to be at all like Europe: it was a New World, wasn't it?

Many of her relatives were older than Miss Batterson, but they were very gratifyingly of a New World; at first Gottfried tried to memorize the best and strangest of their remarks, so that Irene too would know—but it was no use, he would have had to memorize everything: what they said, and how they looked as they said it, and how they pronounced the words, and the tunes they sang the words to. It was all different; he thought with joy, "It is an opera they are performing for me—at last I do not write an opera but am in it."

The relatives' Conversations with a Modern German Composer were, to begin with, very careful. They made some polite remarks about Strauss and Puccini, but soon strayed off to Schumann-Heink and Galli-Curci and Pavlova. Gottfried's German-ness—they made no distinction between Austria and Germany—was more difficult to do anything with; they kept away from Hitler and the Kaiser, and stuck for as long as they could to German literature. This was not for long: if *Faust* and *The Magic Mountain* had not existed, Gottfried felt, American readers and German writers would have had left in common only the *Lorelei*. They talked about *Faust*.

But their *Faust* was Bayard Taylor's translation: when

Dr. Rosenbaum made some remark about doggerel and Hans Sachs, they looked as blankly astonished as if he had said this of *In Memoriam;* and he looked down, embarrassed, and took another big bite of beaten biscuit and country ham. "I have never tasted such ham," he said, and they told him for how many years and over how many cords of hickory logs they had smoked it. His *I have never tasted such ham* was perfectly sincere: it did not seem to him ham at all, but something as exotic as the pemmican he used to read about—if they had told him that it had been made from buffaloes or mustangs, he would have believed them. He asked them if they had ever eaten pemmican, but they never had.

One man was plainly cleverer than the rest, and said things about *Faust* that Gottfried would willingly have understood; but he was from Charleston, and from an old Charleston family at that. He said *gre-ut* and *bo-ut* and *highvey* and *lyĕdy* in magical gobbling tones, like a Negro from the Bahamas imitating a baseball-player from Brooklyn, a cultivated one. Gottfried said *highvey* himself, so that was easy for him; but he missed, in every sentence, just enough words to make it incomprehensible. He gave up the clever man and returned to the ordinary Virginians, who seldom said anything worse than *trahflin'* and *abooot*. They had begun to talk about *Ivanhoe*—it is hard to say anything hard about *Ivanhoe*.

Gottfried, among these people, felt like a polar bear among genteel old foxes; yet he liked them, and felt for them a mocking, uneasy kinship that he felt for few people at Benton. He and they had the Past in common, of course; and these people gave the circumstances of their lives an attention or inattention akin, in some ways, to that he gave his own. What they said had, now and then, the rubbed unobtrusive gloss of their furniture, and they were as old and shaky and delicate as their furniture. They were grotesque, too—but Gottfried was himself grotesque, and did not hold that against them. Yet as he took a second helping of their candied yams, he found himself remembering a tune, a Papuan folk-song, that he had not thought of for many years. There the yams had not been candied. He sat stirring his coffee with a rattail spoon, and felt that there was something half barbaric, half archaic about the place and its people; he felt—he smiled as he invented—that the tenants of Miss Batterson's relatives brought them eggs, and hogs, and the logs to smoke them with, and that the relatives paid the tenants with—with drafts on *Ivanhoe* or *Oliver Twist*, or by promising to represent them next year at Patrick Henry's courthouse; and what money the tenants had stayed under the mattress, and what money the relatives had stayed in mortgages that they had been paying one another interest on since the days of Santos-Dumont. Could these people and the professors of Benton, these people and the girls who skied at Kitzbühel over Christmas—could they really be existing at the same time in the same country? He said to himself, "No, it is not a country, it is a continent." But he listened to what he had said with a distrusting smile: he had seen too many countries and provinces and cities turn into continents with acquaintance.

These old foxes of his had standards of a sort—their own sort—and went by and judged by them, and indicated their judgments with a smile and a look, a sigh and a passing word. Their manners were more formal than their statements; never once did they even lecture Gottfried—so that he heard hovering behind them another, a ghostlier tune, and the words set to it were: *Lightly, lightly.* They were not long for this world, he felt; as they drove him to the bus he saw with uneasiness, hung like a sword above their heads, the dews of evening.

9.

YOU COULD not come up the walk to the Rosenbaums' house without giving an astonished smile. It looked like the child Cecil B. de Mille's notion of the House That Saladin Built, and the snows lay strangely on it, like sherbet. Inside, bronze spears stuck from the beams overshadowing an arch, and the dark beams were hand-hewn—hand-bitten, one almost felt—from California redwood.

Within this idea of Europe and the Past the Rosenbaums had settled themselves. When they had first come to Benton, during the war, they had not been able to find anything better, and after a while they were too used to it to care. Besides, Gottfried liked it, and would say to people: "For de composer Rosenbaum idt iss *ide*al." What this meant, and why he had said it, it was hard for them to say.

Now as he went up the walk from the taxi, he did not notice the tiles and the arches or, inside, the spears; and when his wife got up, looking as people of a certain age look when they are waked at a certain hour of the morning, he did not notice that she looked this way; and as he sat in the kitchen drinking the coffee she had made for them, he noticed neither the coffee, nor the red enamel chairs they sat in, nor the red enamel table they bent over, there in front of the great cream stucco fireplace of their Moorish kitchen. His wife noticed none of these things, but only what he had to say and him. When he had finished describing

Miss Batterson's birthplace, and Miss Batterson's relatives, and Miss Batterson's burial, Irene said to him—and her thin mocking face and his fat clever face looked exactly alike— "Poor old lady!"

It did not occur to either of them that this phrase would have been applied by most people to her, and that the same people would have said about him: "Poor old man!" Were they not exiles? Were they not old?

Dr. Rosenbaum would hardly have known how to reply to this, it would have seemed to him so foolish: perhaps he would have said, with his laugh that sounded like a man saying, in a voice deeper than he had meant it, *ho ho ho*—

But what was there for him to say? The Rosenbaums sat by their fireplace like Baucis and Philemon, and spoke in mourning for this American acquaintance of theirs. They spoke rather sadly, and rather drily, and rather absently; and if, as in a pastoral, the nature around them had mourned, it would have mourned as they did, with a dry and absent sadness. For their house—spears, stucco, enamel, and all— never seemed to you an American house; the air in it was not American air, but was heated differently, moved differently, so that even the curtains hung with a darker and staider and stiller stiffness, as if they had framed, for more years, different things; on the fish-knives pike floated, by weeds, over gravel; the cookie you took, no matter which you took, had a taste you almost, never quite knew—and when you had swallowed it, still ignorant, the cup you put to your lips had the faint odor of some foreign flower. The essence of the Rosenbaums looked above their accident obliviously: as they walked back and forth among the rooms, quarreling fiercely over whether *Falstaff* was better than *Figaro*, Hölderlin than Goethe, laughing loudly in indigna-

125

tion at, lifting their hands in despair over, calling upon all things there to witness, the other's stupidity, you saw that they walked among, called upon to witness, no cities and mountains and rivers of yours, but had brought along with them, when they had had to cross the Atlantic, Europe.

10.

MISS BATTERSON had told me a story that, a few days after she died, I remembered.

During the last years of the Civil War her father had been old enough to take care of the family's cows. The family's farm lay at the side of a big swamp, one with pastures back inside it; the little boy would drive the cows into these pastures, along a sort of isthmus, and then would wait all day at the foot of, or in the branches of, a tremendous oak tree that grew there at the edge of the swamp. He had one pet cow, a heifer named Elfie, that the family had given him while she was still a calf—he said that Elfie always went away last of all and came back first of all.

Miss Batterson said: "I asked Papa, 'Why did you name your heifer Elfie?' and Papa said that he didn't, that he named her Brownie, and that his mother said, 'Brownie's so *commonplace*. Why don't you call the little thing Elfie?' "

The little boy had his lunch with him, and he would eat it in the tree. He spent most of his time in the tree. He was supposed to: from it he could see for a long way out over the country, and if he saw soldiers—it didn't matter what kind—he was supposed to go back into the swamp and keep the cows there. Up in the tree he sang songs, and ate his lunch—a corn pone and a turnip, generally—and watched for the soldiers who would some day come for the cows, and knitted. Every day he knitted, with yarn and knitting needles his mother gave him, a stocking for the army—part of a stocking. In hot weather he wore a straw hat, though he hardly needed it in the tree, and in cold weather he wore around his shoulders an old shawl of his mother's. The leaves were so thick that it was hard for him to see out of the tree, but he had a lookout part that he would climb to, every hour or so, and then he would climb back down to the tree-house part that he stayed in. This part was so much of a tree-house that he could doze off there and sleep quite safely; and one day, after he had slept for longer than usual, he climbed up and looked out and saw some soldiers so near that he couldn't climb down and run to the cattle, barely had time to get back to the thickest part of the tree.

For a while he didn't dare look down at them—he didn't even dare open his eyes. Their voices were very different from any he was accustomed to, and frightened him; and when he at last peeped down at them through the leaves, their new dark uniforms and shiny weapons and big dark beards were more frightening than their voices. It was a relief to him to look at their horses, that were just the same as the horses he was used to.

It was late in the afternoon, almost time for the cows to come back. He had been waiting for the soldiers to go, and feeling uneasier and uneasier inside, and telling himself that next minute they'd surely go; and then he saw that they weren't going to go—they were pitching camp. In a little while the cows came. Elfie was walking in front switching her tail.

The soldiers killed Elfie and another of the cows—the rest ran back into the swamp—and cut them up and cooked them and ate them. Afterwards they talked for a long time in the darkness below; finally they went to sleep, and after a while the little boy went to sleep too. Next morning, when the soldiers had gone, he went back into the swamp and got the rest of the cows and drove them home.

When I would read about, or hear people talking about, the Civil War, it would remind me of Elfie; but this was the first time I had remembered the story since Miss Batterson had died. I thought of her father sitting there in the tree—with his mother's shawl over his shoulders, his knitting needles stuck in his belt—watching the soldiers kill and cook and eat up Elfie; crying for a while, but not aloud, and getting drowsy and dropping off to sleep, and sleeping all night just as the soldiers slept, and leaving after the soldiers left in the morning. I thought of him just as I always did, but I realized that there was something incongruous about him: not the knitting needles, not the shawl, the trousers. They did not go with his face, which—a little smaller than I was used to, a little younger than I was used to—was still Miss Batterson's face.

IV.

Constance

AND

The Rosenbaums

1. Often that year, looking out the window of my office, I would see Gertrude walking down the walk with some teacher or student; she would say something, and then listen intently to the reply. I used to murmur to myself, *Ah, Questioner;* one day I said to her through the window, silently: *Whence comest thou?* and she answered, silently —so I pretended—*From going to and fro in Benton, and from walking up and down in it.* I told my wife this; it amused her. After that we used *walking up and down in it* as a sort of general phrase for Gertrude at Benton.

It always astonished me that people did not realize what she was doing: what could listening—in *Gertrude*—mean but a book? She listened only As A Novelist. In private life she either talked all the time, when she was excited, or else sat in glum, impatient silence, paying no attention to anything. Fortunately for her, she was easily excited. One of the only anecdotes she knew about her childhood, her mother had told her: "When I was three," Gertrude said, "and we had visitors, it would make me so excited I'd run around and around in a circle till I got dizzy and fell down in the middle of the floor."

She hadn't changed; now, though, she didn't fall, but grew drunk and bedazzling with her own words, felt her eyes fill with a light like earthshine. She was all right, then. But as long as the speed of her own mood wasn't carrying

131

her through herself, she felt a restless dissatisfaction with herself, with people, with the world—a dissatisfaction not merely with being but with the possibilities of being.

Even her wit depended on the motion of the moment. Gertrude had all eternity to write her books in, and it weighed upon her lively spirit. The books were crushed down into method: as I read I was so conscious of what was being done that I scarcely noticed or cared what it was being done to—and life and death, men and women seemed to me for those moments no more than the systematic, verifiable abstractions of some galactic Mechanism. But in conversation Gertrude hit you with the poker, the bobby-pins in her hair, your own shoe—you went away murmuring that anger is the mother of invention. Anger is also, as we know from Aristotle, the emotion nearest to reason: no wonder Gertrude's books seemed so rational!

I do not know whether it was reason or anger that prompted a philosopher to make an odd remark about her work. Gertrude had been saying that philosophy is something you read in order to get over philosophy. A little later the philosopher said to her, in a thoughtful, dispassionate tone, that her own novels seemed to him influenced by Spinoza, and that she should, like Spinoza, have given Roman numerals to the paragraphs, Arabic numerals to the sentences.

Gertrude said quickly, "His sentences aren't numbered, just the propositions." The man answered, "Yes, that's so," and laughed. Normally Gertrude would have kept herself from saying this; one could see how much the remark had stung.

Yet Gertrude could have replied, with justice, that she was far more of a moralist than Spinoza. Did he not say that he had "labored carefully not to mock, lament, and execrate, but to understand"? Gertrude had labored carefully to mock, lament, and execrate—to condemn utterly; and to do so it had also been necessary for her to understand, for her to have at the tips of her fingernails the Facts. The world divides into—Gertrude had read—facts; and the facts were what Gertrude knew. Were Memory truly, as the Greeks feigned, the Mother of the Muses, she would long ago have traded all nine of her daughters for Gertrude. Gertrude was as knowing as *Time*. All clichés, slogans, fashions, turns of speech, details of dress, disguises of affection, tunnels or by-passes of ideology, gravestones of rationalization and cant lived in Gertrude as though in nutrient broth; and Gertrude nourished them unharmed, knowing all, believing none.

She made her characters, held them, to the letter of the law. If one of Gertrude's heroines, running to snatch from the lips of her little daughter a half-emptied bottle of furniture-polish, fell and tore her skirt, Gertrude knew the name of the dressmaker who had made the skirt—and it was the right one for a woman of that class, at that date; she knew the brand of the furniture-polish that the little girl had swallowed; she knew, even, the particular exclamation that such a woman, tearing her skirt at such a moment, would have uttered—the particular sin that the woman, in thinking of her skirt at such a moment, would have committed. (The Church itself had no such casuist as Gertrude.) But how the child felt as it seized and drank the polish, how the mother felt as she caught the child to her breast—about such things as these, which have neither brand nor date, Gertrude was less knowing; would have said impatiently, "Everybody knows *that!*"

Gertrude knew the price of every sin and the value of none; and almost everything, to her, was a sin—a sin and a shame, as our mothers would have said. Her books were a systematic, detailed, and conclusive condemnation of mankind for being stupid and bad; yet if mankind had been clever and good, what would have become of Gertrude? Often morality—to parody another definition—is the last refuge of a moralist. Gertrude's good jokes, her good spirits, her not very good income were rooted in, luxuriant above, the vices and stupidities of mankind: when she met someone who was either good or clever, she looked at him in uneasy antagonism. Yet she need not have been afraid. Clever people always came to seem to her, after a time, bad; good people always came to seem to her, after a time, stupid. She was always able to fail the clever for being bad, the good for being stupid; and if somebody was both clever and good, Gertrude stopped grading.

If a voice had said to her, "Hast thou considered my servant Gottfried Rosenbaum, that there is none like him in Benton, a kind and a clever man," she would have answered: "I can't *stand* that Gottfried Rosenbaum."

2.

DR. ROSENBAUM had never, except in Gertrude's dream, come to America in a submarine, but he had been everywhere else in everything else. His immense rawhide suitcase (it looked like the common ancestor of suitcases and safes) had on it labels that went as far north as the North Cape, as far south as Sydney. He had once spent a year and a half recording the songs of the inhabitants of the Gulf of Papua, and was still admired by anthropologists, who would say when you mentioned his name: "Oh yes, the friend of Malinowski." (I said to one of them, when he happened to mention Malinowski, "Oh yes, the friend of Rosenbaum"; he looked at me as though I were insane.) Whenever in one of Dr. Rosenbaum's compositions there was a theme a good deal more commonplace, more nearly diatonic than all the rest, you could be sure it was a Papuan folk-tune.

Long ago, Dr. Rosenbaum's settings of Brecht's most seditious poems—he specialized, in those days, in *Sprechstimme*—had left his audiences troubled and uncertain about the music, the police troubled but certain about the words; when the Germans went into Austria Dr. Rosenbaum escaped, as he put it, at the eleventh hour, by the skin of his teeth, without a garment. His first American work, a secular cantata that used "The Witch of Coös" as its text, had in it the most idiomatic writing for skeleton that I've ever heard—one *ostinato* figure, half glissando xylophones and half violinists hitting their soundboxes with their bows, seemed to me particularly notable; but he had used almost as extraordinary an idiom for the Witch, for her son, and for Robert Frost, and it was hard for an audience to decide which of the four was most frightening. I thought that he had made the skeleton, correctly enough, the most sympathetic being in the piece—to accompany the line *The faintest restless rustling ran all through them* the orchestra played a far-off Bergish waltz-theme, as though spring had come late that year, and Dr. Rosenbaum, Constance, and I would all sniff, Constance quite sincerely. I liked to hear him humming parts of the cantata to himself; it was best of all when he would sing, with tremendous understatement: "*I knew idt. Idt vass de bones!*"

He had been working for about a year on a requiem mass

for Alma Mahler; he would say about his mass, simply: "I vant to haf idt readty ven she die."

He loved hitherto-unthought-of, thereafter-unthinkable combinations of instruments. When some extraordinary array of players filed half-proudly, half-sheepishly on to the stage, looking like the Bremen Town Musicians—if those were, as I think they were, a rooster, a cat, a dog, and a donkey—you could guess beforehand that it was to be one of Gottfried's compositions. His *Joyous Celebration of the Memory of the Master Johann Sebastian Bach* had a tone-row composed of the notes B, A, C, and H (in the German notation), of these inverted, and of these transposed; and there were four movements, the first played on instruments beginning with the letter *b*, the second on instruments beginning with the letter *a*, and so on. After the magnificent group that ushered in the piece (bugle, bass-viol, bassoon, basset-horn, bombardon, bass-drum, bagpipe, baritone, and a violinist with only his bow) it was sad to see an Alp horn and an accordion come in to play the second movement. Gottfried himself said about the first group: "Vot a bunch!" When I asked him how he had thought of it he said placidly: "De devil soldt me his soul."

I have heard him placed with the sentence, "He's a sort of Viennese Satie"; but his titles were not so strange as Satie's, and his compositions were a great deal stranger than Satie's. You did not know how to take them—did not even know how you were supposed to take them.

Some of his transcriptions and adaptations were quite popular, and all of them were admired; and he had published three volumes of an immense work showing how content gets expressed in, and modified by, the forms of its time—three volumes, and there were more to come. The less technical parts were very entertaining and, sometimes, very astonishing; the more technical parts were, I believe, profound—I asked a friend, a composer, about these and his answer began: "It's commonly agreed. . . ." I saved that "It's commonly agreed . . ." for the next question he asked *me*.

Constance told me, "He goes over your piece as if he were you, and the next girl's piece as if he were her—she. He seems to know what you would have done if you could have done it instead of what you did; I just don't know how he does it. And the worst things he says are the ones that encourage you most. It takes the weight of your pieces right off your shoulders."

My wife had heard one girl say to another, "You just haven't *lived* till you've had Dr. Rosenbaum for a teacher." I repeated this to him and, oddly, his face darkened; but then he said with a rueful smile that he was glad his light so shone before the world.

You say, after you have listened to someone talking for a while about music, or painting, or literature; "I see the line you're taking." It was impossible to say this about Gottfried.

It was impossible, that is, where music was concerned. Outside of that he took an extraordinary line—had one, as his girls would have said. He pretended to believe that the sculptures of Henry Moore are predictions of a kind of socialist Utopia, and would say resignedly: "Ve all look like dat, ven de Shtate hass videredt avay." *Ven de Shtate hass videredt avay* was one of his favorite phrases—he seemed to find it inexhaustibly humorous.

Benton's choreographer, a sunny Bachelor of Physical Education somehow derailed into the modern dance, loved Dr. Rosenbaum, and often asked him for dances for her students' recitals; he always assented cheerfully, since he could write a dance for her in fifteen minutes, and indeed would say: "Ven idt take more dan fifteen minutes, *zell me down de river.*" (He liked American idioms; and liked even better insisting that he had learned them, as a child, from the frontier novels of Friedrich Gerstäcker—it was hard successfully to dispute his contention.) The rhythms of his dances made any motions that accompanied them seem timid and constrained; and he specialized in long unexpected rests during which the dancer would stand with one foot in air, waiting, while Dr. Rosenbaum looked at her with twinkling eyes. He himself liked ballet.

Once, along with *Transfigured Night*, he played a class Rachmaninoff's *Isle of the Dead.* Most of his pupils had not seen the painting, so he went to the library and returned with a reproduction of it. Then he pointed, with a sober smile, to a painting which hung on the wall of the classroom (*A Representation of Several Areas, Some of Them Grey*, one might have called it; yet this would have been unjust to it—it was non-representational) and played for the class, on the piano, a composition which he said was an interpretation of the painting: he played very slowly and calmly, with his elbows, so that it sounded like blocks falling downstairs, but in slow motion. But half his class took this as seriously as they took everything else, and asked him for weeks afterward about prepared pianos, tone-clusters, and the compositions of John Cage and Henry Cowell; one girl finally brought him a lovely silk-screen reproduction of a painting by Jackson Pollock, and was just opening her mouth to—

He interrupted, bewilderingly, by asking the Lord what land He had brought him into. The girl stared at him open-mouthed, and he at once said apologetically that he was only quoting Mahler, who had *also diedt from America;* then he gave her such a winning smile that she said to her roommate that night, forgivingly: "He really is a nice old guy. You never would know *he's* famous."

"Is he really famous?" her roommate asked. "I never heard of him before I got here. But gee, before I got here *I'd* never heard of Dr. Crowley."

"I'm pretty sure he's famous—anyway, famous in Europe," the girl replied. Then her eyes brightened and she exclaimed, in scorn at her own forgetfulness: "Of *course* he's famous! He's in the *Britannica,* in the article on Schön-berg."

Mrs. Rosenbaum was twelve or fifteen years older than he, a slight, animated, disquieting woman who had little to do with anyone except Dr. Rosenbaum, a few friends, and occasional visitors of her own—astonishing visitors, gen-erally. She and Dr. Rosenbaum had money of their own, too, and not just his salary: they had a cook, a summer cot-tage on Cape Cod, and a new Simca convertible that Dr. Ro-senbaum looked remarkably funny in, since he had bought it a size too small.

Mrs. Rosenbaum had brought with her, from the Old World, the remains of beauty; jewels—some family, some Jewels; a couple of fur coats which, cut as they were cut, worn with the provisional air with which she wore every-thing, made her look like the Queen-Mother of some tribe of Northern Canadian Indians—one left behind in the snow to die, gaunt but upright, calm, unrepentant. She had dresses of some of the finest vintages, and her new dresses were, almost, as astonishing as the old: she must have had hidden, in a priest's hole behind the spears, a Foreign Seamstress. She dressed in no style to which the faculty wives were accustomed (in no style to which anybody on earth has ever been accustomed, had they only known) but they felt that her clothes were very foreign, very characteristic, and must have been once, to foreigners, very impressive. And they could buy records of her, some of them even *had* records of her, though her name was not Rosenbaum on the records but her own real unsayable Russian name; or rather, Rosenbaum was her real name now, but on the records one found the name that she used to have when, years and years ago, she had been a well-known singer of opera and *lieder*, and not the wife of a respected and fairly ill-known composer.

She looked at the world like a bird, considering; and you too considered; but you could not make up your mind whether she was a Lesser Bird of Prey or simply a song-bird of some dismaying foreign kind. She used too much make-up, her hair was dyed; she had almost frighteningly deep eye-sockets, so that her eyelids were like pieces of porcelain: when she looked at you for a moment with a bright sufficient stare, and then looked past you, you felt that you had been weighed upon her eyelids and found wanting. She judged by standards you guessed at uneasily, and kept her judgments to herself or gave them offhand, as if they could hardly matter to *you:* so that you decided that justice was not going to be done to you, and awaited, like a child, her smile. It was an unqualified, forthcoming, outgoing smile, a smile like spring: you could not believe in it, but it was so.

She said about her husband's compositions for voice, "No, my voice was ruined before I even met Gottfried." The comment was just; still, she could not resist looking mischievously at him as she said it. When I first knew them I noticed that he did little things to placate or mollify her, or to keep her from being troubled or aroused, and I decided that she was the dominant member of their household, but after a while I noticed that she behaved in exactly the same way about him: they were a Dual Monarchy.

Their cook, a Bavarian, was the Witch from *Hansel and Gretel*. She had decided that it is safer to feed than to eat people, but she smiled her old smile—I could never look at her without feeling behind me for an oven. Her smile was like a caricature of Irene's: you didn't believe in it, and it wasn't so. Good, kindly, crochety Else! the Rosenbaums felt; how they could have felt this I do not know.

Else was not a talkative woman—she couldn't think of anything to say—but she talked volubly on one subject: things that man could not find, no, not if he searched for a thousand years, in the stores and kitchens of the Americans. There is a delicious fish, called *fögel* or something of the sort, that dwells only in Lake—I forget the lake, but Else knew it; this fish cannot be found in the lakes, or in the ponds, or in the streams of North America—and when you have said that, what remains to be said of North America? Else thought that Americans are immoral, though childish, and drunk half the time. She had a leather-bound *Hermann und Dorothea* that she had received as a confirmation present; she looked around her at Americans and she saw that they had none—she could not help thinking them uncultivated.

People said about Dr. Rosenbaum's wife that she had married beneath her, and was really a princess of the house of— the houses varied: Hapsburg, Hohenzollern, and Saxe-Coburg-Gotha were the commonest. (I don't understand how they thought a member of any of the three could have been named Letscheskinskaya; perhaps they thought she had married into one and had picked up Gottfried later in life; perhaps they enjoyed saying what they said too much to worry about details.) Gertrude, on the other hand, said that she was Dr. Rosenbaum's mother.

3.

CONSTANCE WAS lonely during her first months at Benton. (She had known my wife and me too long for us to help: we were family, almost.) She made friends with a couple of the girls who worked in the offices at the college, and went on dates with them, sometimes, but they and the dates didn't know much about music—didn't know much about anything. They were hardly better than students, Constance felt; and Constance, now that she was through being a student, was through with students. She had—had always had —a taste for older people, for men and women. These seemed to her real life, not just fooling around. She looked fondly up to them, and they fondly down to her: she knew just how to act, just how to feel about herself, when she was with them.

Her father had said to me about her, when she was twelve or thirteen: "She doesn't want to grow up"; and had concluded, after a pause, soberly, "But she'll have to." I felt that she didn't have to—many people don't; but I was surprised that he knew she didn't want to. He was a remarkably methodical and unimaginative man.

So Constance went along the walks of Benton like Teufelsdröckh, searching for a Man, a Woman. And, for her, Dr. Rosenbaum was one and Mrs. Rosenbaum the other; but along the walks and inside the classrooms of Benton there were others; and Benton's library, its gallery, its listening-

rooms with their two expensive unsatisfactory phonographs
—these too were full of the works of men and women, the
works of man.

But the Rosenbaums were Constance's great find—and
luckily for her, she was theirs. This astonished her and yet
didn't astonish her: grown-ups were always adopting Constance. After a while she lived in and out of the Rosenbaums' house almost as if it were her own. It was full of the
works of man: there were, badly arranged on its rarely
dusted bookshelves, books in English, German, Russian,
French, Latin, Greek—all the languages of the earth, Constance felt; and there were printed scores, photostats of
scores, scores in manuscript, scores in Esperanto, almost. In
the living room, over the fireplace, there was a copy of a
Cro-Magnon painting of a buffalo: Gottfried said that it
showed how American they had become. Elsewhere in the
house there were many reproductions and a few originals:
Vermeer's *Girl with the Red Hat* and *Girl with the Flute*,
the painting of *Degas' Father Listening to Pagans*, several
Cézannes, Delacroix's *Portrait of Paganini*, a real Vuillard,
Kokoschka's *The Tempest*, two real Klees, Uccello's *The
Rout of San Romano*, a Persian painting of a battle between
owls and crows, a sketch of Mahler conducting, water-
colors of Irene in old parts, costume-sketches for the parts,
inscribed photographs of Janáček and Richard Mayr, a
pale engraving of Vivaldi, Beethoven and Liszt letters in
stand-up frames, glass on both sides so that one could see
both sides of the page. There was no end to the confusion
and richness of the house. Constance felt that it was in some
strange way the world: that just as there are Sea-Cucumbers
and Sea-Anemones and Sea-Horses, so there was at the Rosenbaums' the shadow of anything in the world.

The house held, besides its scores, many records: Constance would listen to the records as she worked her way along the bookshelves, pulling out books and thinking which ones she would (and which ones she could) read. As she sat on the floor by the shelves, occasionally looking up to see Mrs. Rosenbaum preparing a sort of High German tea, and Dr. Rosenbaum going jerkily over a student's exercise, lifting his brows in wonder as he marked—as she sat there everything would seem to her a dream: she would close her eyes, and then open them again and look at the Rosenbaums "like puzzled urchin on an aged crone/Who keepeth closed a wond'rous riddle-book/As spectacled she sits in chimney nook."

They were wonderful to her: a real Russian, a real Austrian, a real opera-singer, a real composer, a woman who had really sung with Chaliapin, a man who had really been a friend of Alban Berg's—Constance could scarcely see the Rosenbaums past so much reality; what she would not have given to be, as they were, a part of that reality! She even began to learn German—from a paper-bound *College Outline* of German, from Grimm, and from Heath's *Graded Readers*. (One of these *Readers* had a story by Dr. Rosenbaum's Friedrich Gerstäcker in it, one called *Germelshausen*, that Constance stumbled along in for a while, and then read with such excitement that she could hardly bear to stop to look up the words she didn't know; she didn't eat dinner, that night, till ten o'clock.) Constance felt that she was learning the language almost as well as a German child does: at the end of her first year she'd be able to say several words. But she tried to say them exactly as Dr. Rosenbaum did, and this was, if there is such a thing, a Pyrrhic defeat.

"*Ach, mein Gott!*" said Mrs. Rosenbaum, laughing—
and then laughing harder at Constance's woe-begone face.
"Speak as I do, Constance, with a little lightness—don't
speak like a *German!* If you go on imitating *him*, that Ochs
von Lerchenau, you will in the end sound exactly like
Mariandel." (*Der Rosenkavalier* was one of her favorite
operas; she had played, in Prague and Dresden and Vienna,
Octavian, and had pulled skirts on over her riding-trousers
and pretended to be the chambermaid Mariandel.) All at
once her face changed, she held her whole body differently,
and she sang

> *Nein, nein, nein, nein!*
> *I trink' kein Wein*

in the voice of a soiled dumpling with dreams: Constance
and Dr. Rosenbaum almost said *Gesundheit!* to make sure
her wandering spirit got safely back into her breast. It returned and said mockingly, "Almost as good as Olszewska,
don't you think?"

It was a horrible vexation to her that Olszewska was on
the recording of *Der Rosenkavalier*, and not she; she said,
"Mayr *apologized* to me—apologized in the abjectest tones.
I let Olszewska know what I thought of it." Constance
asked, "What did she say?" Irene said, smiling: "She only
smiled."

She had in her breast none of the rigidity that you find
sometimes in even the softest Austrian or Bavarian one; and
Dr. Rosenbaum's soul was as supple as hers, though grainier.
And Irene had, occasionally, a trace of the peculiar fantastic
wit that keeps surprising the reader of Leonov or Pasternak,
so that a man is described as he looks reflected in the coffee

pouring from a spout into a cup, and the soft dark blanket that hangs in one corner of a room in the slums turns out to be the sky.

4.

OLD FACES are forbidding or beautiful for what is expressed in them; in a face that is young enough almost everything but the youth is hidden, so that it is beautiful both for what is there and what cannot yet be there. Constance's face was a question mark that you looked at and did not want to find an answer for.

But Constance was of no importance, and people—usually without meaning to—showed her that they knew this; it did not bother her, since she herself felt that she was of no importance. (Later on, she felt, who knows?) President Robbins was as informal and democratic with her as though the United Nations were going to give him an award for it; but he was that way with everybody, and was proud that he was: the sun shines on the just and unjust, and on secretaries. Some people treated Constance unusually well because she was unusually beautiful, but President Robbins was not a person of this sort: he had never seen a girl so beautiful as Benton—or for that matter, as Harvard, Yale, or Princeton.

The person who treated Constance as a girl like any other would have treated Cézanne as a painter like any other, I think. When you looked at Constance in a certain light, or when she had a certain look, you kept on looking and stopped because your heart was in your throat. The freshmen getting off the train were not an hour younger than Constance; it seemed unbearable that she should change.

Women so thin and cruel and glamorous that they appeared to have stepped from the illustrations of *Vogue* felt kindly toward Constance: *Poor thing!* they said to themselves, remembering that they themselves had been so once. Ah, but they hadn't. When you looked at Constance you wanted change and chance and choice to *leave her alone:* you were angry at existence, that could think of this, and then temper it into wisdom with time, and then destroy it.

Not every child has, at the age of five, lost a mother; at the age of fourteen, lost a twin sister and a father. This had happened to Constance; or had it? Such events were not in her style of life, which was a dreamy absent innocent style. She had been, somehow, sheltered from things; and when she hadn't been she had managed, like a sleepwalker, to shelter herself from them without ever seeming to. Later on what she knew already would recur to Constance, and this time it would be transmuted: life is, so to speak, the philosopher's stone that turns knowledge into truth.

Since her grandmother had died Constance had been— except for a little money, gone now—alone in the world. She had finished college (a plain old-fashioned college not a bit like Benton) the spring before, and her job at Benton was only a way to put off making up her mind about what she was going to do. Everybody had told her, ever since she was a little girl, that when she grew up she would surely become a concert pianist; but at college she had, as she always told you, "majored in music," and had learned that people don't become concert pianists any more than they become sweepstakes winners. Still, *somebody* wins sweepstakes: Constance practiced faithfully, read and thought about music, composed—as she would say modestly—"a little"; she was a girl ripe for the Rosenbaums.

Before she had known Gottfried six weeks she had be-come—need I say it?—a composer of the twelve-tone school, an exponent of what the French call *la musique sé-rielle et dodécaphonique*. A female exponent, alas! It was discouraging to her, incomprehensible too, that no woman has ever written a very good piece of music; but she was a modest girl, and besides would feel vaguely: Later on, who knows? This phrase, or the attitude it represents, was her form of optimistic assertiveness.

When you heard Constance's current pieces—she would play them for you—you realized that Constance had put in a good deal of time on the works of Berg, Schönberg, and Gottfried Rosenbaum; you realized, also, that she was a young girl. I said to Gottfried, "How *can* twelve-tone mu-sic sound so innocent?" He answered—but I do not indicate his pronunciation any longer: spelling doesn't do it justice, has never done it justice. He answered: "What is done in trust is trust. We shall all sound so, go far enough into the future."

5.

VISITS TO friends, sometimes, are like *Zwieback*, or *frijoles refritos*, or twice-told tales: the friends are themselves still, bondedly so, and you go home sounder and a little subdued, the staple of your life re-established. Visits to the Rosen-baums weren't like this.

I went by one evening for help with the Rilke I was translating. (You can always get a German to help you with the German, but who is there to help you with the Eng-lish?) I rang the bell, and admired the two-foot-high catalpa in a pot on the porch. Irene had succeeded in dwarfing most of our native trees; the Persian, by one, looked like a saber-toothed tiger. She espaliered, too—there were family trees, peach- and pear- and plum-bearing, on half the walls.

Else let me in. Constance was there, as usual; the phonograph was playing, as usual—this time it was a piece that sounded as though it might have been called *Pages from a Dentist's Life;* there was a score on the floor, as usual, with two teacups beside it. (The house floated on tea and Rhine wine.) Constance kissed me, Irene and Gottfried shook my hand; like most Europeans, they gave the impression of wanting to shake hands with the cat whenever it came into the room—to shake hands and utter a short formal sentence that would express their genuine pleasure at getting to see Frau Katze again. Gottfried greeted me with baroque, and Irene with blank, effusiveness. I looked at her and then looked at Gottfried; he nodded.

Normally Irene spoke her mind, shortly and firmly, about anything and everything. But once every ten days or two weeks there was a day of pure unresponsiveness for her, so that she might as well, might better, not have been there at all; you felt as you do when a character in a Chekhov play says, "The wings of the Angel of Silence have passed over us." They would pass for a day, for two days even, and then, thank God, stop passing. Until then you spoke to her, she registered what you said, and after a moment replied to what you had said; she registered, she replied, she did not respond—not so much as by changing the light on the surface of her eyes, even. Her eyes kept their absent, preoccupied, unchanging stare. She was absorbed in something—what, you did not know. If you said something good you thought, "Irene will enjoy this if she remembers it tomorrow."

This was evidently one of the times. Irene subsided into a chair, into unregarding silence; I sat by the fireplace under the painting of the buffalo; Constance and Gottfried sat down beside their cups.

"What is that beautiful thing you're playing?" I asked. But I had to repeat my question; the dentist had struck a nerve.

It was a work by an Italian twelve-tone composer named —well, Piccalilli is the way I remember it, but that can't be right. Gottfried not only wrote and played twelve-tone music, he spoke about it, and spoke not as himself but as a loving propagandist: the sirens couldn't have made out a better case for their songs than Gottfried made for Schönberg's. Sometimes he was so bewitchingly melodious that I wished the recording company had made a photostat of the score and recorded Gottfried.

"*He* would like Schönberg better if Schönberg had also composed *Giselle*," Dr. Rosenbaum said to Constance, looking at me with an indulgent smile. Constance replied that, naturally, I was a little old-fashioned in my tastes; I said in a telling voice, "I like the *Lyric Suite*, don't I?"

We laughed. The *Lyric Suite* was my triumph—Constance's triumph, that is. I had liked *Wozzeck* at first hearing and Berg's violin concerto at the third or fourth: there was no reason I shouldn't like the *Lyric Suite*, as Constance said, and she had made up her mind that I was going to. Whenever she had dinner with us, whenever she came by in the evening, she held in her hand a long-playing record of the *Lyric Suite*, and once each time she played it to us. I would sit and read, sit and talk, sit and dream—at first, I have to admit, I'd sit and suffer; my wife suffered but did not sit—she would say with a vague sidelong smile, "All that darning. . . . Call me when it's over, Constance."

After four or five playings I was getting used to it, my wife did not get up and leave any longer: there were parts we liked very much better than other parts; three or four more times and we liked the other parts—we were, we found, crazy about the *Lyric Suite:* how could any of it ever have seemed hard to us? Constance was very polite, and didn't once say, "When I was young I was the same way about it." So far as the *Lyric Suite* is concerned, we had been foolish and young and Constance old and clever; and we were grateful to her for that best of gifts, a change in one's own self.

But I was willing to thank her simply for existing. She had been for me, always, an almost unmixed blessing; I could have said of her what, in *The Tales of Hoffmann*, the old man says of his daughter: that she is *sage, modeste, et belle.* (I suppose this should have made me distrust my feeling: the daughter that he says this about is, after all, an automaton of his own making.) As a child Constance had seemed to me more of a fairy tale than the fairy tales I told her: there had been about her a dreaming composure, an essential absence or removedness—she saw something you could not see, had never seen. (She didn't really see it, of course; I know that; but she seemed to see it.) She kept this now only as a queer vagueness of manner. She had this vagueness, some of the time, when she played the piano. She played either dreamily, in absent refuge, or merely correctly, or else with a peremptory objective power that astonished me. When I said something about this to Gottfried he replied: "You see that? Yes, it is very apparent; it is one of the things that interested me about her from the beginning."

Constance said now, "Wake up, you'll be sorry to miss this." I looked toward the phonograph, but it had shut itself off; it was Dr. Rosenbaum that she meant. He repeated, with a sunny smile: "I shall tell you, inattentive as you are, anyone but you three I would not tell, what is my real ambition: I want some people to come from another planet and to make me their pet."

I thought that this would interest even Irene; it did not. Gottfried went on: "And you too, of course—all three of you."

I said thoughtfully, trying to do justice to his revelation: "You're big for a pet. But it's hard on you, being cleverer than other people—it *is* your turn to be stupider, I suppose."

He answered mockingly, "Ah, how well you put yourself in my place!"

Constance said: "When I was little there were eight steps out in the front of our yard, where the lawn went down to the street—I thought that if I ran up the stairs to the eighth step, at night, and stopped there, then if you asked me any question in the world I would be able to answer it."

"If Gertrude knew that she'd put it in her book about Benton," I said. "That's where she is, on the eighth stair."

"Is she going to write a book about *Benton?*" Constance asked.

"Of *course* she is going to write a book about Benton," said Irene, surprisingly. "If something happens to you, what good is it to have happened, if you do not put it in a book?"

I said, "Don't say anything about it. It'd only make people uneasy—and poor things, they'll know soon enough. Gertrude—"

Constance broke in just at that minute, "Gertrude will—" and Dr. Rosenbaum said in weary amusement, "Oh, Gertrude! She is just like everybody else, only more so. She is like air in tanks—like com—con—"

Constance exclaimed in uneasy incredulity, "Oh *no*, not like *everybody!*" Dr. Rosenbaum said, relenting: "No, not like everybody. But there is a Gertrude inside everybody." Then he shook his head and said heavily, "No, not everybody, but—" He paused, dissatisfied with explanation.

Irene said indifferently: "She is a principle of things, one of the naked ones."

"I think her husband's very nice," Constance said. "I talked to him a lot, that night you took me there. Mostly he's very mild and meek and sweet, the things he says, but every once in a while he says something perfectly *awful*. I think those are just things she's said that he's repeating, though. They're awfully odd together. Why do you suppose she married *him?*"

Gottfried said: "It is lonely without readers. She wanted company."

Irene replied to Constance, in a voice at once vivacious and oracular—she had emerged altogether from her silence —"Have you never seen it before? He is—he is St. Jerome's lion's lion. He is nothing, absolutely nothing, you see— without her what could he do? He is hers as a baby is its mother's. She is not afraid that he will—will do *anything*. Perhaps he is the first person in her life she has not distrusted. She does not need to be Gertrude, even, to him: if she painted two eyes on her pillow and said to him that it was Gertrude, he would believe it."

"You make it sound scary," Constance said with a little laugh.

"Everyone must have *something*. She belongs to him as the mother belongs to the baby."

I said, "I hate to think what would become of her if anything happened to Sidney."

Gottfried said, though his tone contradicted what he said: "*Hate* to think of it! Where are your principles?"

"What's the good of wasting principles on Gertrude?" I answered; but then I felt disloyal, somehow, and said: "She's a Fact of Nature. I've never known anything like her —oh, I've seen lots of imperfect presentiments of her, but never any more than that. But Irene, you sound as if you'd known hundreds of her."

Irene answered, "She does not exist in Europe, not in quite this state. She is hidden, or distributed among several, or a man, there. This is because it is a society dominated by men." As she said this last sentence she gave a mocking and confident smile, as if a society dominated by men were her meat.

Her smile changed, and she went on: "Sidney and she, I know the situation *so* well—it is a classical situation—and I have known many people who are like them or like parts of them. When you are as old as I, even if you know nothing of people from good sense, you know too much, terribly too much, simply from acquaintance—types and types and types of those types. When I meet a man on the street I think sometimes: I have known you on three continents for six decades. And, too, what talent I have is for such things as this. You told me that your psychologist Henry James—" I said, "No, William, William"—"that he said that if you wish to feel as a man feels or think as he thinks, you must sit as he sits, and walk as he walks, and hold your head as he holds his head. This is absurd but it is *so*—partly so, only partly so, but so. I have made myself so much into other people that sometimes I look at a person and think—oh, it is an illusion—that I not only am that person, I am tired of being, I have been so long: to be him is intolerable to me, it is so familiar."

We were silent for a moment. Constance said to Gottfried, suddenly: "Oh, I forgot to show you the Williams. I cut it out—it's in my bag."

Every day Constance turned first to the comic page of the Mount Pleasant *Courier-Sentinel,* and would look at a picture, different every day, called *Out Our Way.* "In the papers out West," Constance told the Rosenbaums, "they call it *Skull Valley.*" The pictures were pictures of cowboys, soldiers, factory workers, fathers and mothers and their children—of things as they are now, and as they used to be thirty or forty years ago. They were drawn by someone who, Constance said, knew *everything* about Americans. She even converted the Rosenbaums to her J. R. Williams, to such an extent that Convert Gottfried came back coughing from the newspaper-files of the public library. "This is the other America," he said. "In Europe they know nothing of this."

He went on to say that in his opinion it was not the real America exactly, but the real America as it remembered itself: "*He* knows so well that they recognize it all, and it stands for all the rest they know. It is a kind of national ideal, therefore in the past." Constance hardly understood him. He always had a great deal of sympathy for the American past; he said that Americans had tried to do what had never before even been tried—perhaps they had failed because it could not be done. Constance understood this not at all; to her America was ordinary reality, what everyone is born into, and the rest of the world romance. She had fallen in love with it at second hand.

We all looked at the Williams drawing: some overalled or coveralled men were staring like another species of being at the ill-clad beauties, one to a calendar, that lined the wall of their machine-shop. Constance said, "Once I had a date with a boy I'd known in college when I was a freshman, he'd got to be an engineer—he took me to this musical comedy and said that all machine-shops are like that, that if he had a sister he'd say to her, 'Always shut your eyes when you go in a machine-shop.' But I've never had the chance to, I've never been in a machine-shop. Except that musical comedy was quite a lot like one, I thought. It was—"

Constance said like an older woman, "I'll forget my head next. You know it as well as I do. It was that *famous* one, a sort of war love-story on a desert island—you know, the one that had—" Constance hummed part of one of the songs; she had no difficulty remembering the words, which were almost all *I'm in love*. Gottfried laughed, but the song didn't seem to help him to identify the play; Irene said, "In Europe one knows these things, alas, but here, no"; and Constance said, "The words aren't *that* funny, that part of Lensky's aria I'm so crazy about has the same words, they're just in Russian." Then she asked me, "Oh what *is* it, *you* know."

I said, "*South Pacific*."

"*South Pacific!*" said Constance happily. "Of course! *of course!* Well, in *South Pacific* whenever they saw a girl, whenever they *thought* of seeing a girl their mouths watered and so did the audience's, but how could my mouth water?—I was a girl."

"*That* at least is no different in Europe," Irene said. "We are cakes that must think, *How nice to eat me!* There is a

girls' school at Lyons where the students wear long linen
nightgowns in the bathtub, but that is very Jansenist of
them. Here in your country Art and Commerce and Life
are a bitter—no, a sweet pill covered all over with sex; if
Moses had lived among you he would have returned to find
you worshipping not a Golden Calf but a Golden Girl, and
he would have engraved his commandments upon her
stomach. But why should I buy a bridge because in the ad-
vertisement a girl walks over it without her clothes? Why
should I buy a bridge because the man who built it tells me
it is the best of bridges?"

"Why should you buy a bridge?" replied Gottfried. He
walked over to poke the fire. The Rosenbaums had on their
mantel an odd little statuette, a bull cut and twisted from
black sheet-metal, that I kept remembering to ask them
about whenever I was in bed or taking a bath or playing
tennis; now, at last, I saw and asked.

"*That* is because I am a Bull-Painter, a Steer-Leader!" he
answered mockingly. Constance and I looked unenlight-
ened, Irene accustomed, and he told us a story about the
siege, during the Peasants' War, of the fortress at Salzburg.
The defenders, when they ran out of food, kept leading
along the top of its wall their last steer: they would paint it
a different color each time and point complacently to it, till
finally the peasants went home to their haying—no hope to
starve *that* fortress out. While Dr. Rosenbaum delighted in
their stratagem, Constance asked wonderingly: "But how
does that make you a—a Steer-Painter?"

"Because I am born in Salzburg! You mean you don't
know I am another Mozart? Oh but I am, I am! When
people come to my door and say, 'Unless you write us a
song that says I love you, I love you, I love you—' "

Constance said, "No, no— I'm in love, I'm in love, I'm in love."

"When people come to my door and say, 'Unless you write us a song that says I'm in love, I'm in love, I'm in love, we don't give you anything to eat,' I shall say to them, 'First I will eat my steer!'"

He pronounced these last words as if he were Odin playing hopscotch; when we laughed he wrapped around him some injured dignity, with a magnificent gesture, and said reproachfully, "Oho, you don't think they ask me to write I'm in love, I'm in love, I'm in love. Did not they ask Igor Stravinsky to write a polka for the elephants?"

"The elephants?"

"If Stravinsky writes elephant-polkas you think *I* cannot write I'm in love?"

Irene said, "Avenge yourself upon them all—write it this moment, Gottfried!"

"No, I will write another *Civilization!*" This song was the only popular song that Gottfried liked, but he liked it enough to make up for the others. He sang it like Koussevitzky being the Greatest Master of the Double-Bass; after I had heard him singing *Bongo Bongo Bongo, I don't want to leave the Congo*—or, almost better, *Bingle Bangle Bungle, I'm so happy in the jungle*—I hardly minded not having got to hear Paganini and Liszt and Farinelli.

He was beginning on it, in loving tones, when Constance said equally lovingly: "Do you know what I think, Dr. Rosenbaum?"

"No, what?"

"I think that you are a child."

"That is what you Americans think of all of us," Dr. Rosenbaum said soberly.

"All of us? You mean Austrians or Europeans?"

"Zulus!" cried Dr. Rosenbaum. "Zulus!" He was happy in his jungle.

I said regretfully, "Here's the Rilke," and opened it to the poem I was working on. "Can't Constance help?" Irene asked in a useful voice.

"Don't make fun of him," Gottfried answered. "He would not like German half so well if he should learn it. There is no such happiness as not to know an idiom from a master-stroke. And all that we say was once a master-stroke —he has gone back to the first days of the earth."

"Gee, you're mean," said Constance. "I wish *I* knew as much German as he does."

I looked gratefully at her, but it was the worst thing anybody had said. I repeated, "Here's the Rilke," and we got to work. After a while Gottfried said in a wondering voice: "But this is extremely strange. It is not arranged correctly, but—Irene, whom is *this* like that we have talked about to-night?" He read:

Braucht nicht der mond, damit sich sein Abbild in Dorfteich fände, des Fremden Gestirns grosse Erscheinung?

Then he translated for Constance: "Needs not the moon, in order that it may be reflected in village ponds—does not the moon need the strange star's great apparition? It is a little wrong for Gertrude and Sidney, with them it is a case of the strange star needing the moon's reflection in the village ponds, but the whole somehow—"

"Oh, it's right, just *exactly* right!" said Constance.

6.

THOSE DAYS Constance filed, typed, stamped envelopes, did anything else that the President, the President's secretary, anyone else could find for her to do; and while she wasn't filing and stamping and typing, she sat and looked at the circumstances of her life in content. Back before the War, the Revolution, or the Fall, before we grew up or were born, before *something*, we knew the bliss of being without wishes, and would have answered the angel that guarded us, if he had asked, "What is your blessing?"— would have answered: "That things are as they are, not otherwise." What one day didn't give the next supplied: when she woke in the night Constance reached out and touched her life and, comforted, went back to sleep.

Gottfried and Irene were Constance's Fairy Postmen: her days were dappled with letters and packages and post cards, and all the stamps were foreign. She said often, those days: "To think that only six months ago I'd never heard of—" some name would follow. Even Else grew too used to her to mind her much, and the Rosenbaums' Persian would come and roll on her feet and, looking back, walk off toward the ice-box.

She never knew what the Rosenbaums would talk about, or what they would say about it when they did. Dr. Rosenbaum liked being a Steer-Leader, but he talked of the Dual Monarchy with more contempt than nostalgia, saying: "It is my ambition to be unjust to Austria." One night, after reading a kind of Pindaric ode to Metternich, in prose, that he had come on in a magazine, he said to Constance that the author "thinks that Europe has occurred to him, but not to someone else before. That young *Spiessbürger* should get a job with Salazar. And yet, he has reason—he is full of reasons: as the proverb says, *I killed your cat because she ate my cow*."

"Is that an Austrian proverb?" asked Constance eagerly.

"A Rosenbaum proverb," Irene replied, with resignation; Dr. Rosenbaum, like Swift, made up proverbs. Then she said something, in Russian, that Constance did not know the meaning of and that Dr. Rosenbaum did not know the words of, but that was very familiar to him: it *was* a proverb, one that meant *Heaven gives us habits to take the place of happiness*. Yet as she said it she looked almost baskingly at him, like a seal. She often had this sleek animal look; and her eyes would look soulful, but not, then, as if the soul were a human soul.

Dr. Rosenbaum sat uneasily ruminating, his own eyes very human; he began to reminisce about Metternichs. The old Princess Metternich used to buy pastry at a shop across the street from his room, in the days when he had been a student, he told Constance; he described her and described her car, and finished: "In good weather I could look down into the automobile. On a pole that fitted into a socket, there was a standard like the Imperial standard. Their gratitude was not short-lived."

He pronounced this last sentence with an ironic, dismissing smile; but after a little he stirred restlessly, and murmured: "It was a Mercedes, I think." Constance said: "Oh yes," brightly; she had never felt farther from him. Something was going on inside Dr. Rosenbaum, it was plain; he said to her a minute later, "Have you ever looked out of a window and seen, at seven o'clock on a morning of spring, in the middle of an avenue of linden blossoms, an officer in a white uniform coming home from a ball, in a helmet with white plumes? A *blond* one?"

Constance said that she had not; and Gottfried said thoughtfully, "Nor have I. At least, I can no longer believe that I saw it. And I *detested* them—their stupidity was truly more than human. But—but I wish that there were one, on one morning, for you to see. Talleyrand was right, my child: if you have not lived under the old dispensation you have not tasted the Sweetness of Life." Then he laughed at himself.

His wife laughed at him too, and said to Constance, looking at her oddly: "This is not so, *entirely* not so. When we are young we all live for a time under that dispensation. And yet everyone has always felt so about his own age and the ages: nostalgia is the permanent condition of man."

But the Rosenbaums talked surprisingly little about such dispensations. Flo Whittaker had once gently reproved Dr. Rosenbaum for his attitude toward politics. She had done so by quoting to him, in tones that rather made for right-eousness, a line of poetry that she had often seen quoted in this connection: "We must love one another or die." Dr. Rosenbaum replied: "We must love one another *and* die." And he had once ended a long half-hour's political lecture—conversation, the speaker would have called it— by saying to the speaker: "Nijinsky said, *Politics is Death.* Is that right?" The man looked at him speechlessly, and he said: "Is that right? You say politics *is* in English? *Is*, not *are?*"

Once Constance asked him whether he had known that peculiarly Austrian composer Richard Strauss. She had asked him long before, of course, about Berg and Schönberg and Mahler. (He had said to her about the last: "Or Berlioz?

How old do you think me, my child? Yes, Mahler knew me: when he looked up into the topmost gallery of the *Hofoper* I am sure that he could distinguish little Gottfried Rosenbaum from the other *Wunderkinder* who were about to become Mahler.") But now he replied drily: "He knew that I existed. I do not know whether he would have said of me what he said of Schönberg: 'But you have talent— why should *you* compose atonally?'" Then his face clouded; perhaps he thought he knew. But he spoke of some of Strauss's music with great respect, and did not even complain, every time that he mentioned him, of the size of his orchestras. (Dr. Rosenbaum's own orchestras had often been mistaken for quintets.)

Irene talked of the old days more vivaciously, and in *much* better English. Though Dr. Rosenbaum's was pretty good except for the sounds: what it needed was re-scoring. She told Constance once, "I learned English from an Englishwoman in Orel. We had her as one has a cow, for the children. They tell me that I did— I cannot remember not knowing English and French."

She had been radical to begin with. "There was nothing I wanted so much as a Revolution," she said with a laugh beyond either humor or sadness. She had had a long enough and an eventful enough life for Constance to have almost everything in it wrong; Irene would say, "Ah no, my dear, Prague was ten years after Dresden," and Constance would laugh and say—she had said it timidly, the first time—that Irene should have been arranged alphabetically, like the *Britannica*. Anything that Irene and Gottfried did nowadays was only an inconsequential appendix or coda, like that volume of the encyclopedia that is sent to subscribers every five years, to bring them up to the present as best it can;

even Constance could see that, in some real sense, the Rosenbaums' lives were over.

Irene still would sing for Dr. Rosenbaum—would, occasionally, for my wife and me; sometimes she let Constance accompany her. She sang the *Songs and Dances of Death* and *Where the Shining Trumpets Blow* and that other of Mahler's that begins *Man lies in sorest need*, songs from *Eugen Onegin* and from Rimsky-Korsakoff operas that we had not heard even the names of, Wolf and Mozart and Verdi and Schubert and Schumann. She would say apologetically, "It is only to amuse myself. I remember old times."

When she sang you decided that a singer does after all need a voice to sing, but you did not decide this until several minutes after she had finished singing. Even her breathing was unmistakable, so that her hearers would feel, in senseless pleasure: "Who else in all the world would have thought of breathing *there?*" She did what she did because there was nothing else possible to do, and when she had done it she did not know what she had done: or so you felt, hearing. This was a delusion, of course; she once talked for half an hour about Lehmann's, Schiøtz's, and *her* ways of singing the song from the *Dichterliebe* that begins, *Ich grolle nicht*.

In any art there is a Higher Regularity which seems to conventional people arbitrary and to unconventional people commonplace: Irene's singing was of this sort. And of all the singers I have ever heard she was the most essentially dramatic: she could not have sung a scale without making it seem a part of someone's life, a thing of human importance. Yet when the song and her voice said: *We are all dying,* something else about her voice—a quality that could not be localized, that all the sounds possessed together and none possessed apart—said to you also: *Whoever dies?* Over feeling and act, the human reality, her voice seemed to open out into a contradicting magic of speculation and belief, into the inhuman reality men discover or create. Her voice pushed back the boundaries of the world.

She was an old woman and Constance a girl, yet her grace and lightness (when she was light and graceful—often she sat there like a stone) made Constance seem to herself lumpish; and when the older woman talked to the younger with soaring gaiety, with a courage beyond any event, beyond even knowing itself courage, it seemed to the girl that the woman's voice said to her that life is uncreated and will not be destroyed—said softly, without accompaniment: *Believe, believe, my heart!*

7.

WHAT GERTRUDE said about the people of Benton did not trouble me. News was good news: I had listened too long to what *they* had to say. That Dr. Crowley should leave flowers and candy and bon-voyage baskets outside the front door of Dr. Willen's bungalow, watching from the bushes, shyly, as Dr. Willen ejaculated: "Well, I *never*—" that this should happen did credit, I thought, to Dr. Crowley, and to Dr. Willen, and to Gertrude. To Gertrude especially: it was as though I had learned that Gertrude had written *Peter Rabbit.*

What she told people about Constance and Dr. Rosenbaum was different. I would have begged her not to say it, if I had known beforehand that she was going to; and yet what good would it have done? I started to say, "Gertrude, how could even *you*"—yet what good would that have done? What good did anything do, with Gertrude?

When Constance heard what Gertrude Johnson was saying about her and about Dr. Rosenbaum, she couldn't believe it; she would have been no more surprised if Gertrude had said that she was having an affair with Gertrude. Why, Dr. Rosenbaum was old enough to be not simply her father but her grandfather, practically, and he was a—a respected composer. It was the reflection on the Rosenbaums that dismayed her most: imagine saying such a thing about *Dr. Rosenbaum!* She herself was just a girl of no importance to anybody else in the world, and besides—she thought in ignorant confidence—no one would believe such a thing of *her.*

The first time Constance met Gertrude alone on the campus she said hello to her and stopped and waited, expectantly, till Gertrude had stopped. They were two small shapes under the oaks, one of them in a modest tweed skirt and her best cashmere sweater, the other in more bohemian garb. Constance said to Gertrude in a measured voice, the voice of a girl measuring her first shortening for her first cake, the sentence she had prepared: "You shouldn't speak as you do, Miss Johnson—" no, that was wrong—"as I'm told you do, Miss Johnson, about Dr. Rosenbaum."

Gertrude looked at her in stupefaction, and Constance looked back like the Children's Crusade. Then this terrible warrior—who was quite as willing to do anything whatsoever as she was to say anything whatsoever; who had, everybody said, once chased a guest down the steps of her own front porch, striking at the woman with the candlestick she had picked up from the dinner-table; whom you could have deterred from having affairs with all the members of the Cabinet simply by saying, "Gertrude, it would shock people more if you seduced the Supreme Court"— then Gertrude did nothing, said nothing. She seemed to feel almost as a big dog does when it won't fight a puppy: finally she looked Constance in the eyes, smiled, and said indifferently: "Speaking as I should would be quite a departure for *me*." But then she gave a helpless marvelling laugh and said: "Is this *really* your idea of how to— Oh, don't worry, nobody would believe anything about *you*." Constance said, "It isn't—" and Gertrude said, "Oh, don't *you* worry," laughed again, and walked away. But the second laugh had been as queer as the first. Constance thought them both laughs of embarrassment; so, for her, that was the end of that.

But why *had* Gertrude done nothing? She was no big dog, Constance was no puppy. Proust says, in an unexpected sentence, that the commonest thing in the world is kindness: is it so common that, somewhere in Gertrude too, neglected and frustrated and despised, there was a shred of this primitive kindness—a little shame, a little guilt, a little grief? President Robbins had never had time to be human, Gertrude had never wanted to be; but perhaps, like it or not, both of them were human.

8.

CONSTANCE ONCE had asked Irene, "Do you understand why Gottfried—" and Irene had broken in: "Understand? Gottfried? I have never understood him—but then I have never needed to understand him."

Constance did not understand this; after a while she

forgot it. Most of Gottfried seemed to her *beyond* her, of course, but the rest of him she understood or didn't even need to understand, it was so plain. He was as fat and open and goodhúmored as a comedian: he moved in reassuring familiarity, an old joke recollected on a fine day.

It is hard to believe that any other cellist could look as good as the cellist of the Budapest Quartet, but Gottfried looked better: you could see every note. And he looked more like an orangoutang, too. He had that animal's fixed, sorrowful, bottomless stare—though the little incidents of the score would lift his spirits immeasurably, and bring a fleeting smile to his lips, as if his keeper had just brought him a banana.

Whenever Gottfried played the cello I would remember how he looked the first time I ever saw him. He was sitting on a beach in red knitted swimming-trunks, he wore over his shoulders an army surplus blanket, and he stared out to sea. The look on his face was one of passive sadness; his hand, a small hand for so big a man, hung down into the hole he had been digging as though it had never moved, could never move.

He was introduced simply as Dr. Rosenbaum. I thought him some physician saddened by the death of all his patients, but after a while I could see that, patients or not, he didn't care. It was windy in the cottage of our host, but who else would have shut himself into the closet to light his cigars? Even the children seemed to feel that there were the children, the grown-ups, and Gottfried.

His wife arrived that afternoon. I said to Gottfried, "Why, you're *Gottfried* Rosenbaum!" He said, "You *are* musical"; and exclaimed in a voice of solemn grandeur to Irene: "I have lived for a thousand years beneath your shade, you Pyramid!"

"Who remembers Letscheskinskaya?" Irene asked cheerfully. Then she said to me with delicate, confiding, majestic sorrow: "I am old." She gave a wonderful purity to the *o* of *old*.

I laughed: a man watching me through a telescope would have cried out, "There's a delighted man!" Irene gave to her good audience the tender smile of the professional, and I saw that, thin as she was, old as she was, she had kept in the middle of each reddened cheek a dimple.

I heard a woman say about them, later that day: "They're an absurd couple," and this vexed me. But of course they were: Irene occasionally and willfully, Gottfried systematically.

You can do anything with children if you will only play with them, as Gottfried was fond of saying; but he did not want to do anything with them except play with them. His automatic acceptance of everybody was a judgment of mankind crueller, perhaps, than Gertrude's impatient rejection of everybody. She had great expectations for humanity, expectations which any human being disappointed; anybody satisfied Gottfried's expectations. The thought of how he had acquired these expectations was a disagreeable one.

He told you everything, always; Irene was often silent or oracular; after a few years you knew Irene, and had more facts than you knew what to do with about Gottfried, so many more that you wished you could go back to the days when you hadn't known so much, and still had had a chance to understand him. (A man as open as *this* must be hiding something; and something as big as Gottfried, even, could have been hiding behind something as big as Gottfried.) But then—you felt just as Irene did—you did not need to understand him.

He had an extravagant and impartial humor, a relish for telling the truths that are themselves jokes, that was to most people the only disquieting thing about him. It seemed to them, almost, inconsequence or malignity: if he had not been a joke himself, they would have found it hard to forgive some of his jokes. Besides making jokes, he made guesses. As you were telling him what some friend of yours had said or done, he would break in and tell *you*—and he was right disconcertingly often. When I asked him how he did it he replied: "I only make jokes. When people would tell me about their friends, in the middle of what they said I would think of what would be right for a joke, and say it, but it would be true. So now I say it for the truth."

He was one of the best-humored of men, but sometimes his humor was out of gear: at those times he looked at what was without any humor, good or ill, with a joyless transparency, and what was remained what it had been. And he was inhumanly disinterested. Many of us have learned to detach our vanity from our opinions, and to join it to the part of us that discards these if it can see that they are false. But with Gottfried it was more than this: he not only tried to judge himself as he judged others, his works as he judged theirs, he managed to do so. About the killing of six million European Jews, even, he spoke with detachment. He said to my wife and me: "I can understand killing them. We have our faults. Six million Jews are, after all, six million people." But then his face distorted itself into vivacity, and he exclaimed: "But those poor *gipsies!* What had *they* done?— told people's fortunes, stole people's cows. When I heard that Hitler had killed them all, I thought like Peer Gynt, 'Nature is witty, oh so witty—but economical, no, that she isn't!' Imagine! The *gipsies* of Europe! It is hard for me not to say: 'I do not want to live in a world that has killed off all the gipsies.' "

Sometimes as you look at someone who has no notion that he is being looked at, his body seems to be saying, without any help from him, without any expectation of an answer, in passive helplessness: "What am I doing here?" Gottfried's, though, seemed to be saying in half-humorous, half-rueful astonishment: "What am I doing *here?*" He was a remarkably polite listener, and nodded all the time you spoke, as if to make his listening visible. After you had finished he would give a last nod different from the rest, his eyebrows raised a little, his lips pursed a little, his head akimbo like a dog's in a movie: it was almost as if he were waiting to hear something else; then he would reply, or go on to his next joke, or wait a moment for yours. Once as I looked at that final nod I thought of two lines from a poem, a poem about the call a bird gives:

> *The question that he frames almost in words*
> *Is what to make of a diminished thing.*

But what was the thing that had diminished? The world? Gottfried himself? I did not know.

9.

THE RUSSIAN Irene, the Austrian Gottfried, the Bavarian Else, the Persian Tanya—the cat was named Tanya—these and the Simca, a French car manufactured under Italian patents, often made me think of Europe and America, the Old World and the New. To think of such things is a confession of ignorance, and I was not so ignorant as not to know that; but I couldn't help myself. I thought about them, talked about them, even. When Gottfried cut his cantaloupe into squares with a knife and put sugar on the squares, it was as if I had seen Europe buckling into the Alps: I would feel, *How very European!* and then try to recall whether it was European or just Gottfried; the same thing happened with Irene; and with Tanya I must often have felt, *How very Persian!* when really it was only cat.

It was hard to know whether to be just or patriotic. As you thought of Else you could be both: a Tasmanian, as he thought of Else, could have felt proud of the past and confident of the future. But sometimes as you thought about Gottfried you felt your trust in yourself shaken: it seemed to you too late to do anything about yourself—as much, that is, as needed to be done—and you felt that it wasn't just Gottfried, but Europe. Gottfried knew more than you did, and could do more with what he knew; and when you looked for a clause, beginning with *but*, that would end the sentence in your favor, you could not find one.

Yet a way of life is a way of escaping from perception, as well as of perceiving. Here in the midst of your own world you noticed all the things that Gottfried didn't notice, and that you did; that Gottfried didn't distinguish from one another, and that you did. And his godmothers had given Gottfried, along with everything else, a gift for organizing even these blind spots into a system—the last had said to him, smiling: "My child, you shall never be at a loss for long." He made generalizations even when he didn't have anything in particular to make them with; and he understood so well what things necessarily are that he didn't see, sometimes, what they accidentally were. Yet all this was characteristic not so much of Gottfried as of his kind—one noticed it in Irene too; and when Gottfried was least his kind he was most Gottfried.

Their kind was a European kind. In ungracious moments I felt that their minds were traps in which things came to an already-agreed-upon end; and they must have felt that my mind was so open that things streamed through it without coming to any conclusion at all. (*I* felt that they must have felt this: but how easily we give to others the understanding of our own qualities that only we possess!) It seemed to me that the Rosenbaums had made up their minds, and that I hadn't. Sometimes a judgment of Gottfried's would make me think with a despairing laugh, "He's only a European after all." I never thought about any of my judgments, "I'm only an American after all," but Irene and Gottfried may have.

I hated to come to anything so uncongenial, so un-American, as a theoretical conclusion—to anything so theoretical and conclusive as a theoretical conclusion. I felt (to put it in my own terms, which were more than fair to me) that it is better to entertain an idea than to take it home to live with you for the rest of your life. But I sat surrounded by the results of doing the opposite: the light I read by, the furnace that kept turning itself on and off to warm me, the rockets that at that moment were being tested to defend me from the rockets that at that moment were being tested to attack me, all were the benefits of coming to theoretical conclusions; I was a living—still living—contradiction.

Yet when I thought of Irene and Gottfried and myself— or for that matter, when I thought of Else and myself—in the terms of the old American comparison of Europeans and Americans, something was wrong. They were smarter than I, and I was better than they? Their sophistication had, unfortunately, made them bad, just as my naiveté had, fortunately, kept me good? To believe this I would have had to be good and naive. I repeated with mixed feelings the definition of an American I remembered—remembered inaccurately, I imagine—from the novels of Henry James: an American is someone who says *I guess* and is better than Europeans. I liked having my own continent win this moral victory over another, but I wished that it had won in all the novels: in European ones, I remembered, an American is someone who says *I guess*.

And yet—and yet. . . . There was a hardness and matter-of-factness about Europeans, sometimes, an accustomed dismissal of what no one could dismiss—no one, surely, ever become accustomed to—that I was troubled by: they brushed life aside as though they themselves were life, and could afford to do as they chose with it. Marianne Moore has said about New York, that treasure-hoard which Americans lie with their tails around, growling at one another—has said about New York, even: "It is not the plunder but/ accessibility to experience." That said, almost, what I wanted to say about Americans. They had, so far, no armor against fate—for riches and bombers and empire aren't armor, but only fate. There was something helpless and noticing about Americans, a few Americans, which I liked; something happened to them, sometimes, and they looked at it and were at a loss, for long, for long. They did not understand it; and it takes a young and ignorant race not to understand something, when so many different ways of understanding it already exist. The sheltered and ignorant can, sometimes, make concessions, show a kind of tentativeness and forbearance, there on their little strip between the rocks and the stream, that those making a bare living from

the rocks, escaping with their bare lives from the stream—
that *they* less easily can. Yet I had to admit, about some of
the American qualities I liked best, that they were so rare
in Americans that it might almost have been better to look
for them in—but no, that way madness lay!

As you talk about your own qualities you are always
rather a comic figure, and I must have been one as I talked
about the qualities of Americans. There was an *I did not
know what* about American qualities: as you heard me talk
about them, trying to say what it was, you did not think
as usual, *He's a true American*, but were impressed with
how subtle I could be—you could see that, with all our
faults, we Americans were still, in some sense, *better*.

. . . There is no good resting-place between Man and
men: to say that someone is typically anything is an unfavorable judgment, and even the oddest of foreigners cannot help seeming to us, in some ways, typically foreign. We
despair of any nationality except our own, and we don't
despair of it only because we don't take it seriously—we
know that, at bottom, Americans are just people, a little
more so than any foreigner ever manages to be; didn't Adam
and Eve and the snake speak to each other in Standard
American? Adam and Eve and the snake have a different
story, but this is ours. Foreigners tell it with the names
changed, it is theirs, then, but it is the same story. All of us
reason about and understand what people necessarily must
be; we dream about, are bewitched by, what they accidentally and incomprehensibly are.

I decided that Europeans and Americans are like men and
women: they understand each other worse, and it matters
less, than either of them suppose. But I thought of what
seemed to me a way to get a detached, objective judgment

about Europeans and Americans: I asked a Chinese acquaintance of mine. He seemed puzzled by my question; I repeated it; and he replied in a high astonished voice: "There's no difference. No difference at all." He meant to say this; really he said *difflence*.

This left me more confused than ever about Europeans and Americans, but for a moment I was sure about Chinese.

10.

TO CONSTANCE the Good Europeans Gottfried and Irene were never confusing, only wonderful. If they had burned their house down on Midsummer Eve and told her that Austrians always did, Constance would have danced off with the news and stored it under Austrians, Customs of, somewhere in the happy filing-system of her head. It was a strange thing to do, but they were strangers—*her* strangers. When you admire a grandee's mountain range and he says to you, *It is yours*, it is not the gift that matters, not the manners that matter; he might just as well be a bandit chieftan saying to you, *No Kafir has set foot on that mountain since the days of the Prophet!* God is the Wholly Other: that others are now, were, and ever shall be, world without end, *different*—what else is Romance?

Someone at a travelogue cannot help feeling, even if he knows better: "Lucky coolies, to be there in the midst of the romance of the East!" But they aren't in it, they are it, so it is no good to them. In the same way I could not help feeling: "Lucky Constance, to be there in the midst of Innocence!" I did not know at all what it was like to be Constance, and I did not want to know; if I could have found out I might have felt, like the Dauphin in the story:

"Why, if that's so, to be Dauphin is *nothing!*" And Irene was no better; she would look at Constance or at me in surprise and disappointment when one of us responded to something just as she would have responded—she *liked* us different. That the soldiers in the barracks at Chanute Field had called me *Tex* did not seem half so funny to Gottfried as it seemed to my wife and me: how willingly he would have learned that I had been reared by an old buffalo named Cheiron!

Constance loved, as a nice young American student of the piano should love, a book by a nice young American student of the piano named Amy Fay, who lived from teacher to teacher in the Germany of the '70's, and wrote a winning account of Liszt; from Constance's comments about the book you could see that she not only identified herself with Amy Fay, but Gottfried with Liszt. (Amy Fay wouldn't have minded, but ah, Liszt!) Constance could not help feeling that the Russian-ness and Austrian-ness and Past-ness of the Rosenbaums were of the same use to them that they were to her, just as we look at an old photograph and feel that the people in it must surely have had some intimation of how old-fashioned they were, of the fact that their problems were not *really* problems—we feel this even when the photograph is a photograph of corpses, strewn in their old-fashioned uniforms along an old-fashioned trench.

Constance was in love with what the Rosenbaums seemed to be; what they were she might have loved less or loved more.

They were, in the first place, what they seemed to be, just as a beautiful woman in an evening dress is first of all what she seems to be. But underneath her dress, on one side of her stomach, is the scar of an operation for appendicitis; some of the skin below it, of the skin along her thighs, has a grained or marbly look—this came from the strain of child-birth; and her teeth would not be so regular and magnificent as they are if she had not worn braces on them, an unwilling child. There is a reality behind the outer reality; it is no more real than the other, both are as real as real can be, but it is different. All this part of the Rosenbaums: the part that bears and passively suffers and merely exists, so that the other can live and sparkle in the sun; the seamy side, the side with the seams that show how the dress was put to-gether; the seams at which the dress comes apart—all this Constance could not see. Or rather, would not see: she glimpsed it now and then, for the time it took her to catch her breath, but then she would shut her eyes, and open them, and it was as if it had never been.

To Constance the Rosenbaums seemed as wonderful as Life, but really they were only as wonderful as life, that short blanket, that mixed blessing, that, that—

Gertrude had impressed me by talking about a "definition by ostentation"; she said, rather mockingly but rather good-humoredly, that it was just the thing for me. "How do you do it?" I asked. She answered: "You simply point."

"That *is* just the thing for me," I admitted. I felt that a definition by ostentation was almost as good as none.

To Gertrude a definition by ostentation was almost as bad as none; and how often, for how many things, she had had to take it or none! To her the world was one of those stupid riddles whose only point is that they have no point. It was a knot she could not untie; and she was not willing, as many people are, to pretend that she could, but wanted to cut it or, better still, give up and throw it down and stamp on it. A good child will work away at a knot in its shoelace for all eternity. Gertrude was a spoiled one, and knew it, and knew that the world soon stops spoiling children, except in the other sense of the word. In that sense she was a thing spoiled beyond repair, marred forever in the making; and she did not know whether the world had made her or whether she had made herself, so she blamed both.

Gottfried and Irene, unlike her, never had sleepless nights on principle. They had come to accept things, and themselves too, for what they were, though what they were would have seemed to them the most extraordinary thing in the world if it had not been the most ordinary. Gertrude pushed everything away with the nausea of a suicide-note: "The whole thing is *impossible*." "*Yoh*, the whole thing is impossible," Gottfried would have replied in his grainy, wheezing voice. "But what has that to do with it? It is and I am; here I am."

And yet the Rosenbaums found things, often, rather hard. If this seems inconsistent, one can reply: Were they not exiles? Were they not old? Was not Gottfried a man and Irene a woman?

And they did not like America so well as one would have wished them to like it; they were used to different things. Irene, for instance, had a name that is pronounced *i RA ne*, more or less, over most of Europe; here in America she was called I REEN. This became for her a little mocking symbol. She hardly cared what she was called, other things being equal, but she could not help feeling that the world is named *i RA ne* and that Americans call it I REEN.

Irene had once come down to breakfast and found her hostess serving sausages to a famous American scholar, a hearty man who had interrupted Irene's first sentence, one acknowledging their introduction, by saying cordially, "Just call me *you!*"

"*What* shall I call you?" asked Irene, her voice rising.

"Just call me *you*."

Irene looked helplessly at her hostess, who said in a kind voice: "He wants you to call him *you*."

"*You?*"

"That's his first name, *you. H, U, G, H—you*."

Irene gave a long sigh; when Gottfried met her at the station the next day she shook hands with him and said, "How do you do, Dr. Rosenbaum."

Gottfried was puzzled, but went along with her game far enough to reply: "Haven't we met before?"

Irene answered, "In five years I call you Gottfried," and went on to explain.

I have heard Gottfried remark about Travel: "There is no need; wait, and they chase you all the way around the world." But sometimes, to Irene, America hardly seemed the world at all. She believed in (though she didn't usually bother to say them) some of the most familiar clichés of European settlers in America: that American vegetables look better than they taste; that we have a disproportionate admiration for Youth ("you Americans do not rear children, you *incite* them; you give them food and shelter and applause"); that we believe in Education and distrust anybody who is educated; and so on and so on and so on—she would probably have repeated half the things in Toqueville, if pressed. I remember saying to her one evening, when she was talking about American education: "You mustn't judge other American colleges by Benton—plenty of other American colleges are hardly progressive at all."

She replied: "But may I not judge your grammar schools, your—I have forgotten what you call a *gymnasium*—your *high schools* by Benton? I have read that many of them are progressive like it. And if they are, surely in the end the others will be: perhaps Benton is the college of the future."

While I sat staring at this prospect Gottfried told us about a speech which he had once read, a speech which the Emperor Wilhelm II, back during the '90's, had made to the teachers and parents of Germany. Gottfried said, smiling: "He asked—he *implored* them not to make their children study so hard, for many of the children had had their eyes ruined by their studies, and were no more good for soldiers. Your own American education is, I believe, of all the educations that have yet been devised the best for the eyes of the children."

And yet Irene liked America too: as she said to Constance, parodying a line of poetry that had attracted her, "In the United States, there one feels free." But she spoiled it by continuing, "Except from the Americans—but every pearl has its oyster." She stood looking out at the oyster restlessly. She could never bear to sit still for long, to sit for long: sitting down reminded her that her occupation was gone. Then she said to Constance in an elegiac voice: "We at least have the memory of having had a world that respected us; that respected us—as a symbol, perhaps—whether or not it knew what we were doing." She was old and entered into things hardly at all, and looked around her with unsympathizing eyes; her eyes were disinterested, but they were also rather uninterested.

And yet sometimes as one listened to Irene her voice seemed to say, as the voices in one of Mahler's pieces say (after a long pause, softly): *Believe, believe, my heart!* But

it was only the believing of the heart she believed in: her
Believe! was without accompaniment, was for the human
voice accompanied only by human voices. Perhaps these are
enough; perhaps, enough or not enough, there is nothing
else to have; but for her they were not enough.

She said about singing: "When you have learned to sing,
it is too late. . . . These American singers are right to sing
as they do, it saves them years. Centuries perhaps." She
particularly delighted in a singer called Thomas James
Joseph, or James Thomas Joseph, or something equally
apostolic-sounding; she said of him, "Ah, poor un-Doubting
Thomas! He is not even a bull, he is a cow: he *moos*." Then
she mooed; and old and delicate and mocking as she was,
for a moment she was that sober, homely, undoubting cow.

She said to me about American compositions: "There is
a picture that one sees, a picture with an old man, and a man,
and a little boy—they have drums and he a piccolo, and
they are all ragged. I do not know its name."

I said, "It's called 'The Spirit of '76.' "

"The part that I like least in your American compositions
is the part where these people come into the piece. Why
should a piano concerto, or a ballet, or a description of how
dawn comes over your American prairies, need always a
little march with a piccolo?"

I said, "It's put into the piece to show that it's an American piece." Irene replied, "Ah, no doubt. It is like that little
sign *Made in America* that one sees on objects—without it,
perhaps, the piece could not be exported."

There were three or four American singers she was fond
of—she had records of them and went to their concerts—
but she did not let these spoil the fine sweep of her remarks
about American singers. She said: "What you should do

with American singers is to send them to Europe when they
are about, I think, five. After all, they are only people—
they would make singers like anybody else, *nicht wahr?*"

When Gottfried said, "My wife was considered a very
good and a somewhat—somewhat *difficult* singer," you
could see what he meant. But the fine arch of her eyebrows
broke, her hand—raised in her own version of the gesture
with which the *danseur noble* points out the accomplish-
ments of his partner—fell to her lap and stayed there, and
she said in a different voice: "Here you truly think—no, it
is worse than that, you not only think, you *feel*—that you
can find what is beautiful, or right, or true, by asking everybody, and some people will say one thing and some another,
and what the most people say, *that* is what is beautiful and
right and true. So in the end there is no more true, no more
right, no more beautiful, there is only what the most people
say." But she made her indictment indifferently—and
smiled, as she finished, a smile of settled and indifferent discontent. Her daemon no longer possessed her: it had not
left her, but had nothing to do and nowhere to go, and it
and she sat together all day wearying each other.

She found, now, nothing by which she could be possessed. But she still looked; some days she spent looking—
looking silently, seeing nothing except what she did not see.
She was a bow waiting, in dust and cobwebs, for someone to
come along and string it; and no one came, no one would
ever come.

V.

Gertrude

AND

Sidney

1. Though Gertrude's grammar, syntax, and punctuation were perfectly orthodox, though her style made everything sound as if it had been dictated to her by the Spirit of Geometry, she was admired by the most experimental of writers, men who, since high school, had never so much as used a comma, except perhaps to put one after every word of a book of poems. But she was (and they felt this, even if they couldn't say it) as excessive as they: her excess was moral, spiritual, and cut far deeper into life than anything they had managed themselves. Grammar and capital letters are conventions, the last twigs on the tree of life; it was the roots that Gertrude sawed patiently away at. So even the farthest-flung picket of Experimentalism (poor *verlorne Feldwacht!*) loved Gertrude's work, and forgave it its hysterical blindness toward him and his for the sake of its vision of the rest of reality. With them and Gertrude it was a case not of deep calling to deep but of chaos calling to chaos: they were all members of the *Sons and Daughters of Old Night*, a lodge as strange, in its way, as Florian Slappey's *Sons and Daughters of I Will Arise*, another lodge of which one used to read.

Gertrude pointed at the world and said, her voice clear and loud: "You see! you see!" But as you looked along that stretched shaking finger you didn't see, you saw through. Her vision was too penetrating. She showed that anything,

anything at all, is not what it seems; and if anything is not anything, it is nothing. How Gertrude did like Swift! His work, that is: in his life, she felt, he was always fooling around with his friends, gossiping, trying to help the Irish, making up proverbs and jokes and riddles, writing letters in baby-talk to that silly woman. In his work only one thing puzzled her: why had Swift liked the Houyhnhnms? Whenever she thought of *Gulliver's Travels* she felt a faint impulse to sweep the last piece off the board, to write an article exposing the Houyhnhnms.

Gertrude could have taken the Houyhnhnms for granted; to anything except a bust of Cato, they expose themselves. But Gertrude hated for anything to be latent or tacit or implicit: if there was an inexpressible secret to the world—or one unexpressed because taken for granted by everybody—she would express it or die. So her books analyzed (besides the sun, the moon, the starry heavens, and the moral order) the dew on the cobweb and the iridescence of Titania's wings; and they did not murder to dissect, but dissected to murder. The blush on the cheek of Innocence is really—one learned this from Gertrude—a monomolecular film of giant levorotatory protein molecules, and the bonds that join them are the bonds of self-interest. She said to the Universe that she accepted it, for analysis.

Of any thousand pigs, or cats, or white rats, there are some who eat their litters and some, a good many more, who do not. Gertrude understood the first, the others she did not understand; she explained everything in terms of the first. They would all have behaved like the first except for—this, that, the other. She saw the worst: it was, indeed, her only principle of explanation. Consequently she seemed to most people a writer of extraordinary penetration—she appealed to the Original La Rochefoucauld in everybody. People looked up to her just as they look up to all those who know why everything is as it is: because of munitions makers, the Elders of Zion, agents of the Kremlin, Oedipus complexes, the class struggle, Adamic sin, *something;* these men can explain everything, and we cannot. People who were affectionate, cheerful, and brave—and human too, all too human —felt in their veins the piercing joy of Understanding, of pure disinterested insight, as they read Gertrude's demonstration that they did everything because of greed, lust, and middle-class hypocrisy. She told them that they were very bad and, because they were fairly stupid, they believed her.

It is partly our own fault—the fault of a great many of us, at least—that writers like Gertrude come into being and stay there: the baby does nothing but cry because, each time he cries, we go upstairs with a bottle, and bounce him on a tender knee. Gertrude was not, alas, a good woman; Gertrude had a style in which you couldn't tell the truth if you tried—and when, except when it was a shameful one, had Gertrude ever tried? But how many of her readers cared? Most of them went on admiring her in the tones of butchers from Gopher Prairie admiring the Murderer of Düsseldorf; they could not mention that style without using the vocabulary of a salesman of kitchen knives. If Gertrude had written another *Remembrance of Things Past,* they would only have murmured disappointedly that it wasn't the old Gertrude. They wanted her to tell them the worst about themselves, and after they had met her they whispered to one another the worst about *her.*

But as a writer Gertrude had one fault more radical than all the rest: she did not know—or rather, did not believe— what it was like to be a human being. She was one, intermittently, but while she wasn't she did not remember what it had felt like to be one; and her worse self distrusted her better too thoroughly to give it much share, ever, in what she said or wrote. If she was superior to most people in her courage and independence, in her intelligence, in her reckless wit, in her extraordinary powers of observation, in her almost eidetic memory, she was inferior to them in most human qualities; she had not yet arrived even at that elementary forbearance upon which human society is based. Most of the time Gertrude was not an ordinary human being but an extraordinary human animal. Her hand was against every man's and every man's was against hers; she had not signed the human contract when the rest of us signed it. She was, like the man in the poem, "free, free!"— free to do anything she pleased; and of all freedoms this is the most terrible.

She was free to destroy Sidney too, if she wanted to; she just, just—just didn't want to. . . .

Sidney kept Gertrude alive: without him she would have gone on functioning drearily, striking at anything that came in reach, but she would hardly have *lived;* yet Sidney, and the part of Gertrude that lived because of Sidney, never got into Gertrude's books at all—she would have been ashamed and embarrassed to see them there. Gertrude, unlike many writers, really did have a private life, one that she never wrote a word about.

So because of all this—of all this, and so much more— even the best of Gertrude's books were habitat groups in a Museum of Natural History: topography, correct; meteorological information, correct; condition of skins, good; mounting of horns, correct. . . . Inside there were old newspapers, papier-mâché, clockwork. And yet, *mirabile dictu!* the animals moved, a little stiffly, and gave the calls of their species, a little thinly—was it not a world?

It was a fairly popular world, even. Gertrude's readers did not understand things, and were injured by them; now for a few hours they injured and understood—and understanding was somehow the most satisfactory injury of all. They did for a while all that fear and pity and ordinary human feeling kept them from doing ordinarily, and they were grateful for it: if Gertrude had had sweep and sex (her method was microscopic, her sex statistical) she might have been considered a Great American Novelist. As it was, she was always called "the most brilliant of our younger novelists." *Brilliant!* People had called Gertrude brilliant before she could talk; she had been called brilliant so much that, five seconds after you said it, she couldn't remember whether you had said that or hello. It seemed to Gertrude that she had been writing for several centuries: weren't people *ever* going to stop calling her a younger novelist? But enough raw woman survived in her for her to be pleased in spite of herself with the word *younger*.

The world was the arsenal Gertrude used against the world. She felt about anything: If it's not a weapon what am *I* doing with it? and it turned out to be a weapon. She knew that people must be, at bottom, like herself, and this was enough to justify—to make imperative—any measures she could take against them. And if everybody had been, at bottom, what Gertrude thought she was, she would have been right to behave as she behaved, though it would have been better simply to curse God and die.

If you were one of the ordinary lumps of dough, sacks of

flour, that made up the human landscape of her world, you were safe from her; but if you moved or spoke, were for some reason, from the beginning, extraordinary, she slapped you in the face, pointed out to people the marks of her fingers on your flesh, and characterized your response in terms so cruel and funny that people laughed at you and were ashamed of themselves for laughing. If you rejected Gertrude it was because of the slap, if you accepted her it was in spite of it; she had arranged things so that she could never be rejected for herself alone.

If you didn't hit Gertrude she thought you were afraid of her. To her generosity, tenderness, good-humored indifference were unaccountable except as fear or caution, and she herself was willing to know neither fear nor caution: she stripped off all her armor for the fray, her pale eyes blazing, her lips grey with sea-spume—or was it foam? She was willing to go herself, if the rest of things went with her.

It seems to us so hard to be even fairly good—for either it is hard, or else when it is easy we do not think we are being good—that we cannot help feeling that the bad are as much happier than we as they are worse. If the bus companies could have sold conducted tours of Gertrude's head, it would have done more for ethical feeling than all the moralists since Kant.

2.

ONE DAY Gertrude met Derek out walking with one of the Afghans. She said hello to him in a friendly though rather lifeless voice—after all, he was in the book. He didn't say anything. "Out walking with Yang?" Gertrude asked.

After a minute he answered gravely, tightening his hold

on the dog's collar: "He's not Yang, he's Yin. Yang is a *bad* dog."

This was what Gertrude didn't like about children: they didn't act like grown-ups. She couldn't understand why they didn't act more like grown-ups—a little more like, anyway; it seemed to her almost affectation on their part. Sometimes when we see a poor fat old woman in the bus, we think incredulously: "Was *she* ever a child?" In the same way Gertrude looked at Derek and thought: "Was *I* ever like that?" She could not believe it.

She had not had as much childhood as most people, and could remember almost none of what she had had. It was queer that she couldn't: she remembered everything else. Her books had all the details of childish existence that they needed, of course—accurate foreign details that she got, taw by aggie, from other people's rememberings; but children not only bored her, she felt that she was right to be bored by them. The double standard that people employ for children and grown-ups seemed to her a grotesquely disproportionate one.

Derek said, "I went to John's."

Gertrude said, "Oh, you did?"

Derek said, "Yes, I did. He told me I could. He's thirteen. He showed me all his turtles."

What can you *talk* to children about, Gertrude thought despairingly; but she said, looking as interested as she could: "And his snakes too?"

"Fern said they would hurt me. Huh, snakes won't hurt me, I have lots of snakes."

"You do? Where do you keep them?"

"In bed at night. Sometimes they wake me up." He started to say something, and stopped. Then he said, in an unexpectedly grown-up voice: "That Fern!" He laughed, and told Gertrude rather confidingly, "She showed me the hole she buried her doll in."

"Buried it?"

"The one Santa Claus bringed her. She took its clothes off, and she broke its arms, and its legs, and its head, and she buried it under the tree where the turtles all are."

"Why did she do that?"

"She was mad, she didn't want a doll. She wanted Santa Claus to bring her a baby with real wax in its ears." Gertrude had enjoyed this section, and filed away that *real wax*; but then Derek said, almost without pause: "I met your husband at the bank."

"Oh, you did?" said Gertrude, brightening at the mention of Sidney.

Derek said, "He let me blot his check. He's a nice man, I believe."

Gertrude had the feeling that would have been expressed, a generation ago, as *Bless his little heart!* Derek went on: "Were you married to Sidney when Sidney was a little boy?"

"Oh no, little boys don't get married."

"*I* think they do," Derek said. Yin was pulling at him, trying to get on with their walk; Derek gave him a tremendous yank, so that they both almost fell down; then they stood there waiting for her to say something. There was a silence: Derek did not say anything and Gertrude, for once, could think of nothing to say; the mention of Sidney seemed centuries away. Yin sat down.

"What grade are you in this year?" Gertrude said at last.

"I don't go to school, I just go to kindergarten," Derek answered. Then he said, looking at her in an odd way, so that he rather squinted: "You look like my mother." He didn't say "You look like Pamela," as Gertrude would have expected him to; he said, "You look like my mother."

Gertrude hated to be compared to anybody; anybody would have hated to be compared to Pamela Robbins. She said, "I don't think so really, do you? She's got black hair and mine's quite fair."

"Yes, that's right," Derek said, but he didn't look convinced. He pulled Yin up and said, "Well, goodbye, Mrs. Bacon."

"Goodbye, Derek," said Gertrude. She walked away feeling almost miserable, she didn't know why. It had been a depressing conversation.

4.

GERTRUDE DIDN'T eat much, and Sidney had accustomed himself to not eating much. There were many things that she couldn't eat and more that she wouldn't eat: all her childhood aversions had persisted, and she joined to them the unwomanly but thinly feminine trait of being able to get along on crackers, a sucked lemon, and the last lettuce-leaf in the back of the vegetable-drawer of the refrigerator. *What women eat when they live alone!* a doctor has said—and that is what Sidney ate. Gertrude, as she would say, hated being held down by housework: she floated over the apartment like a balloon, and a few dust-motes from it sailed up past her in the sunlight.

She especially disliked most Southern foods; she said in her rough way, "Grits! I'd as soon eat boiled grubworms as grits," but then her face paled at the thought of the grubworms, and she wished she had spoken like a lady. Mashed potatoes, oatmeal, boiled or poached eggs, almost all soft bland foods were repulsive to her. The foods that she liked were clear green independent standoffish foods: she belonged in our Age of Salads. There was something faintly nauseating to her about the thought of chewing—or, worse still, of eating something so soft that it didn't need to be chewed. She loved sweet things, though. She and Sidney bought a box of candy every week, at one of those candy-shops where you can make up your own box: they would divide the box in half, and each seriously select his own kinds and amounts. "You mean you're not going to get any *black walnuts?*" Sidney would say in astonishment; and Gertrude would answer, "Black walnuts! I'm sick of black walnuts. I got five of them last week—don't you remember, I got so tired of them I traded you the last one for one of your mince-meats."

Her psychoanalyst had told Gertrude that finding so many foods nauseating was "part of her whole pattern of rejection." Admiring as he was, it had not taken him many months to become another part of the pattern. Gertrude was ingenious at finding some way of rejecting—of dismissing as beneath any conceivable consideration—anything or anybody. One fabulist, a black, smiling, Irish creature who said that Gertrude's books were "a Barmecide feast given by a fireworks company," was fond of telling people (Gertrude felt that he did nothing else; Gertrude felt that people *talked about her all the time*) the plot of a play he was writing, a play of which Gertrude was to be the heroine. The play had many characters at the beginning, but as Gertrude told each what was wrong with him, and broke with him in the sort of scene of which an actress-manager dreams (the audience whispered, *What a moralist!*—they had seen nothing like her since Savonarola), the cast got smaller and smaller: toward the end only Gertrude was left, and she told herself, sternly, smiling her nasty, jerky, imploring smile, all that was wrong with her, and then broke with herself forever—her hand, flung out toward the darkness of the wings, was that of an Etruscan Fate.

People responded to this story in different ways. Some of them had read something like it in a book; some of them had heard someone say something like it; one of them said, "Why, it's simply Haydn's *Farewell Symphony*"; quite a lot of them—these were the ones with bad memories, I suppose—laughed and let it go at that. The story's wit lay in its exaggeration, all of them would have said. But the story was not exaggerated. Until Gertrude had found Sidney the story had been exactly true; if anything were to happen to Sidney, the story would again be exactly true.

Some nights Gertrude would lie patiently waiting to go to sleep, thinking of anything and everything, shifting her limbs to another position, patiently, till she would remember what, she had read, someone once cried out upon the scaffold: *O God, if there is a God, save my soul, if I have a soul!* Instead of these two things there were herself and the people in the world: she thought of herself, of them, of what they had done to her, of what she had done to them, of what they say and feel and *are*—and it was unbearable beyond belief, worse, surely, than any nightmare. She had never had a nightmare; this was her nightmare. She looked at the world, and *saw*, and cried out, her voice rising at the end of the sentence into falsetto: "Why, it wouldn't fool a *child!*" And why say so?—she had known as long as she could remember; God knows that *she* was used to knowing!

Her thoughts went on in their accustomed round. They

had worn for themselves a rut, a ditch, a canyon, too deep
for them ever to climb out of; so deep that it was hard for
Gertrude to distinguish, far down in the darkness below,
their dark shining—and sometimes she would have to say,
as you say when you recite to yourself, in the darkness, a
poem you know too well: "Where am I now?" Then for
an instant even habit was no help, as she identified her anger
—or was it anguish?—was, for the instant, her anguish.
Sometimes she would move her arms and legs and bump
them against Sidney, and his slow, stupid, sleepy *Wha, wha
is it, Gertrude?* was good and dear to her as she said that she
was sorry, she must have been dreaming. (Not even Sidney
knew that Gertrude did not dream.) But sometimes in bed
beside her sleeping, her perpetually sleeping husband, she
felt herself shaking so that, faintly, with a little steely sound,
the springs of the bed shook: she said to herself, in wondering agony, *Why am I so angry?* She was *right* to be so angry; and yet, why was she so angry?

5.

ONE DAY, as I went by Gertrude's office, there was a fat,
dark, pretty girl in ski-trousers standing outside the door.
She started away, came back, started away, came back,
twice in thirty seconds; Gertrude wasn't there for their conference, she said, and she absolutely had to get her story in
because it was a week late already, and she couldn't be at
her conference next week because she was going to be at
Dartmouth that day, and this was the last day of the week
that Gertrude had conferences on, and she *couldn't* get her
story in *three* weeks late. "I ought to have it in so she can

read it over the week end," she said. "That's when she reads our stories. She reads *awfully* fast. Sometimes when she's reading one of my stories—she just glances them over again so they'll be fresh in her mind—she reads a page at a look. She says that when she gets all worked up to a big bunch of our stories, and has to waste herself on only three or four, she feels like the Blatant Beast." She laughed; so did I. Something came up from the clear dark depths of her untroubled eyes, a thought, a memory, something, and she exclaimed, looking rather as you do when you meet the postman blocks from home, and he may have a letter for you: "Who's the Blatant Beast?"

"Something in a long poem that none of *you*'ll ever have to read," I said, smiling at her. She said in astonished pleasure, "Do you know, that's *exactly* what Miss Johnson said to me when I asked her. But what is it really?"

"Oh, a dragon all full of pamphlets—he's the Pope, too. He's in the *Faerie Queene.*"

I couldn't make up my mind whether or not the name meant anything to her, but my sentence certainly did; she exclaimed, more pleased than before: "That's an extraordinary coincidence. You know, that's—well, anyway, in some ways, that's *very* like my story." When she said *my story*, she glanced down at it; it came in a pretty blue cardboard folder. She looked at it in hope, and said: "I'm *sure* it's the best story I've ever written. I hope she thinks so. You never can tell with her, though."

"What's your story about?" I asked.

"It's about a bug that turns into a man."

"Really?" I said. "That sounds very unusual."

"Oh, it *is*. It's—it's influenced by Kafka," she said, looking down shyly. Then she said, "You don't remember meeting me, but I've met you—I met you last year at the tea for the juniors. My name's Sylvia Moomaw."

I said that I remembered meeting her very well, but that I hadn't remembered her name. (This wasn't so: I had remembered her name but had forgotten her.) She said, "Ever since I can remember I've wanted to be a writer when I grew up. Did you when you were young?"

"No," I said, "I wanted to be a physicist." She laughed, thinking that I was joking. She was a sort of student familiar enough to me, a soft, gentle, officious, trudging sort, as good as dough; I said in vague amity, "Just give me your story and I'll give it to Gertrude on my way home—I go right by her place."

She asked, astonished at my rashness: "Do you think I ought? She says a writer's home is her castle."

"It's all right," I said. "She won't mind."

She was pleased, but still doubtful. "Do you know her *that* well?" she asked.

"I've known her quite a long time. Is her class fun for you?"

"*Fun?*" she said. "It's just out of this world! I've never *had* a teacher like her—not the least bit like her."

We talked a moment longer and parted; but she came back after a few steps and said, "You can read it if you want to."

I said that I'd like to very much. I read it as I walked along to Gertrude's. There was a part where the man said, "Could I have ever *really* been a bug?" Waves and waves of the queerest, most mixed-up feelings went over me; I would have cried out from their depths, *Alas, poor Moomaw!* except that . . . except that this would not have done justice to the facts of the case. She had adjusted herself—as she would have said—to Gertrude, to Kafka, exactly as if each had been Sylvia Moomaw; and I had not yet entirely adjusted myself to her—*Alas, poor you!* she could have said to me.

I shivered: it was not as if she had been walking over my grave, exactly, but more as if . . . I felt that a Moomaw was walking through my ruins, and looking their date up in her guidebook.

6.

AFTER I had rung the doorbell and after Gertrude had come to the door, we looked at each other and saw that we were not exactly ourselves. She looked tired and distracted and irritable. I held the story out to her wordlessly, and she said after a glance: "That dope!"

I said, "Once upon a time there was a princess who lay down on seven mattresses, and slept like a baby all night through, and when she woke up in the morning she said, *I dreamed there was something under my mattress,* and they looked and there was a horse."

Gertrude said, "Do you want me just to give your story a grade, or shall I go over it with you and tell you what's wrong with the point of view? Yeah, she has that effect on me sometimes. But you don't give her enough credit: *she* knew there was something under the mattress."

I said helplessly, "Yes, it's like that proverb of Dr. Rosenbaum's: 'The goose said to her daughter, *You are a perfect goose.*' It'd be so much easier if she were worse. There isn't a—a mean bone in her body."

"Or any other sort," Gertrude said, snorting. She recited

in a hard firm voice: "Blessed are the poor in spirit, for they shall inherit the earth. . . . Over my dead body they will. Come on in."

"You're working."

"Come on in anyway. I don't feel like working. I haven't got three sentences done all morning."

She looked haggard and jumpy, and the apartment was in remarkably bad shape—for once it didn't look bare but cluttered. The sofa was covered with magazines, most of them *Partisan Review*. "I was looking up something I was sure was in *Partisan*," Gertrude said, "but I can't find it there or anywhere else." She pushed some magazines away to make herself a place to sit, and a pile of them fell on the floor; she made a cross, impatient, helpless noise, like a child who's been hurrying so much that he's lost his temper, and burst out: "I just can't concentrate today." Then she said, dropping her voice: "I suppose we'd better not talk so loud —Sidney's asleep."

"Sidney's here?"

"Yes, he couldn't go to work. He's been sick ever since Tuesday. Maybe he's awake now—I'll look in and see. You'll be a distraction for him. He doesn't feel like reading."

She opened the door of the bedroom, very softly for her, and peeped in at Sidney. "No, he's still asleep," she said. Her face softened, as your face softens when you look at a cat and her kittens, in a box in a closet. "Look at him," she said.

He lay there in unhappy sleep. He had two pillows propping up his head; the noise of the cars in the street or of Gertrude's typewriter must have bothered him, for he had put another pillow over his head, a tremendous ochre one from the living room. A wan segment of his face showed from

under it, like a mouse lying under a loaf of bread. I felt sorry
for Sidney. The devil, come to drag Sidney's soul off to hell,
would have felt sorry for Sidney. His body was curled into
a miserable (yet somehow homey) mound, and his pajama'd
arm was clutched around—no, it wasn't clutched around
anything, and yet it looked so much as if it were that you
could almost tell what the thing was: it was either a teddy
bear or a cloth duck, and I stared hard at it, trying to make
it out—but it was no use. "He feels pretty bad," said Gertrude. "He said to me, 'Gertrude, I feel so bad.' "

I said, "Poor thing! What is it that's wrong with him, do
you know?"

"Something he ate, he thinks." My thoughts were mostly
a mother's thoughts, as I looked at him, but I couldn't help
thinking at *this:* "I'll bet it was." The things Sidney must
have eaten!

Gertrude went on: "And he has a cold, of course—a bad
one. We think he's generally run down. He's been forgetting to take his vitamins—well, to tell the truth, I forgot to
get any more when the last bottle ran out. I've just got too
much on my mind—the book, and all these students, and I
do most of the shopping, here. Sidney does it all at home.
Life is more difficult out here, that's all there is to it. You
just *have* to live in New York if you want your life to be
convenient."

A voice from the bedroom said feebly, "Who's that, Gertrude?" Gertrude told him, and he was feebly glad to
have me there, and asked me, feebly, to come in. I talked to
him for a little, but it was hard for him to pay attention to
what we were saying; he nodded as amiably as ever, though,
and said yes as politely as ever—but oh, so feebly. Finally

he said with weak hope: "Gertrude, may I have some lemonade?"

"You can if you'll take it hot without any sugar."

"That's just not lemonade," Sidney said disappointedly.

"Oh, all right," Gertrude said to him. Her voice wasn't grudging, really, but gracious, and she said to me in an undertone, as she squeezed the lemon: "The least I can do is give him some lemonade. There's so little you can do for someone when he's sick. . . ."

I said, "Yes, they live in a different world. I think the Scythians, instead of deciding everything once drunk and once sober, should have done it once well and once ill."

Gertrude wasn't listening, and said mechanically: "The Persians. I'd a lot rather be sick myself. It's so easy when *I'm* sick." She went on absently, "I don't worry about myself when I'm sick."

It was so: she was the best of patients. I remembered getting to hear her say to Sidney when *she* was sick, "It simply hurts, Sidney, and there's no use your making a fuss about it. No, I don't want anything to eat, and I've already had two aspirins, and if I can't sleep I'll read. You can play the radio if you don't turn it up too loud—just shut the door and let me alone and I'll be all right in the morning." Not even sickness could make an ordinary human being out of Gertrude: she was indomitable.

Not even sickness—but Sidney's sickness seemed to be a different affair. I said, "Gertrude, after I've left why don't you take a nap yourself? Maybe you can get something written after you wake up."

"I'm going to," Gertrude said. "I'm *exhausted*." She took the lemonade in to Sidney, and Sidney sat up half way in bed and drank it in weak gulps and, when it was gone, said in a troubled voice: "I feel bad, being such a nuisance for Gertrude; she's hardly got anything done since I've been sick."

"Don't you worry, Sidney," said Gertrude. "I could do *this* book with both hands tied behind my back."

7.

SIDNEY WAS well in a week. But Gertrude took longer to recover from his illness. One night of that week she got up to go to the bathroom, drank some water out of the faucet —her mouth tasted bad, and the water had the sweet, pure, insipid taste of water drunk at such a time—and as she straightened up she saw herself in the mirror over the washbasin. It was still only half past two; her head ached, her red eyes stung with sleeplessness, and as she looked uncomprehendingly into what seemed to her worthless, her own face, she had a queer fraction of thought: two thoughts going on at the same time, one over the other. "What would I do if something happened to Sidney?" was the top thought, and appeared infinitesimally sooner, and the thought under it was: "How long will Sidney go on being Sidney?"

Gertrude was afraid of nothing. She said to the world: "If you can do without me I can do without you"—she wanted, almost, to get rid of it so as to prove that she could do without it. But could she say, "If Sidney can do without me I can do without Sidney?" There in the middle of the night, rubbing her hurting eyes, staring into the scrambled flaccid face that had not yet even made itself into Gertrude, she felt an abject physiological certainty that she could not. Without the sweet, pure, insipid taste of Sidney in her mouth she would—she didn't know what she would do.

She had trusted Sidney entirely because Sidney needed her entirely: how could Sidney possibly get along without *her?* But now that she saw she could not possibly get along without Sidney, her trust was shaken. When Sidney found out that she was in his power—if he found out, her heart substituted hastily—what would he do? How could you trust *anyone* with such power?

It didn't occur to Gertrude that she had had such power for a long time, and that Sidney had trusted her and had been right to trust her. All power corrupts, and absolute power corrupts absolutely, Gertrude was fond of quoting —though she, of course, quoted it correctly and said *tends to corrupt.* (And she always said *to paint the lily:* she knew that this was a commonplace phrase and that the memory of mankind had transfigured it, and she was contemptuous of people who said *to paint the lily*—just as she was contemptuous, in a different way, of people who said *to gild the lily*—but she couldn't bear to have anyone think that she didn't know which one it really was. She didn't care how you misjudged her, as long as you knew that she *knew.*)

In the world there were people who were bad to her and people who were good to her, people she was bad to and people she—and Sidney. Sidney was what Gertrude could be good to. From the black steel of Gertrude's armored side there opened a kind of door, and from it a hand emerged and held out to Sidney a glass of lemonade—cold, and with sugar in it, even if it was bad for him—and the hand, seriously and with interest, watched Sidney drink the lemonade. Then the door closed; but still, it had been open for that long: for that long there had been nothing between the world and Gertrude but a hand holding a glass of lemonade.

It always surprised Gertrude that people, ordinary people, could take themselves seriously; surely even they must see how ridiculous they were! But as she watched Sidney drink the lemonade she did not see how ridiculous he was, but watched seriously and with interest, taking him on his own terms.

Gertrude knew that she herself was a very exceptional person, a person ordinary in no sense of the word. Yet this did not help her to think that Sidney would continue to need her, continue to love her. I heard her say once, in vexed impatient wonder: "People just aren't *loveable*." Love—or affection, or tenderness, or good-humored acceptance—seemed to her a precarious state arduously maintained; if Sidney had come home from work some evening and had said to her, "I'm not interested in you any more, Gertrude," she would have thought this a disastrous but perfectly reasonable, perfectly predictable thing for him to say—he would simply have come to his senses.

She thought about Sidney; she thought, for some time, about how difficult it must be for Sidney, being Sidney— *keeping on* being Sidney! The complaints he didn't make! the retorts he didn't utter! All the admiration he gave instead of getting, all the triumphs he walked in chains at the tail of, barefoot, without even a slave to whisper in his ear what he had never had the opportunity to forget: *Remember that you too are mortal!* She realized for the first time how hard things were for Sidney, as she for the first time put herself in Sidney's place. She put herself into it as she would have put herself into the skin of a cinnamon bear, and as she walked along being Sidney she could have been recognized—as Gertrude, that is—at an astronomical distance.

She went slowly, with soft thoughtful steps, back into the bedroom; as she started to get into bed Sidney stirred, with a little whimpering sigh, and she looked down at where he was, in the darkness, and said to herself, "No, I might wake him." She went out and closed the door. She got the last two blankets from the linen closet—I wish we had more *blankets*, she thought—and, feeling absurd, went to the sofa with them, made a cozy bed for herself, and lay down in it: but not, alas, to sleep.

How much Sidney had to put up with! She thought about it for a while, putting herself in Sidney's place; but she wasn't used to doing this, and got tired of thinking the same thing over and over. . . . But luckily, Sidney wasn't clever, so people interested him. She herself could have said, "People just aren't *interesting*." She hadn't for many years even expected them to be. She *knew* what people are like, had known for so long that it was almost as if she had always known, and yet she still couldn't reconcile herself to the knowledge. If she had been allowed to pick one word for what people are, it would have been: *irritating*.

Once John Whittaker had told me the plot of his favorite science-fiction story. It was a rather sad, nostalgic story about a man of the future, one who is retiring from his position, an important one, at the age of a thousand. I said, "Did they think he was so old he was about to die, or what?" John answered, "Oh no. But they can't use them in jobs any more after they're a thousand: they get too irritable."

Sometimes when I was with Gertrude I would think of this story: she was a thousand years older than other people. Yet irritability is, as I remembered from biology, one of the primary properties of protoplasm. Gertrude was as protoplasmic as they come. She didn't suffer fools gladly; and as she looked around at this fools' purgatory in which we live, a rational malice at everything, an impatient dismissal of everything would overcome her, and soothe a little as they overcame—she was like a magic sword that is content only as it comes shining from the scabbard.

She dismissed the world generally, but writers, competitors, people who mattered, particularly—death or a bad book was a joy to her, and the world's swift forgetfulness best of all. She thought often: Well, that does for him. If she had learned that not seven but six cities had competed for the honor of being Homer's birthplace, it would have given her a little thrill of pleasure.

Lying there on the sofa under the blankets, she kept walking aimlessly around and around in the maze of herself, suffering sometimes, triumphing sometimes, sometimes only walking, and at about the time she could see dawn over the walls her steps slowed and she fell asleep. But she knew about Sidney and herself, now; and until the newness of her knowledge had worn off, things were harder than usual for Gertrude. And harder, alas, for Sidney. She felt that she must not at any price let Sidney see what she had seen—just mustn't give him a *chance* of seeing; how glad she was that Sidney wasn't smarter! Some of her usual absentminded good humor toward him disappeared, though only for a few weeks. Sometimes when she had some slight cause for vexation, and sometimes when she had none, she spoke to him more severely than she had spoken to him for a long time: she *had* to, it was for his own good, if he only knew. Sidney would look at her uncomprehendingly and try to figure out what he had done, and when he couldn't, he knew that he didn't know because he did not understand things as well as Gertrude, but that she knew. One evening this response was so plain on Sidney's face that Gertrude's heart failed her, and she said, "Oh no, I didn't mean that, Sidney. I—I don't know what could have come over me."

He smiled at her in gratitude—the dark day had turned fair—and said that she'd been working on the book so hard that week, all that new part about Mrs. Whittaker, and she was tired. "That's a *wonderful* part about her and her little girl—what's her little girl's name really?"

Gertrude said, looking at him gratefully: "Fern." Her whole heart was in that *Fern;* as she stared at Sidney she repeated, without knowing that she had done so: "Fern." After a moment she heard the sound, the sound made her think of the name, and the name made her think of the world. Brought back to it from whatever place she had been, she thought of it—and from the midst of her own accustomed, exasperated, despairing thought, the oldest and deepest of her being, she said, dropping her head on Sidney's shoulder: "Oh, Sidney, people are such *dopes!*"

8.

HOW BEAUTIFUL the school was as, in glade and in grove, it lay there in the level light of evening! more beautiful, more composed and eternal, than later in the diminishment of moonlight; all things seemed steady there beneath the sun. In those moments, in all the moments of those spring days, it justified everything that Gertrude Johnson had said of it. She had said it—read it, rather—to a predominantly scientific Committee on Aims (her Chorus of Elder Sociologists of Thebes, she used to call them) to which she was unfortunately and unwillingly attached. .

Gertrude believed that people hoarded and fed and slept and knew not her; it was her strongest belief, and she took all the measures that she could to strengthen it. As she began to read, the Sociologists looked narrowly at her enthusiasm for Benton, moving their necks in their collars—it was one of the only signs of liking she had ever shown. But when she had finished they looked at her with friendly dazzled eyes, thinking *Why, that's beautiful;* it sounded to them like Veblen or the Bible. Gertrude had read them a passage that began by calling Benton a home of lost causes. But it went on to say that the causes were not lost: "No, we are all seekers still! yet seekers often make mistakes, and I wish mine to redound to my own discredit only, and not to touch Benton. [She paused.] Beautiful spot! so young, so lovely, so unravaged by the fierce intellectual life of our century, so serene!

'There are our junge Mädchen *all at play!'*

And yet, steeped in truths as she lies, spreading her gardens to the moonlight, and whispering from her towers the first enchantments of the Future Age, who will deny that Benton, by her ineffable charm, keeps calling us nearer to the true goal of all of us, to the ideal, to perfection—to beauty, in a word, which is only truth seen from the other side?—nearer, perhaps, than all the science of M. I. T. . . . Adorable Benton!—" It went on so, with a few necessary judicious alterations, to the end.

When she finished Gertrude said apologetically that out of its context it might seem a little abrupt or—or too lyric and old-fashioned; but they did not feel that this was so.

They had not known that Gertrude was so good a writer; and they felt better, too, about Gertrude's soul.

In the moment that Jerrold congratulated her upon "the elevation, the almost Victorian eloquence of her style"; in that moment, as in many more—though not in so many as she could have wished—the pain under Gertrude's right breast, just beneath two of the lower ribs (though sometimes it was higher, sometimes lower), was gone . . . or if it was still there, she had for the time forgotten it. It was a pain almost like the stitch in the side that runners get, and was faintly nauseating in the same way: a knotting or fluttering or gnawing of muscles, or the memory or anticipation of this, that was always there: Gertrude's flesh catching its breath. Or rather, it was an idea that Gertrude's body had had, and could not get rid of; it was the fixed idea of her flesh. Sometimes it was bad, sometimes it almost was good, but good or bad, like weather, it was there.

Gertrude had been afraid of it when it first came, and had gone to her doctor with questions about ulcers and cancer and tuberculosis: there was nothing; and from then on Gertrude did not mind it, hardly remembered it when it was gone, would pay no attention to it when it was barely there —she could bear anything, feel safe with anything, that was "merely functional." She did not mind it because she understood it: it was part of the price of being Gertrude.

Did not mind it, medically speaking, intellectually speaking; yet sometimes as she lay awake in the darkness, without any world there to distract her from herself, the stitch in her side grew and grew until it seemed to her bigger than the world, a sea of boredom and nausea upon whose swells she and the earth floated in vexed, unending, senseless misery. It did not seem possible to her that she had ever been without it, and to be without it seemed to her happiness; and when she shifted herself or wadded her pillow against it so that it grew smaller, she seemed to herself to have two hearts, one on the left and one on the right; and the last, her real heart, was a heart of pain.

She lay there in the darkness. If Gertrude hit out at the world when she and it were together, it got its own back from her when they were apart: it had taken its own back, that is. Nothing nice had ever happened to Gertrude in bed. There applied to her, in a much more general sense, the words in which the Bible tells the story of David and Abishag:

"Now King David was old and stricken in years; and they covered him with cloths, but he gat no heat. Wherefore his servants said unto him, Let there be sought for my lord the king a young virgin: and let her stand before the king, and let her cherish him, and let her lie in thy bosom, that my lord the king may get heat. So they sought for a fair damsel throughout all the coasts of Israel, and found Abishag the Shunammite, and brought her to the king. And the damsel was very fair, and cherished the king, and ministered to him: but the king knew her not."

The world was very fair, and cherished Gertrude, and ministered to her: but she knew it not. She lay there beside that homely negligible extension of herself, that fifth limb, Sidney Bacon, and cried to the men and women of her world, those *divinités du Styx:* "Far be it from me to implore your cruel pity." She went on to say—so to speak, so to speak—that she died unmoved; and that, dead or alive, she was Gertrude Johnson still. . . . This formula was first used by Medea, but Gertrude repeated it with as much relevance and grace.

And the next morning, lying back in the bathtub watching her husband, that Constant Reader, shave, she said to herself in the dreamy voluptuous spirituality of being in hot water up to her head: "My destiny is accomplished and I die content." How often she made such quotations as these, said or felt or was them! For just as many Americans want art to be Life, so this American novelist wanted life to be Art, not seeing that many of the values—though not, perhaps, the final ones—of life and art are irreconcilable; so that her life looked coldly into the mirror that it held up to itself, and saw that it was full of quotations, of data and analysis and epigrams, of naked and shameful truths, of *facts:* it saw that it was a novel by Gertrude Johnson.

9.

YET, UNDERNEATH everything, there must have been in Gertrude some uneasiness about her books; the terms she was on with the world were not terms she wanted to persist. The world put her in the place it had found for her—Gertrude's Place, it was called—and it was the most special of places, of cases, but still it was a place; and Gertrude knew there was no place in all the world for *her.*

When she told me the plot of her book, it was a Real Plot. It could have happened anywhere—anywhere except, perhaps, Benton. None of her other books had had anything that approached this; I varied my invariable resolution about life with Gertrude, and disagreed with her. I said, "Gertrude, has anything happened to you since you've been at Benton?"

"*Happened* to me?" she asked with an odd expression.

"No, no, I don't mean have you changed any. I mean, has

anybody tried to kill you, or proposed to you, or left you his fortune, or—has anything *happened* to you?"

"I should say not. Never had less happen to me in my life."

"Or to Sidney?"

She laughed.

"Or to Flo? or to Jerrold? or to the President? or to my wife? or to me?"

Gertrude laughed in a different way; she saw what I meant. Her quick eyes shifted from side to side, looking up in Benton, down in Benton. "Well, Miss Batterson died," she said at last.

"In Iowa."

Gertrude looked at me uneasily, clutching her plot to her breast. I said: "Nothing ever happens at Benton, Gertrude."

But after a day or two Gertrude quite recovered. She said to me when next we met: "How about Manny Gumbiner?"

I laughed: it was so; but I said, "He's the exception to all laws, Gertrude: if you held him out the window and let go of him, he wouldn't fall."

She took this as fun, not argument, and went on with her argument: she talked, as always, about the difference between life and art, and the necessity of giving life form— form, in this case, was her plot, and you could see that having been given that plot was the best thing that had ever happened to Benton. And the fact that nothing much ever happened at Benton made her even more impatient with Benton: it was not simply raw, but dead unresisting, material. She felt justified in paying no attention to it except as a giant nursery of facts, facts that would cover, with their mild academic ivy of verisimilitude, the girders of a plot that could have supported the First National Bank.

And I didn't argue. I wanted her book to be a success. I *wanted* it to have a plot that would bear up under the weight of hundreds of thousands of readers, a plot that higher critics could call crude and that bewitched families could pad over in house-slippers. The Rosenbaums had talked to me for half an hour about what success would do to Gertrude: Constance had looked in joy at her Big Friends and all they knew, and I had been convinced against my will—not much convinced, that is. Irene had finished, waving her hand: "All she needs is for everybody to be Sidney."

"That's all any of us need."

"But of course, of course—Gertrude is no different from the rest of mankind."

Constance cried, "You always keep saying that Gertrude isn't any different from the rest of us. But that's just not *so!* . . . Is it?"

Irene replied, "That is something of which I should not speak to you, and of which I should not need to speak to *you*—" nodding at me. We looked at each other. She did need to speak to me, but it would have done no good—I was on Constance's side.

The successful Gertrude, as Irene pictured her, was really mellow. She described an analogue, a Czechoslovakian writer named Jiří Vlček-Krkonáček: evidence named Vlček-Krkonáček is almost irrefutable. Still, we objected with feeble stubbornness: "You mean that Jiří—that that man, before he was successful, used to say worse things than *Gertrude?*" She replied, "Gertrude is not worthy to touch the hem of his garment."

Gertrude's success in the future was certainly having no effect on her disposition in the past. This was her—and Benton's—Time of Troubles. It was safer not to go out to dinner, those weeks. Every other day reports of some new quarrel came in: she didn't ask people, now, she told them. *Her* Benton had come into autonomous existence, and the men and women and girls, the lawns and flowers and trees of Benton were of no more use to her—she could pay them back, now, for all the looking and listening she had had to do. After her new quarrel with the President the President thought numbly about the old: "How could I have thought a little thing like *that* a quarrel?" And there was one person less in the universe for Flo to oversee, nowadays; she felt that she was no longer in any sense responsible for Gertrude. Jerrold said to me, in a mild observant voice: "She found a perverse delight in taking Florence's finest traits and making a kind of *indictment* of them. It was a deplorable thing to do. And yet one had to admire the ingenuity with which it was done, perverse though it was. I do not myself hold it against her—verbal aggression of some kind is inescapable in such natures as hers. But I do not blame Florence for wishing to have as little as possible to do with her. She *is* an—" here he gave a delighted smile at the phrase that had come to him—"an uncomfortable bedfellow." Flo and Jerrold looked a little alike, as husbands and their wives, people and their pets so often do; but at that moment there was a kind of humor in his eyes that I had never seen in Flo's.

Gertrude was an uncomfortable bedfellow even for the Spring. Yet how could anyone have behaved so, those days? why didn't Gertrude's beige limbs burst out into appleblossoms? Benton looked as if Nature had whispered to man: "Beyond Me you cannot go." People from New York City—born New Yorkers, men whose earliest images were of asphalt—got off the train, looked, and realized that, plays and concerts and Culture or not, they could never go back. As the tendrils of the ivy felt a way along their limbs [or if it wasn't ivy, it was Virginia creeper: everything at Benton was covered with one or the other, and you were glad that it was so—you felt that all the Parthenon and Santa Sophia need is some ivy] they knew that New York is a terrible place to visit, and that they couldn't live there if they tried.

But Benton was like this all year. In Spring the air was full of apple-blossoms, and Benton was like—like Spring everywhere, *but more so*, far, far more so; in Winter the air was full of snowflakes, the red-cheeked snow-booted girls stood knee-deep in their pedestals of snow, and the frost-crystals of their windowpanes were not frost-crystals at all but cut-outs, of Matisse's last period, that had been scissored from the unused wedding-dress of Elaine the Lily Maid of Astolat; in Autumn all Benton was burning, and the students walked under the branches of the fire—how was it that they walked among flames, and were not consumed?—and picked the apples the blossoms had grown into and threw the cores on the tennis courts, where Yang and Yin and the Rosenbaums' blue Persian played with them.

But in Summer it was best of all: it was dark, cool, and green under the great trees, and in the hush of desolation (even the President was gone) the secretaries shot with the school's bows and arrows on the shady lawn—if Robin Hood and Johnny Appleseed and Uncle Wiggly had come up behind them and kept score for them, how could they have been surprised? The secretaries, the assistant to the Di-

rector of Admissions, the girl who sent out remembrance
and admonition and entreaty to the alumnae: these sweet
mice, all the old cats gone, yawned for bliss, danced for joy,
and played seriously in Saturday afternoon round-robins
with the mothers and fathers and vacationing college-chil-
dren of Mount Pleasant, winning for themselves ash-trays
and cans of tennis-balls and golden opinions; and behind
the dark gold of their faces, Summer was turning gold.

Nature did her best for Benton. . . . And Nature, and
nurture too, had done their best for the girls of Benton.
When the freshmen arrived in September it was as if Benton
had been transported to the wondering Antipodes to have,
alone among earthly places, a second Spring: wasn't it the
buds, the hawthorn blossoms, and the first curly leaves that
got off the train and made arrangements about their bags
and worried over how much to tip the taxi-driver?

At Benton, as you looked at the old sober certain evenings that were teaching the young mornings to turn into
them—into *them!*—you resented Necessity. And, soon, the
girls would change before your eyes: they got older and
sadder and wiser, and the professors never got any younger
or gayer or stupider; you felt that the girls had (as Dr. Rosenbaum, that widely ranging reader, quoted) *turned in all
their gold/For the banknotes of the one unwithering State.*

Dr. Rosenbaum one year, in one of the experiments characteristic of Benton, taught a class of freshmen. The girls
were so pretty that they always made him blink his eyes: he
said, sentimental Austrian, that all they needed was Salzburg
behind them and you wouldn't even know Salzburg was
there. This class would file into a classroom being vacated
by a more advanced class: an odd class: one girl very fat;
one very tall—American girls are getting larger all the time,

and she was a woman of the future; one a Hindu, very dark; one lame, poor thing; one very athletic; and three *very* advanced in dress, make-up, opinions, everything—they looked like the Three Graces of Dada.

Once when they had all gone, Dr. Rosenbaum exclaimed, complacently smiling at his beautiful girls: "Next year when you are educated—next year *you* will look like that." Classes laugh at almost anything, and they laughed hard at this; Dr. Rosenbaum laughed harder than any, except, except. . . . When everyone had stopped laughing he said, "I will quote you from Goethe. *Man would not be the best thing in this world if he were not too good for this world.*" As he said this his face was half-sad, half-glad, and altogether Dr. Rosenbaum's face.

Their education was, for a good many of the girls, what they themselves would have called a traumatic experience. Two of the psychologists of the school talked of education not simply as therapy but as shock therapy: "The first thing I do with a freshman," one of them said to Dr. Rosenbaum, "is to shake her out of her ignorant complacency." Dr. Rosenbaum knew one of her freshmen, a cheerful scatterbrained girl who was neither cheerful nor scatterbrained about *her;* this girl said viciously, "All she does is *pry.* She thinks I'm a bourgeois prejudice and she wants me to get rid of myself." But he said nothing of this, and muttered under his breath, in German: "God spare us our ignorant complacency."

If Benton had had an administration building with pillars it could have carved over the pillars: *Ye shall know the truth, and the truth shall make you feel guilty.* Just as ordinary animal awareness has been replaced in man by consciousness, so consciousness had been replaced, in most of the teachers of Benton, by social consciousness. They were successful in teaching most of their students to say in contrition, about anything whatsoever: *It was I, Lord, it was I;* but they were not so successful in teaching them to consider this consciousness of guilt a *summum bonum*, one's final claim upon existence. Many a Benton girl went back to her nice home, married her rich husband, and carried a fox in her bosom for the rest of her life—and short of becoming a social worker, founding a Neo-Socialist party, and then killing herself and leaving her insurance to the United Nations, I do not know how she could have got rid of it.

The demands American education could not meet—that it give a continent a college education—had forced this portion of it into regression: Benton was in its second childhood. It had sloughed off the awful protean burden of the past: of Magdalenian caves and Patmos and palm-leaf scriptures from Ceylon; of exiles' letters from Thrace or the banks of the Danube; of soldiers' letters from the Wall—the Roman Wall, the Chinese Wall. Benton did not see that it is we who ride upon Proteus, and that without him our journey is weary and our way unfriended. So, most of their burden flung off, the people of Benton went light and refreshed on their way, their broad smooth concrete Way; and when, soon, their legs got tired, they said to one another that it is the destiny of man to get tired.

The people of Benton [Gertrude would have sung *Men of Benton!* to the tune of *Men of Harlech!* if she had only known the tune] had not all been provincial to begin with, but they had made provincials of themselves, and called their province, now, the world. And it was a world in which almost nothing happened, a kind of steady state. Benton was a progressive college, so you would have supposed that this state would be a steady progression. So it had been, for a couple of decades; but later it had become a steady retrogression. Benton was much less progressive than it had been ten years before—but somehow this didn't bother people, didn't make them feel less progressive, didn't do anything to them. Is an institution always a man's shadow shortened in the sun, the lowest common denominator of everybody in it? Benton was: the soldiers, as always, were better than the army in which they served, the superficial consenting nexus of their lives that was Benton. The people of Benton, like the rest of us, were born, fell in love, married and died, lay sleepless all night, saw the first star of evening and wished upon it, won lotteries and wept for joy. But not at Benton.

VI.

Art Night

1. My wife and I were Gertrude's only old acquaintances at Benton; sometimes we were sorry that this was so. She called one morning to ask whether we could come by for her that night—it was Art Night; "Sidney's in New York," she said, "and I feel that As A Novelist I ought to go." I replied senselessly: "That's odd—my wife's in New York too, with the car. Do you suppose she and Sidney have run off with the car?" Gertrude was silent for a moment; she didn't like jokes about Sidney. Then she said, "That's silly." I tried to think of something to say that would make up for what I had said: that my wife certainly wouldn't have run away with *Sidney*, that *Sidney* certainly wouldn't run away with anybody, that—I said, "Yes, that was silly," and told Gertrude that I could come for her anyway, that someone was taking me.

It was Dr. Rosenbaum. When we got to Gertrude's I jumped out of his car and then paused, transfixed. Gertrude's apartment was on the second floor; it had a little balcony; Gertrude was sitting on the balcony holding in her hand an enormous Mexican glass; inside her apartment a phonograph was playing, louder than I had heard a phonograph play before. Gertrude held up her glass, waved it— quite a good deal spilled—and called out to me, "Look, Jack Daniel's! Mama sent it to me for my birthday."

I said, wonderingly: "Your mother! For your birthday! I didn't even know you had one."

"Didju think they found me under a cabbage-leaf?" Gertrude asked, laughing girlishly. Something about her laugh attracted her; she repeated it. She was all dressed up: her voice, her flushed smile, everything about her gave an impression of reckless but secure gaiety. "Come on up and have a drink," she said.

"You come on down; we don't want to miss any of *Art Night.*"

"O.K.," said Gertrude; "be right down. Just let me finish this drink." She finished it in three swallows, without visible effect; I watched without belief; but when she repeated, "Be right down," she had become for the moment a contralto.

As she walked to the car the music came to a climax: the orchestra itself seemed to have turned into a drum. I said to Gertrude, raising my voice: "I believe you've left the phonograph on."

She answered, "It'll turn itself off; it's automatic." Then she said—but she didn't make it the first time, stopped, and repeated carefully, in a voice of real elevation: "And what if it does not?"

The time had come. I said, "Gertrude, say hello to Dr. Rosenbaum; he's going to drive us over to school."

Gertrude stopped. She stopped as a tribe of Indians, walking in single file through the forest, stops when its chieftain sees a snake. She stared into the Simca.

Dr. Rosenbaum said in a terribly deep voice, *"Guten abend, gnädige Frau!"* Gertrude said nothing. I opened the door of the car; after a moment I said, "I'll—let me sit in the middle."

Gertrude said, "Pray do."

Dr. Rosenbaum said, "There is no middle." This was so; between the two bucket seats there was only the gear shift. I could have asked Gertrude to sit in my lap, and yet. . . . I got myself into the space behind the seats; there was room for everything but my head. Gertrude sat down and folded her hands in her lap; I reached over her shoulder and shut the door.

We started away; for a while the strains of the music followed us. I said, "What is that, Gertrude? It's very impressive."

She answered, "It's—" Then she paused, and said surprisedly: "I can't remember."

"It's *Ce qu'on entend sur la montagne*," said Dr. Rosenbaum; "what we call the *Bergsymphonie*."

"That's right," said Gertrude. Then she said, "That's *right*." She was silent for a moment, collecting herself. Then she began to talk. At first it was hard for her to pronounce some of the words, but from the first what she had to say was witty and coherent—by the time we got to Benton her mother might as well have sent her sachet. No liquor could influence Gertrude like an audience.

2.

WHEN WE got inside the gallery, the first thing we saw was Sona Rasmussen. Miss Rasmussen was half Japanese, half Norwegian; she came from Honolulu. She was a fat, tiny, shiny woman: with a different paint job, and feelers, she would have looked exactly like a potato-bug—I used to think of her as part of a children's story in which there were

Reginald Chipmunk, and Dorothy Thrush, and Sona Potato-Bug, and many other innocent, foolish, and agreeable
creatures.

Miss Rasmussen made welded sculpture. Her statues were
—as she would say, smiling—untouched by human hands;
and they looked it. You could tell one from another, if you
wanted to, but it was hard to want to. You felt, yawning:
It's ugly, but is it Art?

Miss Rasmussen also designed furniture; but people persisted in sitting down in her sculpture, and in asking "What
is that named?" of her chairs. This showed how advanced
her work was, and pleased her; yet when she laughed to
show her pleasure, her laugh sounded thin and strained.
Gertrude said about her work, "She was a shipyard welder
during the war, and the sculpture just naturally followed."
When this was repeated to Miss Rasmussen she said hotly,
"Oh, *that* again! It was an aircraft factory—and besides, I'd
thought of it *long ago*."

She liked Benton, and Benton liked her; but she had had
difficulties during her first term. President Robbins said to
her, after two of her freshmen had burned themselves severely: "A welder's torch is *not* a thing with which just
any freshman can be entrusted, Miss Rasmussen." Miss Rasmussen said that you couldn't shelter students forever, but
after that she had her freshmen stick to wood, mobiles, and
Cold Iron. Her advanced students were a different affair:
she and they, in their goggles and masks, looked wonderful,
like racetrack-drivers about to give a *Nō* play.

Gottfried and Gertrude and I arrived, first, at the wooden
half of the sculpture. All the statues, to show that they were
statues, were mounted on little black pedestals. Off to the

side there was one statueless pedestal; Gertrude looked at it a long time, in silent admiration; I had to persuade her to leave it.

Some of the statues looked like improbably polished *objets trouvés*, others looked as if the class had divided a piece of furniture among themselves, lovingly finished the fragments, and mounted the result as a term's work. The passing sculptors—and Miss Rasmussen, who did not pass, but stood there like a sentry—found Gertrude's voluble admiration for their works offensive; she exclaimed about the one she liked best, "Why, you can *see* yourself in it! What I wouldn't give for that in bird's-eye maple!" She went on to say to Miss Rasmussen: "How *do* you and your pupils get this *wonderful* finish?" Miss Rasmussen did not reply: she looked as if she were half Japanese and half Ethiopian. Gertrude continued artlessly, "I always use linseed oil and rottenstone, myself; but to tell the truth, Miss Rasmussen, a little old-fashioned elbow grease is what it really takes." She said this with a cheery laugh; she was enjoying herself, and if people didn't know enough to get out of the way, they would have to suffer for their ignorance.

After looking at ten or twenty of these statues you muttered to yourself, "I wish wood didn't *have* any grain"; a few more and you were sorry that there is such a thing as wood—were sorry, that is, until you came to the Ores and Metals section of the sculpture. First came the mobiles—and they were mobile: if you breathed hard that part of the gallery looked like dawn in a cuckoo-clock factory. Then came the welded statues: they were made, apparently, of iron twine, with queer undigested knots or lumps or nodules every few inches, so that they all looked like representations of part of the root-system of an alfalfa plant, or that of almost any legume. Sometimes a statue had four legs and was an animal; sometimes it had two legs and two arms, and was a man. But sometimes it had neither arms nor legs, and was an abstraction.

Gertrude said softly, though not so softly as I could have wished: "Why don't riveters do sculpture, too?" But when she applied the word *fragile* to a statue with less than its share of lumps, Miss Rasmussen broke in stormily: "*Fragile!* You couldn't break that with a hammer! Let me tell you, every joint in that is *welded*."

Gertrude gave her a surgeon's smile; you expected Gertrude to say, "More ether, nurse. This woman is conscious." Then she remarked in a speculative voice, "Have you ever stopped to consider, Miss Rasmussen, just *why* your statues are so thin?" By now the patient, poor fat thing, was beginning to be sorry that she had come to; I said before Gertrude could go on: "I love your statues, Miss Rasmussen," not even crossing my fingers as I said it; and Gottfried said that *dey madt him feel goodt ven he lookedt at dem*. Gertrude looked at me for a moment; then she looked at Gottfried for a moment; then she laughed. It was a placing laugh. When the ripples of this laugh had died, she quoted clearly: "Kind hearts are more than coronets, And simple faith than Norman blood."

Miss Rasmussen began to tell Gottfried and me about her statues. Some of what she said was technical, and you would have had to be a welder to appreciate it; the rest was aesthetic or generally philosophic, and to appreciate it you would have had to be an imbecile.

230

3.

WE CAME to the paintings next. There had been quite a
good painter at Benton the year before, a mild, absent, indifferent man, with hair like a string bag; when he resigned
he said genially, "You don't need *me*." He had been replaced by a painter who painted animals in marshes—or
jungles: all glowed. This man stood looking out over his
herds, the ringstraked, speckled, and spotted; he wore a
turtleneck sweater and a black beard, and smiled a complacent smile, as if he had just said to you in an English novel,
"I thought you'd ask that."

The paintings varied, though not much. The students
loved their teacher, it was plain: there were a great many
beasts of prey, in forests and marshes, all looking like feral
Florence Nightingales. I said to Gertrude, finally: "Gertrude, for God's sake stop saying *Tiger, Tiger, burning
bright!*" Then I said to Gottfried, "Say something!" He
said, "What can I say?"

The animals were recognizably animals, and that was
about all you could say for them—but it was something you
could not have said for any of the other paintings there.
The students had learned all the new ways to paint something (an old way, to them, was a way not to paint something) but they had not had anything to paint. The paintings were paintings of nothing at all. It did not seem possible
to you that so many things could have happened to a piece of
canvas in vain. You looked at a painting and thought, "It's
an imitation Arshile Gorky; it's casein and aluminum paint
on canvasboard, has been scratched all over with a razor

blade, and then was glazed—or scumbled, perhaps—with several transparent oil washes." And when you had said this there was no more for you to say. If you had given a Benton student a pencil and a piece of paper, and asked her to draw something, she would have looked at you in helpless astonishment: it would have been plain to her that you knew nothing about art. By the time a Benton artist got through exploiting the possibilities of her medium, it was too dark to do anything else that day; and most of the students never learned that there was anything else to do.

Gertrude had begun an animated conversation with the painter; her first sentence was, "Tell me, have you ever thought of doing illustrations for *The Jungle Book?*" I thought it unfair of her to talk so much of the suppressed aggressions that manifested themselves in his work, since it was plain from his part of the conversation that he was not a man who suppressed aggressions. Against many conversationalists he would have had quite a good chance: he spoke not as the scribes but with authority, and was untroubled by any of the doubts that intelligence brings in its train. He looked truculent to begin with; within five sentences he was looking baffled and truculent. To Gertrude's extended, unfavorable, but really quite brilliant comparison of his jungles with those of Max Ernst and the Douanier Rousseau, he retorted: "I'm not interested in other painters' paintings."

Gertrude looked at him with delight, and said: "You're from the West Coast, aren't you?"

"What do you mean?"

"Well, aren't you?"

"How did you know?"

Gertrude said modestly, "Oh, I just knew." Then she said, "I'll bet I can tell you who your favorite writer is, too."

"Who?"

"Henry Miller."

The painter laughed triumphantly, and exclaimed: "Wrong! D. H. Lawrence."

Gertrude smiled and said to him, "You're older than I thought"; and to me, "Well, it's a moral victory, anyway."

I said, "Gertrude, don't you think we ought to be finding some seats for the performance?"

She answered, "Christ, you're a—a sobersided man. We can always sit in Dr. Rosenbaum's lap." Then she said to the painter, winningly: "You come too." He said, "Well, I—" But Gertrude, staring at him thoughtfully, murmured: "D. H. Lawrence!" Then she said to me, aside: "Still, I suppose he's doing well to *have* a favorite writer. I think Cézanne was right about painters, don't you?—*le peintre est en general bête.*"

Gertrude's French was so bad that anyone could understand every word of it. But there was no light, either of comprehension or of increased anger, in the painter's glittering eyes; they went on looking intense. Gertrude said again: "D. H. Lawrence! . . . But don't you *really* think Giono beats him at his own game?"

I said, "Gertrude, the seats, the seats!"

Gertrude was opening her mouth; before *D. H. Lawrence!* could come out I pulled her away. She went reluctantly, calling back to the painter a feeling goodbye.

We found two seats, though with difficulty; Gertrude and Gottfried sat down, and I lowered myself to the floor beside them. I noticed that as Gottfried sat down in his seat, and as I sat down in the aisle, we gave a soft strange sigh. Had we too once, long ago, made jokes, said unkind things, been hushed by our worried responsible fellows? We sat there like unleavened Sunday School superintendents, and Gertrude sparkled to the rows around; unsuspecting children would come up to talk and we would tense ourselves, making ready to push them away before Gertrude could go off in their hands.

4.

THE LITTLE auditorium was already full, but a third of Benton remained to be seated. Girls sat in girls' laps; girls sat on the floor, as if at a party; standing girls lined all the walls; athletic girls sat on the hall's Tudor rafters, swinging their shorted legs. (There was disagreement on how to dress for Art Night. Half the girls dressed as if for a date, and were unrecognizable to their teachers, who had never seen them except with their shirt-tails out, in shorts or blue jeans; the rest came with their shirt-tails out, in shorts or blue jeans.) The audience discussed what they had seen and what they were going to see; they pointed, called greetings, rustled like leaves; but, mostly, they giggled. Great visible waves of giggles would sweep across the hall; the girls looked like the choir and furniture of Heaven, but they sounded like bats.

The President sat in the front row, his leg over the arm of his seat, his good profile turned toward his audience; from time to time his laugh would soar up under the giggles of the girls—an unaffected laugh, full of spontaneity and enthusiasm and boyish artless life. He was going to get his thirty-seventh merit badge tonight, Gertrude told her row; some were silent, some gave a shocked and wicked laugh.

The program was already twenty minutes late, but behind the curtain you could hear things being dropped, things being dragged across the stage. But finally a messenger came to the President; he rose; he—

Just at that moment Mrs. Robbins came in. She appeared at the back of the auditorium; she was dressed in—well, she always seemed to be dressed in what she called *a tea gown*, but this was a tea gown with a fringe and sequins. There was a long delay while she made her way to the seat beside the President. I mean this literally: there was no way there, she *made* it. You felt that she had signed a compact with the devil to stumble over or to step upon, to say *Sorry!* to, every person sitting in the center aisle. Mrs. Robbins was always one to apologize, necessarily or unnecessarily, and you could see how she felt: it was a pity to leave unused for even an hour a *Sorry!* so superior as hers.

The President was greeted with loving silence. He said that we had already seen what Benton could do in painting and in sculpture, and now we would see what Benton could do in drama and in the dance. The Department of Drama was going to perform a new adaptation, made especially for us by Mrs. Caraccioli, of Strindberg's *The Spook Sonata;* and the Department of Dance and the Department of Music would give a dance-drama called *The Life of Nature*, with a score especially composed for it by Benton's Composer in Residence, Gottfried Rosenbaum. (Gottfried smiled guiltily.) Last, to sum up the significance of all that we had seen that night, we would have the privilege of hearing a distinguished visitor, Charles Francis Daudier, speak on Art and the Democratic Way of Life.

Mrs. Caraccioli had adapted *The Spook Sonata* according to her lights, the lights of Benton: it was a nightmare still, but a nightmare with social significance. And yet, where *we* were, it was pure delight. As an actor said to me afterwards, "There was one part of that audience that, I don't care what we said, they laughed." Gertrude's improvised variations on Strindberg, sketched out in a rapid whisper, had the seats around her helpless with laughter; as they had giggled once, so, now, they laughed. Gottfried muttered to me—and his voice was almost loving—"Oh, but she is good! I have underjudged her. She is a *truly* witty woman."

When the play was done, Gertrude looked around at her audience in wordless triumph; during the intermission she received congratulations smilingly. It was during this intermission that the President spoke with so much emotion, to the Head of the Department of Literature, of Camille Batterson. He even went on to say: "And this fall we were, perhaps, too hasty."

"Too hasty?"

"In giving up Mr. Gumbiner so soon, I mean." But then he said—and he smiled like the newly created angels, who cannot yet believe their bliss—"Only twenty-three more days!"

But Gertrude was tired, now; after a few minutes of *The Life of Nature* she said surprisedly, "Why, it's a child's point of view ballet"—this was so—and a few minutes later she said that the prima ballerina had "a bottom of good sense"—whether this was so I don't know, but she did stay on all fours most of the time, like the animals—and that was all Gertrude said; we sat and dully watched the dancers. We missed *The Spook Sonata*.

The girl who was a girl—all the rest of the girls were creatures of the forest—had been hurt by life, and the plants and animals helped her to understand. You saw everything through her Awakening eyes. I tried to, to name the birds without a gun, and to be all right because it was almost over—I told myself this over and over—but mostly I tried to find something to *do:* I would have played Ghosts, I would have played Lotto, I would have played Animal Grab. It seemed to me that generations of me would be born, and live their lives out, and die gladly, and still not have got through *The Life of Nature*.

After a while *The Life of Nature* ended: the girl, awake now, was borne off on the shoulders of the forest, and the President introduced Charles Francis Daudier.

Mr. Daudier spoke to us for—for some years, we felt. It was the speech a vain average would make to an audience of means. Gertrude had heard him give the speech before; so had I; Gottfried never had; yet Gottfried knew it better than we did, because Gottfried was older than we were, and had heard that speech more times than we had.

After a while I could no longer hear what Mr. Daudier was saying, and I just looked at him. There were waves like heat waves in the air of the auditorium, so that his face would get big and indistinct, and then small and indistinct; sometimes I would realize that it had disappeared altogether, that I hadn't seen it for minutes, and I would grope my way back to seeing it.

It was a wonderful face. Mr. Daudier—the name is pronounced *Dody*er—came from a Huguenot family that had settled in Massachusetts very early, and become a sort of example to the Puritans. Gertrude used to call him Old Rocky Face. The name suited him: compared to *him,* Dante looked like Little Black Sambo's mother, Black Mumbo.

Mr. Daudier had been pushed up and down New England several times, head-first, by a glacier; this face was what was left. (Or, from another point of view, New England was what was left.) And yet he kept talking about Love; it was always *Love*, never *love*, and when he said *Love* a strange light would come over his face, and make you want to hate your neighbor. He looked *much* more like a stone than stones do: he not only knew that he was right, he knew that he was good—and he recognized the fact that other people weren't; his face had a look of such grave, muted, self-righteous complacency that it seemed a seventeenth century engraving designed to illustrate Socrates' *Nothing can hurt the good man*.

I kept looking into this face while it weighed itself; then a hand wrapped it in some paper, paper that looked like grey moss, so that I said to my wife, who had come back from New York with Sidney: "He's got a haircut." My wife and Sidney and the face began to applaud; the girl in the aisle beside me gently shook my head—it was in her lap—and said, "You've been asleep." They turned on the lights in the auditorium. I was confused, and as I sat up said foolishly: "Thank you for taking care of me." The girl answered: "I've been asleep."

The audience got up slowly, and walked away uncertainly—the girls to their dormitories, the teachers and their wives and husbands to the President's, to meet Mr. Daudier. "Come on," said Gertrude; her face was that of the characters in the *Lays of Ancient Rome* when they swear something upon the ashes of their fathers.

5.

THE FURNITURE of the President's house had been picked by Mrs. Robbins and an interior decorator, and looked as if it had been picked by two interior decorators. Except for photographs and a teddy bear of Derek's, the house was institutional. Mr. Daudier stood in front of the fireplace waving off compliments on his speech, and trying to repress a smile of justified complacency. The President stood by him, alertly beaming. He and Mr. Daudier got along well: they had everything but their views in common.

When the President started to introduce Gertrude to Mr. Daudier, Mr. Daudier halted him, and exclaimed affably, "Why, Gertrude and I are old friends—we've met half a dozen times."

Gertrude replied in a bleak voice, "I'm sure we must have; I just don't remember."

Mr. Daudier was taken aback. He began to remind Gertrude of occasions; Gertrude visibly did not listen, and after a moment broke in, "You remind me of *some*one, though. Haven't you a brother?"

"I? A brother?"

"I could have sworn you had a brother. You mean every time I see the name Daudier it's you?"

Mr. Daudier said that of course Daudier was an old name, a fairly well-known name in New England, but that—

"You're the poet?"

Mr. Daudier said, in the deprecating tone in which Americans refer to poetry, that he *had* published several volumes of verse. Gertrude murmured softly, "*Several!*" and went on to ask him about some anthologies. They were his. Some people are great strawberry-fanciers, or soccer-fans, or stamp-collectors. Mr. Daudier was a great anthologist: he made anthologies all the time. Once a man wrote that we see many men with a passion for gambling, but none with a passion for running gambling-houses; I think that Mr. Daudier, by his anthologies, disproved this remark. And he was a prominent literary critic: he had a column of criticism, every week except the last two weeks in August, in the best-known literary weekly; he was a director of a club that picked books for readers who didn't know what to read; there are radio-programs which have several critics blame, and several critics and the author praise, some recent book, and Mr. Daudier was generally on one side or the other; during the school year he would lecture to colleges, and when the school year was over he would make commencement addresses to them or get honorary degrees from them; he was the chief reader of a publishing-house, he was one of the vice-presidents of the American branch of the Académie Francaise; you saw one-act plays by him, if you fell among anthologies of one-act plays; he even wrote informal essays. ("*Now* I know who it is I've been confusing you with," cried Gertrude; "Christopher Morley!" "*Who?*" "Christopher Morley. Oh, I know you haven't any beard; I was just confused. It was those informal essays.") But mostly he talked about great books—about a hundred of them; I don't know why he stopped at a hundred, but he did, and let the rest go; he must have made up his mind that it was no use trying to get people to read more than a hundred. There were two things he was crazy about, the thirteenth century and Greek: if the thirteenth century had spoken Greek I believe it would have killed him not to have been alive in it. He didn't know anything about, or care anything for, science, unless it was several hundred years old—or several thousand, for choice; he loved it then. He would say, "What do *we* know that Aristotle didn't know?" But he wouldn't let you tell him; it was a rhetorical question. He had diabetes and used to get an injection of insulin every day, but I don't believe he ever got one without wishing it were Galen giving it to him.

He wasn't a Catholic, just a fellow traveller, but he did the Church more good than half a dozen ordinary *monsignori*. He couldn't talk for five minutes without mentioning Aquinas—Aquinas, or Thomas Jefferson. He would say it was sad how rusty your Greek got when you'd been out of college as long as he had; but if he read it a tenth as much as he talked about it, I don't see how his Greek could have got rusty. (I think it must have got worn away with use, the way a beaver's teeth do.) And he loved to read the *Divine Comedy* aloud to you, especially if you didn't know Italian; he would translate it to you as he went along. And he could tell you what Aristotle thought about *anything*. He was a liberal education in himself—a conservative one, I mean.

But it was his novels that seemed to interest Gertrude most. She said in a queer tone, the tone a mother uses when she doesn't want to wake her baby: "I was very interested in what you said about the failure of the modern novel, and about the modern novelist's needing to go back to Fielding."

"You were?"

"Oh yes," replied Gertrude. "I've read one of your novels; that was why I was interested. It was a novel named—named—"

"*The Firmament of Time?*"

"No."

"*The Greatest of These?*"

"No, not that."

"*A Cock for Aesculapius?*"

"No, some other."

"I haven't written any other."

"It must have been one of them, then. It was a novel about—about—well, it's been some time since I've read it, but I remember thinking that the critics had been *most unfair* to it."

Mr. Daudier had a queer look on his face, as if he were a box of mixed nuts, but mostly peanuts; but you could see that he agreed with *this* remark down to the last cell of his toenails.

"Now, *I'm* a novelist, and naturally I'm prejudiced: I want a novel to be *by* a novelist—you know, a real professional job; but I don't think a *critic* ought to be like that, do you? It's his duty to make allowances. *He* ought not to judge a—an unpretentious novel by a beginner as if it were *War and Peace*. I think he ought to judge it by the *spirit*, not just by the letter, and forgive it all those little technical errors an amateur just naturally makes."

I had read that if you let a seed grow for a while it can crack a boulder; and I could see, now, that this was so. We all looked at Mr. Daudier and thought: "He's not half so insensitive as he seems."

Gertrude paused, to give him a chance to say something; but as he did not say anything, she went on: "The moment I started your book I remember feeling—it was such a refreshingly *different* feeling: why, this is the sort of book I used to read when I was a girl, a real *old-fashioned* novel. I felt as if I were just about to curl up in a window-seat with *Little Women*. And that's the sort of thing you can't fake —I'll bet *you've* often curled up in a window-seat with *Little Women*."

The President, looking as if he were worrying about Mr. Daudier, tried to take him off to the others, but Gertrude seized Mr. Daudier by the arm and said firmly: "I know everybody wants him, but I want him first. There're simply *thousands* of things Mr. Daudier and I have to say to each other. You know, little trade-secrets. For instance, what you said about the ideal education being manual labor and Greek. Now, I was interested in that. I'll bet all of us were interested in *that*. I've seen it somewhere else, though. Who said that first?"

Mr. Daudier said that he thought he'd said it first, though he might have read it somewhere else and forgotten; my heart was hardened, and I said: "I think it's Auden." Mr. Daudier looked at me like Pyrrho the Sceptic. Gertrude said, "Yes, that must be right," and gestured towards me, saying: "*He* knows Auden by heart, practically." Then she got back to business: "What you said about manual labor and Greek, that they're the ideal education, that made me think of Cassandra. I mean, when the Greeks captured her and made a slave out of her, she could have cheered herself up by thinking that at least she was going to get an ideal education. And that was so about *any* Greek slave—any slave that was a foreigner to begin with, and didn't know Greek. But there's one thing that bothered me: how could any *Greek* get an ideal education? *They* already knew Greek."

Gottfried said, helpfully, that *dey didtn't needt an ideal edtucation: DEY vere Greeks.*

Gertrude said, "Now take St. Thomas. Did St. Thomas know Greek?"

The President's eyes lit up. He said quickly, "I've read something interesting about St. Thomas—oh, I just happened to come across it in some history or other I was reading—that, that interested me very much because it's so different from people's ordinary idea of him. Did you know that St. Thomas Aquinas was so fat that they had to cut out a hole for him to sit in, at the dinner-table?"

"Of course," said Gertrude. She continued, fixing Mr. Daudier with her absorbed stare: "Now take you. Do you think readers like *you* so much because you know Greek?"

Mr. Daudier said, "Well—"

Gertrude waited for a moment, to let him go on; when he didn't she went on herself: "No, sir! [Here she gave a strange little smile. I think that she was amused at herself for having said *No, sir:* it was overdoing it, but who would see or care? She had the contempt for her audience that the real virtuoso so often has.] The common man likes you," exclaimed Gertrude, "because he feels that you're speaking directly *to* him."

Mr. Daudier looked rather pleased, but surprised, too.

"And why shouldn't he?" cried Gertrude. "*You*'ve never lost the common touch—I think you *are* a common man."

The look on Mr. Daudier's face was so complicated that I was sorry I had ever thought him simple. But also—but also, for a moment, he looked like a poor stupid old man; I thought, "He hasn't a chance."

"Yes, that's the way it is," Gertrude exclaimed. "You know, Swift once wrote to Pope—or Pope once wrote to Swift, *I* don't care—that there's one sure sign of a true wit: all the dunces are leagued against him. You take a writer like you, and nobody's leagued against him: they're *for you*. And the reason for *that* is, you never say one single word that they couldn't—that every one of them wouldn't say himself. Oh, I know a lot of people think you're a reactionary, but they don't hold it against you. They know that at heart you're exactly the same as they are. It was a good idea to get you to talk on art and democracy—anyway, on democracy: I think you're a really democratic writer. . . .

Now take what you said about all modern novels being bad."

Mr. Daudier said that he hadn't called, and didn't think, *all* modern novels bad.

"Oh no," replied Gertrude, "just all except yours."

But a wail from the staircase interrupted Gertrude. It was Derek. He stood there in his pajamas, staring out at us unseeingly; his neck and shoulders were hunched like an animal's. "Poor dear, has he had his nightmare!" cried Mrs. Robbins; she went to him and, with surprising awkwardness, tried to console him. He seemed unable to see or hear her, but her touch comforted him; after a little he stopped trembling and allowed himself to be led back upstairs to bed. I felt so sorry for them both, at that instant, that I cursed myself for noticing that she called him *Pammy's little boy*. During the whole time he never said a word.

Mrs. Robbins didn't come back for some time; when she returned Gottfried and I said goodbye to her, explaining that we wanted to get back to Irene, who hadn't felt too well that evening. Mrs. Robbins was uneasily gracious to us. Gertrude was staying; as we walked to the door she came up to me and, drawing me aside, said happily: "I've always meant to have a little heart-to-heart talk with that guy."

I said something, I don't know what, but my voice was so halfhearted that Gertrude's face fell. I thought, "No, it isn't fair; she doesn't know any better." I felt as you do when your cat brings you a bluejay it has caught; the cat knows no better and the bluejay deserves no better, but just the same. . . . I thought, *Poor Gertrude;* I realized that, in a funny way, I was fond of Gertrude. I said, "You were really good tonight, Gertrude. Did you hear what Gottfried said about you?"

"No, what?"

"He said that you are—" and I imitated his voice—"a *truly vitty voman*."

She tried not to show it, but she was pleased; she said goodbye, and as she went off to find new audiences, new victims, I said after her: "Goodbye, Gertrude. I'll see you soon."

I had been living in another world—a dream world, as they say—for a couple of hours, and had awakened from it. I went out dejectedly. Gottfried seemed depressed, too. I suppose that at that moment, for us, Miss Rasmussen and the painter and Charles Francis Daudier and Gertrude were only Dereks. The world had reminded us that, underneath anything any of us could say about it, it existed.

The Rosenbaums had in their living room one of the longest sofas I have ever seen; when we got there Constance was asleep at one end of it and the cat at the other; Irene was reading. She said, "How was it?" I said, "Awful, awful."

"What was Daudier like?"

"He's a—he's a poor stupid old man," I answered.

We sat down, got ourselves something to drink, talked a while; it was quiet outside, quiet inside; the light fell on the Persian's rumpled fur, on Constance's sleeping head, and it was more peaceful than, for a while, I could believe. Irene kept on reading.

The cat was thirsty or else just dreaming: she lapped for a moment and then stopped lapping. But she had stopped with her tongue out of her mouth, and it made her snore; finally she woke, jumped up, shook herself, and walked out of the room.

Gottfried said to Irene—he spoke, absentmindedly, in German—"What readest thou?"

"A poet—an English one. I've come to a part about a singer."

"A singer of opera?" I asked, smiling at her.

"I think of *lieder*. I will read it to you.

> *I have oft heard*
> *My mother Circe with the Sirens three*
> *Amidst the flowery-kirtl'd Naiades*
> *Culling their Potent hearbs, and balefull drugs,*
> *Who as they sung, would take the prison'd soul*
> *And lap it in Elysium, Scylla wept*
> *And chid her barking waves into attention,*
> *And fell Charybdis murmur'd soft applause:*
> *Yet they in pleasing slumber lull'd the sense,*
> *And in sweet madness rob'd it of it self,*
> *But such a sacred, and home-felt delight,*
> *Such sober certainty of waking bliss*
> *I never heard till now."*

Gottfried said, in amazement, "Why, it is better than Hölderlin, almost"; I repeated silently, *And O poor hapless Nightingale thought I,/How sweet thou sing'st, how near the deadly snare.* "Let me see it, Irene," I said. "There's something further on that I've often thought is—that I want to read to you." I found what I wanted and read it aloud:

> *The leaf was darkish, and had prickles on it,*
> *But in another country, as he said,*
> *Bore a bright golden flower, but not in this soyl:*
> *Unknown, and like esteemed, and the dull swayn*

Treads on it daily with his clouted shoon,
And yet more med'cinal is it than that Moly
That Hermes *once to wise* Ulysses *gave.*

All of us had, I think, the same rueful smile; Gottfried repeated, "And yet more med'cinal is it than that *Moly* /That *Hermes* once to wise *Ulysses* gave"; and Irene said soberly, with the little mock-pedantic intonation she had gained from her life among the Germanic peoples: "Yes, this is so."

I yawned—it seemed to me that Gertrude, and Mr. Daudier, and Miss Rasmussen, and *The Life of Nature* were thousands of years away—and said contentedly to Gottfried: "Take me home. And I guess we'd better wake up Constance and get her home—she'll be having to go to work in the morning."

"There is no need," said Irene. "I do not want her waked. I will cover her with a blanket and set the alarm-clock, and in the morning I will make breakfast for her and take her to the school."

I said goodbye to Irene, and as Gottfried and I left she went upstairs to get the blanket.

VII.

They All Go

1. And so the last day came, and the last hour of the last day. Gertrude said goodbye to the President, and the President said goodbye to Gertrude, and Gertrude and the President said goodbye to Constance; and Constance was left alone. And now after a few minutes Constance's work was done, her goodbyes were over, all was over; she closed the outer door of the office (*almost I/Regained my freedom with a sigh*) and walked away with slow queer luxurious steps, her body feeling as it had always felt when the last examination was done. She saw nothing—she was feeling; but when somebody called to her from the swimming pool as she walked by it, she called back and waved. It had been the President's friendly goodbye.

The President was already in swimming. (He went swimming as easily as other people light a cigarette.) Next day summer would scatter the Robbins to the winds. Derek was going to a summer camp that took *very* little boys; Mrs. Robbins was about to make one of her summer visits to wintry South Africa, there to be the envy of her relatives and friends and any poor Hottentot or aardvark or aasvogel she could catch in her deadfalls and convince of her enviability: strangers are best to fool, but home-folk are the nicest to show off to. The Afghans—as President Robbins thought of this the skin around his eyes did not crinkle, but crackled, with joy—the Afghans next week would be eating their foolish heads off at the nearest boarding-kennel. The President himself was glad to be leaving for two months American educational life, which is as difficult as it is challenging; the Rockefeller Foundation was sending him to make a survey of Progressive Elements in European Education. (Gertrude said, "It's like sending Zuleika Dobson to make a survey of Snakes in Ireland.") And Gertrude Johnson—as he thought of it Dwight Robbins bounced up and down on the loved familiar diving-board of the Benton pool, *his* pool—Gertrude was going, going, almost gone: tomorrow she would be gone, gone forever, never to bother Benton and its President again.

(How could he know that even at that moment she was thinking of him, her eyes alight: that in just a few months now he would be the curly-headed English sailor in that *auto-da-fé* she had been collecting faggots for so long— had already christened, in her hard heart, *Act of Faith?*)

People walking by stopped to watch the President as he did a one-and-a-half-gainer-from-a-sitting-start, or some such thing. If you could name it, he could do it; he was still in almost professional form—would go down into the water smoothly and purely and come up from it sleekly, flinging his dripping hair to the side with a practiced jerk of the head, a gesture as occupational as that with which a mermaid runs through her golden hair her golden comb. He really did feel good: Nature's kaleidoscope had cracked his everyday world to pieces, and had put together from its crystals a moment like a moonbow. He climbed back to the top of the diving-tower, and this time did a swan dive: he went very high into the air and stayed there, his arms outstretched—stayed for so long that you could not believe it, before he began to fall. He looked so beautiful, suspended there in a confusion of shadow and sunlight, that you forgave him everything, were ashamed that it was necessary to forgive: there slipped from his shoulders, in a rain of little drops silvery as dew, the weary weight of this intelligible world. Intelligible? Surely. "What's there unintelligible about it?" he would have asked, if he had told you the truth that was in his heart. As someone says, it's knowing what to do with things that counts: he knew.

As he hung there his dazzled, accustomed, almost dreaming eyes were suffused with the blue and green of the water below them, the bright darkness that held at its center a white increasing shape. He did not see at the other end of the swimming pool the Afghan, Yang. Yang, having finished drinking, stuck into the water a first tentative delighting paw, and did not look toward his master, hung there upon the Wheel of Things.

2.

AFTER SHE had said goodbye to Dwight Robbins, and spoken to Constance like a lady, and danced—kept herself from dancing—home through the streets, Gertrude tried to settle herself, to get down to packing; but her spirits were too good. Even her arms and legs felt that by leaving Benton they were causing it quietly to wither away. She had almost Berkeleyan views about other people: that away from her they didn't really exist, except that—it was a contradiction, like Life—except that away from her they were *talking about her all the time*.

Her Guggenheim Fellowship had been renewed, and she had got a thousand-dollar advance for a travel book: she and Sidney (he had said to his employers, *I have to go, Ger-*

trude is leaving; they had said, *All right*) were going to Peru or Chile or Ecuador—I forget which, the one where you can live like a prince on practically nothing. There Gertrude was going to write not a travel book—this wouldn't have surprised her publishers, they knew her—but the conclusion of her novel about Benton. She felt about each book, always: "This one is going to be different. This one will do it!" About this one she didn't feel it, she *knew* it.

Safe at home with Sidney—Sidney had got down to packing—Gertrude walked through the rooms like a leopard that has just been fed and is just about to be fed: if she had known how to purr she would have purred, if she had known how to sing she would have sung. Elation ran through her veins like a newer, better, carbonated blood. Her fears about Sidney had for days and weeks, months almost, been quieted—were almost forgotten, now. They lay there inside her waiting for a dark day, a white night, and somewhere inside her there was even the knowledge that they were there; but it lay there as silently as they. "How could he do without me?" she would say to herself. "He *depends* on me."

Now, walking back and forth watching Sidney pack, handing Sidney things, saying things to make Sidney laugh, Gertrude looked contentedly at the row of books she had written (she would sometimes say to herself, almost as though she were the President: *I've written seven books*); then she said to Sidney, turning to him with the freshness and lightness of a girl: "I'll be so glad to leave this ———ing place." She ordinarily used such language only at parties—how could she shock Sidney any more? besides, why should she shock her Sidney?—but she forgot now, in her joy.

She shocked others, herself she could not shock; and alone

among humorists, she was less amused by her jokes than other people were. So, away from their laughter, their held breath, their widening repudiating eyes, Gertrude felt: *Am I*—was she what?

She felt: *Am I? Am I?*

But now she would have said to that questing interminable self, a self that delighted not in man, no, nor in woman, no, nor in Gertrude Johnson neither: she would have said to it, her eyes sparkling like Dr. Rosenbaum's: "What do you mean, *Am I?* Here I am!"

She had once been to a musical comedy in which people had sung over and over, with questing, interminable, primordial insistence: "The *FUture!* The *FUture!*" The words of this song came to her now; and as the words *The FUture! the FUture!* danced themselves out in hope, in Hope, there in Gertrude's blissful head, a strange thing happened to Gertrude Johnson: she heard, for the first time in her life, a tune.

3.

THE NIGHT before this last day at Benton Dr. Rosenbaum had said to Irene and Constance, making a gesture that included all three: "They can do without us." His *they* referred not to Benton but to the World. He looked at them soberly and went on: "They didn't know, but now they know."

But after a moment he said with a gay rueful smile, in a voice that got both more dramatic and more incoherent than it usually did, perhaps because of the Josephshofer Auslese they had drunk:

"You think Joseph and Maria, the *Emperor* Joseph and

Maria, you think they *wanted* that poor old dull old Metastasio? Why, they went to sleep! Let me tell you, they thought they *had* to have him—*and* to learn Greek and to go to *opera seria* and to go to Mass every Sunday. They all believed that they must. And so did all the courtiers and all the merchants that were just like the court, they did believe —they all did too.

"And then one morning a man came to them—I don't know who, I think he was perhaps an advertising agency— *ja*, an advertising agency advertising *spinning-jennies*—he came to them and said in a little low voice, just like the King in *Alice in Wonderland*, he said: 'You are all pardoned. *From now on you don't have to do a thing.*'

"And from then on they didn't go to operas any more, they went to Betty Grable; they didn't learn Greek, they all played football—no, that's wrong, they all went to watch the footballers; and they went to Mass *real fast* and then they went to the Stork Club. And they said to the young man, 'We was—we were in chains and now we are free, and it is *all because of you!*' "

Irene and Constance, throughout the course of this speech, had got more and more amused at Dr. Rosenbaum; they laughed, went on laughing, and couldn't stop laughing; and Dr. Rosenbaum looked at them benevolently, laughed as he took off his glasses and benevolently wiped them with his handkerchief, and then said with pride, his voice sounding more or less like distant thunder: "*Speise ging von dem Fresser und Süssigkeit von dem Starken!* . . . How does it say that in English?" Constance had been able to understand some of the words of the German, but none of its sense; when Dr. Rosenbaum translated it she said: "Oh, that's the honey out of the lion: *Out of the strong*

*came forth sweetness, and out of the eater came forth
meat.*"

"*Ah so!*" said Dr. Rosenbaum. "Is not that what I have
been for you tonight? I have made you a bedtime story
from the Evening of the West. But it is too early to go to
bed: Irene, Constance, I will play you *Falstaff* on the
gramaphone."

Falstaff was his favorite opera, and he played it so much
that Constance knew even the little themes that come in,
flicker their wings once, and are gone forever. But after it
was finished, as he was driving Constance home in the
Simca, he said to Constance something that saddened her
for him, though not about him. What he said showed, quite
plainly and indiscreetly, that he did not consider himself a
good composer. Constance argued as well as love for him
and delight in what was his could argue, yet she too could
see—and how she hated seeing!—that when you listened to
Wozzeck or *Le Sacre du printemps* or Bartok's quartets
something happened to you that was different from anything that happened to you while you listened to even the
best of the works of Gottfried Rosenbaum. *If you are afraid
of wolves do not go into the forest*, the Russian proverb
says. We all live in the forest, and there is nothing to do but
get used to the wolves: Dr. Rosenbaum sported with the
pack, and cracked jokes, as if in a nutcracker, between
many slavering jaws.

Dr. Rosenbaum said equably: "Failure is the common
condition of composers—of common composers; I am no
different from my kind. In the textbooks I shall perhaps be
—should surely be, if only I played the violin—a second
Tartini. You will see. They will say about me: he has raised
the very devil."

Constance laughed. To most people Tartini is the composer of a single piece, the Devil's Trill sonata, and to most people Gottfried Rosenbaum was the composer of a tone poem called *Lucifer in Starlight*. The more advanced orchestras played it almost as the less advanced played *The Sorcerer's Apprentice;* it was a piece no audience had any difficulty with. The audience would read the little poem which was its program—how the devil one night flew up from hell, saw the stars "which are the brain of heaven," and fell to hell again—and would settle themselves to listen.

The devil was a yearning, Faustian, chromatic devil, but orchestrated in a style that made the orchestration of a Mahler scherzo sound wholesome and straightforward: each combination of instruments in which the devil's pride or lust or longing was expressed (he was a *very* affectionate devil, and there was no one like him in all the universe for him to love) was a combination of the instruments wrong for it, the combination that could most ingeniously and conclusively disgrace it—and when you had seen that it was entirely disgraceful, and when it had seen that it was entirely disgraceful, it grew louder, it went higher; this happened to each in its turn: it was as if the devil's heart had been cut from his breast and turned inside out before you, and it did not mind that any more than it minded anything else, it laughed at itself without meaning its laughter, and in complacent, yearning, abject shamelessness, went on beating. Then the stars came in.

They were the brain of heaven, but they made no sense. They moved to a thin, muted, march-like succession of notes—it was not a tune exactly—that went around and around and around in eerie, mechanical, incomprehensible infinitude; you felt that you were overhearing the sound of something that had gone on a long time, seeming to change sometimes but changeless, a machine that as it kept running made little sounds that—the sounds were as small and far-off and inhuman as they had been in the beginning, but their repetition had come to seem to you, almost, a kind of sense; come to seem to you, almost—but the piece was over.

The audience would give a long sigh and burst into applause: they had been able to tell where the stars came in, and where Lucifer went down, as well as if both had been the herd of sheep in *Don Quixote*. The devil had been very human, but since he was the devil they did not mind; those who had been following the score showed their neighbors the tone-row the composer had selected for the stars, and pointed out the most unusual of the mirror-effects in the counterpoint. But the piece had given these people, so used to "coping with reality," a different intuition: that the world is too much for even the devil to cope with, but also . . . But also what? They could not say; the piece ended, *But also . . .*

4.

TARTINI HAD sent Constance to bed momentarily forgetful of Dr. Rosenbaum's bedtime story and of Dr. Rosenbaum's—*secret*, as Constance phrased it; but when she got back to her room late the next afternoon, done with Benton, she began to think about both. She worried for a moment, and then was impatient with herself for worrying: she had sense enough not to worry about the world, and to worry about Dr. Rosenbaum seemed, somehow, just as silly. Both would disappear some day; but while they had been here they had been here. And she felt too good to worry: joy, like alcohol, works well on a half-empty stomach and a half-sleepless head.

She repeated to herself what she had repeated to herself for weeks—as a bird repeats to itself its best call, its only call; as Gertrude would repeat to herself, *I've written seven books;* as the President would repeat to himself, *I'm President of Benton.* What she repeated was *her* secret: that she was going to live with the Rosenbaums; to be—happiness beyond any dream of hers!—Dr. Rosenbaum's secretary; to leave day after tomorrow for Cape Cod, to stay with the Rosenbaums all summer, and in the fall to come back with them to a transcended Benton, a Benton to which she would be forevermore an outsider. If a great group of red-hatted Cardinals, all attended by Swiss Guards, had come to Constance and told her that she had been chosen to be Pope Joan II, she would have said, wondering at their innocence: "Oh, but I can't. I'm going to be—" then she would have hesitated, not liking to boast to them—"Dr. Rosenbaum's secretary."

Mrs. Rosenbaum had asked her to be. She had come to Constance's room, looked at the books, praised the pictures, and then had begun with a sort of timid voluble brusqueness —nobody is ever quite so old as he thinks: "There is no point, no point whatever, Constance, for you to sit all day in an office like—like Akaky Akakiyevich Bashmachkin. It is only Gottfried's silliness that he has not had a secretary many years ago. I said to him: If Stravinsky can write polkas for elephants, is Gottfried Rosenbaum to have *nothing?* I said to him: When the state has withered away, what composer will be *then* without his secretary? His *secretaries?* Gottfried admitted that my arguments could not be answered at all. And, Constance, you will be able to be of more use to him than you believe—his book is all looking up and copying and writing out and once more looking up, there is nothing he does not do a dozen times. Your training is excellent, you know our ways and we know—know you. And if you were no use to us we should still like to buy you from yourself, we wish to hang you on a Christmas tree. We can pay you so that you may live in the style to which Benton has accustomed you."

Her gesture included the studio-couch, the rug worn by earlier generations, the elm at the window, the quadrilateral of street beyond the neighboring roof. She continued, "I have not seen a member of my own family since in 1938 I saw one nephew: trust that one to survive! He was attached to a Russian restaurant in Nice—if I had been that restaurant I should have *served* him. And Gottfried has no one. I have read this speech in books, bad books, too many times to make it, and Gottfried is a composer, no *père de famille;* but you are—" and here she paused, and then managed by a little leap of recollection and empathy to put it almost in Constance's own terms—"you are *really and truly*, Constance, all that a daughter would be for us if we had a daughter."

She had gone on talking for so long, in a style so different from her usual style, because she wanted to give Constance time to recover: Constance was beyond words—though not beyond tears and, later, many words. But Dr. Rosenbaum, when she saw him next, behaved as though it had been understood beforehand, long ago, and talked stolidly about the details of what she was to do.

The Rosenbaums had talked about it long ago—with me, two months before. Irene finished, "It is only for a while: a daughter is nothing to keep. Someday in a year, or two, or three, she will want to be a grown-up." She smiled, and her smile drew her lips down oddly. I said joyfully, "Don't you want to adopt me too? You can tell me you're hiring me as a librettist." Irene said that they had adopted me long ago, and sometimes were glad that they had; and Gottfried remarked in a dry voice that he was delighted to see that somebody else shared his ambition to be the pet of visitors from another planet.

The Rosenbaums made Constance's practical arrangements for her as easily as they did anything else of the sort: such things, having no interest, are to be got over with. They saved their time for Life. (What they meant by the word, though, would have seemed notably unLifelike to most of the people of Benton.)

So there was nothing for Constance to do as the last long day ended. She wanted to leave the Rosenbaums to themselves while she still could: the privacy they were giving up seemed a great sacrifice to make for *her*. It was too early to pack—they did not leave for two days; it was too early for dinner—Constance liked to eat late, as continentals do. She decided to make herself study her German lesson, as continentals do also—young ones particularly. The Grammar and the Graded Readings, which had got to a Topographical and Industrial section, were more than she could bear. She got down her two Grimms: one in English, a loved possession—the illustrations had been done by a medieval draftsman born out of his time, Josef Scharl; the other, half as tall and twice as thick, a bag-pudding of a book, was in German, and was stuffed with black-and-white illustrations that were *very* German—or as Constance would have said, *echt deutsch*. One illustration had even been forced out to the beige cloth binding of the book; in the open air its black had turned ink-green and horseback-brown, but there it was, pipes and tailors and matchlocks and geese and all. Inside one found, in modified Gothic type, *Kinder- und Hausmärchen gesammelt durch die Brüder Grimm, Gesamtausgabe mit 447 Zeichnungen von Otto Ubbelohde*.

Constance had made her way through these *Kinder- und Hausmärchen* like a glacier, a glacier generally in love with the *Berg* down which—up which—it is moving. She never skipped any ordinary story, no matter how hard: that way Not Knowing German lay. But she had left out for a time, as the Rosenbaums smilingly advised her to do, the stories in dialect. She turned now to one of these: perhaps by now . . . It was 47: *Von dem Machandelboom*.

Machandelboom! It was like a depth bomb. Constance thanked God for the English Grimm: normally it only saved looking up every fourth word in the *Wörterbuch*, but this word would be in no dictionary of hers. But when she looked in her own green Grimm it meant only *Juniper Tree*, the *boom* was no more than *baum*.

Von dem Machandelboom was from the beginning a burden greater than Constance's childish German could bear. *Twe dusand Johr* was, plainly, two thousand years, and *Kinner* was *Kinder* and *Dag* was *Tag*, and *wöör* must be *war*—how *silly* it looked; but how about *ryk*—oh, *rich*. Two thousand years ago there had been a rich man and his wife, and they had had no child; the woman prayed for one night and day, but none came—and she wept. But one winter's day, standing under the juniper tree paring an apple, she had cut her *Finger, un dat Blood feel in de Snee*. It's *lots* more like English than regular German, Constance thought rashly; but what was *hoog*? a hog? Surely not; but what was *füfted*, no, *süfted so recht hoog up?* The woman had sighed right heavily, and had looked at the blood on the snow, and had wished for a child *so rood as Blood un so witt as Snee*. And then she "felt just as if that were going to happen. Then she went into the house, and a month went by and the snow was gone, and two months, and then everything was green, and three months, and then all the flowers came out of the earth, and four months, and then all the trees in the wood grew thicker, and the green branches were all closely entwined, and the birds sang until the wood resounded and the blossoms fell from the trees [but by now Constance was shamelessly reading the English; the *Kinder- und Hausmärchen* lay on the couch beside her, without even a finger to hold the place], then the fifth month passed away and she stood under the juniper tree, which smelt so sweetly that her heart leapt, and she fell on her knees and was beside herself with joy, and when the sixth month was over the fruit was large and fine, and then she was quite still, and the seventh month she snatched at the juniper-berries and ate them greedily, then she grew sick and sorrowful, then the eighth month passed, and she called her husband to her, and wept and said: 'If I die, then bury me beneath the juniper tree.' Then she was quite comforted and happy until the next month was over, and then she had a child as white as snow and as red as blood, and when she beheld it she was so delighted that she died.

"Then her husband buried her beneath the juniper tree, and he began to weep sore; after some time he was more at ease, and though he still wept he could bear it, and after some time longer he took another wife. . . ."

When Constance read *and when she beheld it she was so delighted that she died*, the tears that had been gathering in her eyes were too much for her to hold back any longer;

she read the last sentence crying openly, and was scarcely able to distinguish its words over there on the other side of the blurring, warping windowpane of her tears—she let her head fall to the harsh pillows of the couch, and wept. She had sighed right heavily—for what, she knew not; for what was to come. The story was to Constance in some way her life, but there was in it something else that she did not understand; and she wept in joy for herself and her happiness, and in grief for her own stupidity and the world's. The story held for her the tears of things, and she murmured in childish—or, perhaps, human—anguish: "Oh, I wish I had more *sense!*"

The tears kept trickling from her eyes, ran down her nose and fell on the faded pillows of the couch, but by now she was not really crying; she said, pulling herself upright, beginning to laugh at herself and everything else, she was so happy: "It's a wonderful world!" She wiped her eyes with her forearm, and stopped laughing because she had to yawn; her nose and eyes were still full of tears; she was sleepy: no longer conscious of the world except as the brimming margin of herself, a boundary that was not a boundary, she gave a soft wondering laugh—then, bathed in her own being, she repeated vaguely, in dreaming trust: "Oh, it's a *wonderful* world!"

5.

MY WIFE and I took Gertrude and Sidney to the train. They were accompanying, or being accompanied by, a family of new plastic suitcases, and Gertrude's tweed stole was the largest I had ever seen; "It's lucky Flo didn't see it or she'd have stolen it," I said thoughtlessly. I meant for the house, not to wear, but Gertrude took it the wrong way. My wife said, "Peru! I've always wanted to go to Peru— or else it's Ecuador. . . . Let's us go to Peru some vacation, darling."

Sidney said, "It'll be a vacation for *me*—Gertrude will be working harder than ever." As he said this he looked at her. For that look you forgave him everything—and after all, what was there to forgive?—you even forgave Gertrude everything; or, at least, were willing to consider the possibility of making the attempt, foredoomed to failure as it was.

Gertrude, waving her hand widely, said in boisterous good humor—she looked so girlish that you expected her to go out and buy a middy blouse— "Oh, it'll be nothing! I could finish *this* book with both hands tied behind my back." It was her customary phrase about the book; it gave me, always, a queer vision of Gertrude finishing the book with just her teeth. Then she said to my wife and me, as we all prepared really to say goodbye: "Sidney and I will *miss* you-all. Having you two here has really helped. Not that we haven't had quite a pleasant time. Living in a quiet dull place like this where nothing ever happens—there's something very attractive about it for a few months. Sometimes Sidney and I felt just like—" here she smiled—"just like Paul and Virginia."

I could have said, "Sometimes we felt just like Martinique." My wife and I were going to miss Gertrude and Sidney, and we told them so. The joy of travel overcame Gertrude, and she flung one end of the stole up over her shoulder as though she were Lady Stanhope, and the porter stepped back respectfully.

"Are you going to live in a *pension* or what?" my wife asked. "Is the—are the native dishes nice in Ecuador?"

"They have *mole* sauces," said Sidney. "They put chocolate on turkey, because the Incas did."

"The Aztecs, Sidney; and that's in Mexico. We're going to get a little apartment and just cook our own meals, most of the time. It'll be interesting to try out some of the native recipes."

"Oh, you don't want to bother with *recipes*," said my wife. I said, so speedily that admiration for myself almost overcame me: "You ought to write a travel book sometime, Gertrude—one about Peru. I'd like to see what you think of Peru." But this made me think, longingly, that I'd like for Peru to write a book about her: what would Peru think of Gertrude?

"I may, I may," answered Gertrude. "I don't know *what* I'll write about next. For a while I've been thinking. . . ." She looked away from my face into my wife's, and away from my wife's into Sidney's, and away from Sidney's into the porter's. Then she said pensively, in an almost demure voice: "I've often thought of writing a book about a—" here, for the smallest part of a second, she hesitated—"about a *writer*."

Sidney, and my wife, and the porter looked at Gertrude all unmoved. . . .

The Rosenbaums' departure, at nine on a blue morning, was a different affair. The witch had left on the train; the summer's books and clothes and scores and records and phonograph were packed away in a canvas-covered one-wheel trailer that, looking very incongruous, stood hitched to the rear of the Simca; the Simca's top was down, and Constance, a scarf around her head, sat crossways in the space behind the two red leather seats; Gottfried sat half behind and half over the wheel, looking alertly around in the last moment before his pit crew brought him his goggles. Irene sat there comfortably in a long blue leather coat and a sort of Bulgarian tam-o'-shanter. The cat sat in Irene's lap, lashing its tail; occasionally it would mew piteously.

I said, "What will Constance do if it rains and you have to put the top up?"

Constance said doubtfully, "I don't know. The top's too low for me to stay back here then, isn't it?"

Irene said in a firm voice: "If it rains you will sit on my lap half the time, and I on your lap half the time, and Tanya will sit on both of us all the time. But how could it rain? Absurd!"

Gottfried said, "Goodbye, goodbye, we shall see you in August." We all kissed or patted each other and made our goodbyes, and the car and the trailer and Gottfried and Irene and Constance and the cat disappeared into the distance, looking—for as long as you could see them at all—simply extraordinary.

It had been silly of us to see them off (they were going only as far as Cape Cod, and we would be visiting them in August) but we had wanted to, somehow, and we had enjoyed ourselves. I said about them, remembering Gottfried's remark about his Bremen Town Musicians: "Vot a bunch!"

"Which does the cat count as?" asked my wife. "European or American?"

"Just human."

My wife said, "I know how you feel about cats, but—"
I said, "Just Persian, I meant to say."

My wife said slowly, "They looked so well off, didn't they? One almost . . ." Her voice trailed off, and she gave a queer smile. And my smile must have been the same smile: as you had looked at them you had wished for them simply to be left as they were.

My wife drove me to my office and left me there. Those days I was throwing away: going over magazines and books and papers and trying to get rid of all I could. I was leaving Benton. My new job was a better job, and it had been foolish of me to stay at Benton as long as I had stayed; but just the same. . . . It meant leaving the Rosenbaums, and Flo and Jerrold, and Constance, and—and Derek and Yang, I thought with arbitrary sentimentality; and the absurdities of Benton were so absurd, and I myself was so thoroughly used to them, that they had come to seem to me, almost, the ordinary absurdities of existence. Like Gertrude, I cherished my grievances against God, but to some of them I had become very accustomed.

President Robbins had spoken so as to make me feel disloyal, leaving Benton, but really it had been disloyal of me to stay. Now Benton would be rid of one uncomfortable citizen, one piece that didn't fit into the puzzle that Benton —that Benton wasn't; and in a few years, when Gottfried and a few other such pieces had gone, Benton would at last be—

No, there would always be new ones; and if I were gone, and Gottfried and the others gone too, and if they let in no new ones like us, still it would do no good, some of the old ones would become like us: man is an uncomfortable animal.

Sitting on the floor in the midst of my great dusty lopsided piles of books and magazines and papers—sitting there in the Cave of the Years, now reading a little, now throwing away a lot—I felt dusty and lopsided myself, and a senseless restlessness and melancholy overcame me. Outside it was all white and blue and green; inside it was only black and white, only grey. I felt that it was the wrong day for packing. I went out and walked aimlessly around, looking at things on the campus. If somebody had looked down at me from a window he could have said to me: *Whence comest thou?* and I could have answered: *From going to and fro in Benton, and from walking up and down in it.*

There was not left in the dormitories one student. The library was gloomy and echoing, and smelled of floor wax; and the two librarians there had the satisfied look that librarians have when nobody is using the books, just as the keepers watering the tennis courts had the satisfied look that keepers have when nobody is using the tennis courts. Nobody was using Benton, you felt. At the President's house all the shades were drawn, and there were no Afghans by the garage, there was no Derek by the sandpile; how I should have loved to see, peering suspiciously from a window, Mrs. Robbins' dark wooden face!

I was beginning to feel that I was a ghost and that the rest of the people of Benton were not even that—and then I met John Whittaker, cutting across the campus on his way to the woods. His starched shorts ended high on his legs, and I marvelled at how big he was getting. The Whittakers were going to the Grand Canyon, he told me. (The worst journey, made by car, was a joy to them: Flo and Jerrold and John and Fern—Fern was two then—had gone through twenty-four states and British Columbia in three weeks, and had never slept except on an air mattress, never eaten except from a tin plate.) John was radiant: "To think of getting to see so many species of *Crotalus*, of *Sistrurus*, there in their own habitat," he exclaimed, thrusting farther into the earth, in his excitement, the pronged stick he held in his hand. "Is Fern excited about the trip?" I asked. He said, "Well, no." His face had fallen: Sister, little Sister, took the bloom off *Crotalus*, off *Sistrurus*, even.

"It looks queer to see it all so empty, doesn't it?" I said. He evidently had been thinking something of the sort himself; he nodded twice, and said softly, "I used to think every summer, they won't come back, *this* fall."

I had certainly thought something of that sort myself; I said, "It's always seemed the most improbable thing in the world to me that they can fly out all over the country, all over the world, climb mountains and write books and get married and—and despair and go to Lichtenstein, and then every September the fifteenth all arrive here on the hour. It's stranger than the swallows. To come back *here!*"

John gave me a still, matter-of-fact smile, the smile of a boy who has read science-fiction since he was seven. He said: "They always return. And do you know why? They can't help it."

"Can't help it?"

He said, "Haven't you noticed how they all talk just the same, and dress just alike, and read the same books, and—and leave the same day and come back the same day? And I've never talked to a one of them that didn't say to me, 'What grade are you in this year?' And do you know why?"

"Why?"

"They're androids."

I too had read science-fiction, and I knew that androids are synthetic human beings, robots who look just like you and me. I laughed delightedly, but said: "You're kidding me." He laughed too, and said, "Yes. When I was younger I believed it, though. It explained a lot of things to me. It was a great help to me."

I answered, "Yes, I can see that. But in the long run it's a greater help not to."

He said, "I've read that you—" here his voice took on a warmthless precision—"that you shouldn't multiply entities needlessly. Have you ever read *The Analysis of Matter?*"

I answered, looking at him wonderingly: "Yes. Have you read any other of—" then I saw that this was a foolish question, and asked instead: "Is it one of the books of his that you like best?"

"Oh yes," he answered. "It's one of my favorites. It's my hope to read all of Russell's books. . . . Do you think if you say they're androids you're multiplying entities needlessly, or that you are if you say they're not?"

I said, "I never saw the android I didn't need: have you forgotten, I'm an android myself. Did I really ask you what grade you were in?"

He said kindly, "You just weren't thinking. It was only— what is it they call it when you say something you don't mean, just to establish communication?"

"Phratic communion, I think—something like that, I'm not sure."

"It was only that. Dr. Rosenbaum never has, though. It's interested me."

I said: "Leaving out the question of what grade you're in, what do you think of school generally?"

"I don't think I'm a fair one to judge," he answered. "It's not bad for the majority of them. Of course they don't learn much."

I said, "Do you?" He answered, astonished: "Do *I? I* don't learn anything at *school*."

We talked a little more, said goodbye to each other, and walked away; but after a few yards I thought of something I wanted to ask him. I said, "John, do you remember what it was that got you interested in snakes?"

He said with an embarrassed laugh: "I haven't any idea. It's—it's an odd interest, isn't it?—you wouldn't think anyone around here would be interested in snakes. When I grow up I'm going to be a physicist."

I said thoughtfully, "When I grew up I was going to be a physicist. . . . Goodbye, John. Because of you I'll never again ask anybody what grade he's in."

He said: "Now you'll always have to say something about the weather."

It was so. I went on—meeting John had brought me luck, and now and then I met somebody else. I met a girl who worked in the admissions office: from a distance she looked like Sylvia Moomaw, and I thought of Sylvia Moomaw; and I saw a cat in one of the apple-trees, and that made me think of the Rosenbaums and Constance; and I saw Dr. Willen and a janitor carrying a tachistoscope out to her car, and that made me think of Miss Batterson. The lunch I hadn't eaten, the shadows I stepped on, and the barred walks shining and empty in the sun, all the absences that were present there, came together into a kind of elegiac listlessness: everything had for me then too faint and strange a life even to need to perish.

I sat down on the grass by the building in which the painters and sculptors and dancers lived and flourished: but there was nobody working away at a block of mahogany, nobody pouring paint onto canvasboard, nobody standing with her leg out in the air as though dislocated, her face fixed in the grimace of her trade. People eat and sleep and live all year, but they are educated only nine months of it.

Someone called to me from the second floor: it was Sona Rasmussen. Art Night had placed me, had placed Gottfried, among old admirers of her work. She was in coveralls—was goggleless, though—and her dark round face was shining with sweat. She said for me to come up, there was something she wanted to show me. As I went up the stairs I repeated to myself what she had said, trying to get into my voice the half-Japanese, half-Scandinavian sameness of internal organization that one heard in every sentence of hers.

When I got into the big studio it looked different: most of the statues were gone, the acetylene torches had been put away into a corner, and a great mound of clay stood naked against the wall, without even a cloth over it to keep it wet. At the other end there was a statue I had never seen before. "It's my new one," Miss Rasmussen said shyly. "It's—it's made from part of a railroad tie." You could see that: the tie had been fixed so that it revolved, like a weather-vane, on the brass rod that supported it.

I looked at it a long time. Finally I looked at Miss Rasmussen with troubled eyes; she asked uneasily, "Don't you like it?"

"I like it very much, Miss Rasmussen," I said. "It's a wonderful one. It's quite a different sort from your others, isn't it?"

It was more different from her others than you would have believed possible—how could I ever again be sure what you could believe possible? The railroad tie had become a man, a man who floated in the air as the foetus floats in the womb; his pressed-together arms and legs, his hunched-up shoulders, his nudging face were indicated in broad burnt lines or depressions, so that you could hardly tell whether the man had been drawn or modelled: he was there. He fitted into the rectangle of the railroad tie as a cat, fast asleep, fits into the circle of itself. Whether or not he slept you could not tell. He was part of the element he inhabited, and it and he moved on together silently: his limbs, blunted by their speed, were still. Even his nuzzling mouth and pressed-flat nose were still, so that I remembered *The arrow in its flight is motionless;* and remembered, as I looked into his flattened face, the proto-Mongolians of a German historian's grotesque theory, *Ur*-men who, many thousands of years ago, were parasites of the wild horses of Asia, clinging to their sides and nursing like foals, or opening a vein and drinking from it and closing it—and all the time the horses ran on, never stopping.

"He's the East Wind," Miss Rasmussen said. She was right; he was the East Wind. There was about him a sinister and conclusive peace: one sank into him, as one looked at him, as one sinks into sleep. I told Miss Rasmussen over and over again what a wonderful statue it was; my shame at having misjudged her so—for to me she not only had looked like, but also had been, a potato-bug, and I had been polite to her exactly as one puts the little thing on a leaf and tells it to fly away home—made me more voluble than I should otherwise have been. She was pleased and grateful, though she was still too dazed with her statue to find my words anything more than the echo of her own veins. She talked to me about the statue for a while, and I saw, not in dismay but in awe, that to appreciate what she said you still would have had to be an imbecile: she said about the East Wind exactly what she had always said about those welded root-systems of alfalfa plants that the storeroom of the studio was full of. She was a potato-bug who had been visited by an angel, and I decided—decided unwillingly—for the rest of my life to suffer potato-bugs gladly, since angels are not able to make the distinctions that we ourselves make between potato-bugs and ourselves.

She too had had no lunch, and we went and ate it together. To me she wasn't Miss Rasmussen any more, but the maker of the East Wind, and I handed her a paper napkin as I would have dropped it from a window into air. As long as her work had been bad she had been a visible fool, and now that her work was good she had disappeared into it. This was an unjust fate; and yet she wouldn't have thought it unjust, I didn't think it unjust—I would have vanished willingly into the words of the East Wind.

As I walked back through Benton to my office I hardly looked at Benton. I felt that I had misjudged Benton, somehow—for if I had misjudged Miss Rasmussen so, why not the rest of Benton?—and yet I didn't feel repentant, only confused, and willingly confused; and I was willing for Benton in its turn to misjudge me. I signed with it then a separate peace. There was no need for us to judge each other, we said, we knew each other too well; we knew each other by heart. Then we yawned, and turned sleepily from each other, and sank back into sleep.

I worked hard for the rest of the afternoon: I threw away and threw away and threw away, because after all—as I told myself to make things go faster—the part of Benton that had belonged to me I could not get rid of by throwing away; and Benton mumbled to me, stirring a last time in its sleep, that now there would be an empty place in the puzzle, and that it would be hard to find an uncomfortable one that would fit into it so well and so comfortably as I. When at last I went downstairs everything was hollow and silent; my steps echoed along the corridor, as I walked down it looking at the sunlight in the trees outside. There was nobody in the building—nobody, I felt, in all the buildings of Benton. I stood in the telephone-booth on the first floor, dialed the number of my house, and my wife's *hello* was small and far-off in the silence; I said, "Can you come get me now, darling?" She answered, "Of *course* I can. I'll be right over."

A NOTE ON THE TYPE

This book was set on the Linotype in Janson, a recutting made direct from the type cast from matrices made by Anton Janson some time between 1660 and 1687.

Of Janson's origin nothing is known. He may have been a relative of Justus Janson, a printer of Danish birth who practised in Leipzig from 1614 to 1635. Some time between 1657 and 1668 Anton Janson, a punch-cutter and type-founder, bought from the Leipzig printer Johann Erich Hahn the type-foundry which had formerly been a part of the printing house of M. Friedrich Lankisch. Janson's types were first shown in a specimen sheet issued at Leipzig about 1675.

Composed, printed, and bound by KINGSPORT PRESS, INC., *Kingsport, Tennessee.*

Designed by HARRY FORD